Strength & Honor:
Book One

Strength & Honor:
Book One

Justice

Author Contact Information
Justice
justcreate11@yahoo.com. 6123888197

Contents

BOOK ONE

BOOK ONE

In the darkness will come the light that will blind
the many and allow the few to walk forward.

CHAPTER ONE

Give them an inch, and it all falls down.

A GUN. A shiny, nickel-plated forty-five was handed over from an older, scruffy-looking Blackman with bloodshot red eyes to a youngster that couldn't be no older then fourteen. The black boy with no facial hair visible, after receiving the weapon of choice that swallowed up his hand, handed over the paper with presidents' faces on them and then turned and ran away in clothes that looked like he had slept in them for the last week. The older man cracked a sly grin as to say, 'don't hurt any one but I really don't give a fuck as long as I got paid'. He turned away as the boy's footsteps could be heard no more and counted the money in his palm that he then shoved in his pocket and strutted off, down the dark and lifeless sidewalk.

Move some miles over from the weapon transaction that armed a baby with a piece he was unable to wield correctly, and onto a vehicle that moved down a shadowy and isolated street in one of the various neighborhoods that was situated right on the border were the suburbs and the inner city merge into one. A rusty, gray colored caravan crept down the residential street in search of the desired house that was looked for. The 1986 Dodge caravan continued to move at a deliberate pace as the search continued. It rounded the corner and sped up just a bit down another street that all looked the same. You know how the suburbs are – cookie cutter material. Then the vehicle, with mismatch hubcaps, spotted the house from half a block down, which caused the wheels to pull to the side, the lights to cut off and the vehicle to roll to a stop. There it sat, unnoticed, for a moment in the tranquil darkness were all that was heard was the sound of chirps, whistles, and squeaks from the various animals and insects that infested the area. There was not a body on the suburban avenue to be seen.

Inside the caravan, Mobb Deep's *'Hell on Earth'* ushered out from the cheap stock tape player.

'The projects is frontline, and the enemy is one time.'

Malik, a corn-rowed, twenty-something year old Blackman with a thin but muscular, lean build, leaned to the window side and observed the area closely and low keyed to make sure things were clear. He gradually shifted his eyes from the quiet row of well-manicured yards and over to the passenger seat. There sat Lars Rollins, a powerfully built Blackman around the same age as Malik with a tight fade haircut, a long white-gold chain that had a medallion attached to it and a gold stud earring placed in his left ear. He lounged back with no care and puffed away on the full marijuana blunt that he had just rolled. Malik kept his eyes focused on Lars for a brief moment. He ignored the straight-faced glare coming from Malik and continued to draw back on the blunt and release the herb smoke.

"Are you going to show any love with that B?" Malik said with a sharp point in the words that demanded to be heard.

Lars refused to be interrupted in his quest to get high as high can be, with a full dime wrapped up in a Philly blunt that the saliva from the tongue kept fastened together. Lars raised his eyes what little he could and started to zone off to the verse being spit by the voice of the lyrical artist Havoc that seemed to him, to fill the vehicle with those words he uttered that penetrated his every pore.

Malik's glowing brown eyes surrounded by the clean whites left Lars' site with the blunt in hand clutched tight. As he caressed his lips to moisten them with his tongue, he checked his beaten up metallic-silver cell phone that had just vibrated on his hip. He showed no reaction to the number that flashed on the screen that was coolly recognized. It was just one of the many lady friends that Malik had across the city, north side and south side. He refused to answer, and placed the palm-sized phone in the glove compartment with no thought. There was only one thing on his mind at this moment in the night.

Lars took one last drag on the blunt that was now past half way smoked up. He kept his eyes low with the head constantly moving up and down to the beat. With his concentration on a specific house, he extended his arm to his left side, with the blunt held by his thumb and index finger, and offered what was left to Malik that was nonchalantly taken notice of.

Malik, with his long fingers that revealed his clean and manicured finger nails, took the blunt in hand and placed it in his mouth with a smooth-like ease. Lars looked down at himself and checked the ashes that had fallen on to his black sweatshirt and oversized jogging pants. He brushed them off with a deliberate stroke that made sure the ashes didn't mush into the garments and stain any part of the material that would become most visible in the all black. Malik sat back and let the blunt dangle from the corner of his mouth. He puffed away, inhaling the weed smoke that was released from out the nose. "You sure about these candy kids?" Malik asked in between the tokes inhaled with his eyes pointing toward the house that was the object of their desire.

Lars let the question pass by with his total focus on the words that spilled out from the tape player. To him, Havoc and Prodigy's voice seemed to be speaking directly to his soul. He was in full attention, with ears open, to hear each statement, each piece explored, and each experience expressed fully with nothing held back in raw fashion. He was living what they were speaking and he knew what each verse truly meant.

Malik, with what was left of the blunt still dangling from his mouth, moved up in his seat and reached for the volume dial. He slowly, with purpose to draw Lars' attention, turned down the music then sat back and took one last drag on the blunt and put it out in the small ashtray underneath the tape player.

A frustrated Lars turned and stared directly at Malik who was waiting to meet up with his eyes. The two young men, in all black, locked pupils for a moment in the silent caravan. Lars and Malik had known each other ever since they were hardheaded little boys, running around the neighborhood, scarring the peter pipers and raiding the candy men. Lars was the type that always found himself in some sort of trouble in some sort of way, and he loved it. Whether it was beating up a boy for his free park lunch, splashing the girls at the city pool, or stealing blow-pops from the corner market. Lars was attracted to mischief and loved bringing grief to adults.

Malik, on the other hand, was always active in organized activities and enjoyed watching the television. He played sports, loved the girls and the game '60' that he played late nights with them, and he was known as one of the illest break-dancers in the city. Both Lars and Malik were attracted to and respected what the other lacked in them self while respecting the strength both of them possessed in their own way.

"Yo nigga, are you on your period tonight or what? What the fuck?" Lars questioned with a playful force that searched to instigate.

"What's the deal with these kids? What's the story?" Malik quizzed as he ignored Lars' attempt to dig at him.

Lars turned his eyes from Malik and to the back of the house where they had parked near by. His eyes glowed with an uncontrolled urge on the doorway that was lit by an outside light. "What I say?" Lars threw back with an agitated tone. Then with a testing attitude, he looked Malik up and down with his low-hatched eyes. "Don't bitch out on me now B."

Malik cracked a small grin of amusement from the corner of his mouth as his hand moved up to his chin and gave a rub over his well-groomed goat-tee. "Bitching out huh," Malik repeated as he faced forward. He detected the seriousness in Lars.

As Malik spoke the words, Lars scanned the area, checking out what was what and were the house was situated. "Check it. I inspected, checked and double checked this piece," Lars lifted his hand and pointed thru the bubbling up window tint. "This is the spot, I'm telling you, so stop your bitchin'." Lars wanted to pull this job – bad. He had spent the last couple weeks watching these kids go thru their daily activities and how they went about them. And to pull this off, he knew he needed Malik to make sure all bases were covered. This was no fuckin' game.

Malik shifted his eyes from across the street where they were parked at and to the side entrance of the house and joined in on the close observation. He was well aware that this was going to have to be lightning quick. "Aright baby boy, but if these kids are on some monopoly money type shite – ."

Lars had enough of the questions and concerns. He moved up in his seat and reached underneath it for something as he cut Malik off from speaking. "Shut the fuck up with all that Minniee-me shit."

"You just better know what the fuck you're doing," Malik shot back.

"Ah nigga, you just stop acting like a little bitch and let's do this," Lars threw back with a small smile that broke out on his grim face as he took off his long chain. This was not your average argument. These two young men who had known each other ever since they could walk, grew up together, shared each other's clothes, and slept over each other's home. They did everything together and were as close to blood brothers as can be defined. And from this developed a stable bond thru the years that was sustained thru loyalty to their differences as well as their similarities and the respect that was demanded. Even when Lars had to go away for a couple years, he didn't drop Malik's name to the arresting officers. Instead, he kept his mouth shut and took his medicine. And as close as they were, they were just as different. Lars was emotional. Malik was analytical. Lars was quick to crack a loud mouth in the head. Malik wanted to know why, then if it was worth it. More importantly, Lars was married to the street life, and for Malik, it was just his hoe. He knew there was something more out there then heists, drugs, guns and quickies. For Lars, that's all there was, and he was content with that and satisfied to live just that, unlike Malik.

Now, here the two sat, inside a beat up caravan being pumped up by Mobb Deep to do an average nights work for them. Time to punch in.

Malik lifted his black ski mask into view that he set in his lap. He pulled a black nine-millimeter gun from under his seat, slipped the clip out, checked it, popped it back in and slapped the hammer back. Lars had clapped his back already and placed it in his waistband. He reached to his side and pulled out a black ski mask. While doing this, the two continued to trade short and direct remarks that poked fun of each other in an attempt to find that soft spot that could be used when the next round commenced at another time. It was a way of playing with each other while at the same time it helped to reveal if one needed toughening up. The young men's nights were filled with robbing dealers, hustlers, businessmen, pimps, car jacking athletes and spoiled women just to make that paper that sustained them until the next job. It was the outlaw lifestyle and it was far from easy work. Malik was once dragged for about a block and a half when a ball player in a Benz decided to be Bruce Willis. There was various gun battles, wrong drop spots, little money and unaccounted for surprises. Credit cards had made the hustle somewhat more difficult and so cash businesses were bulls-eyed.

Lars and Malik moved out of the vehicle quietly and with purpose. They each shifted their heads from one side to the other, like on a swivel, as the words died down. You never knew who laid low in the bushes or who stepped out from the dark cuts. Your eyes always had to be open. As they disappeared into the blackness of the backyard that led to the house, they each placed the black ski masks on top of their heads. Malik took one last look behind him and down the road, both ways, as he reached into his waistband to adjust the gun's placement.

After a half-hour wait in the shrubs on each side of the entrance, the screen side door to the house opened and out came two Blackmen dressed in baggy jeans, football jerseys, chains, big-face watches and ball caps. Laughter and joking filled the night air as one of them boasted about getting his dick sucked by a young lady he messed with the past night. They both laughed at her on how she gave head to him and her facial expressions. With no time wasted, as the chuckling street dealers hit the stairs, Malik and Lars were on them with a quick and firm movement that seized them before they could think. Malik and Lars raise the black guns to the young men's temples. Their young skin felt the hard steel press deep without any care to the feeling it produced.

Lars leaned into the face of the larger of the two to get his attention. "Get your bitch ass in the house," Lars demanded in a forceful like nature. "Don't eye ball me nigga. Move!"

Lars gave a hard shove with the barrel of the gun that pushed the youngster back into the house. Malik pointed to the other to follow in behind with no words, just actions.

Malik disappeared inside. The door closed shut with a thud and the outside light turned off.

Lars and Malik threw the dark-skinned young men to the floor with a violent and hard thrust that splashed them down, face first and spread eagle. The young street dealers were well aware of the purpose of this visit. It was just a matter if the masked men who were robbing them knew who they worked for that would save their lives and their work.

Malik, with hand and foot, delivered a number of blows to the curled up young man on the floor. Lars pointed the gun rocked in his right hand at the shook teenager as he searched, with unrelenting force, the body for what he came for.

Malik stood up from a crouching position and delivered a couple more solid shots that held the young body down on the floor. He rose up from the delivered beating and held the gun over the face down young man. "Stay your bitch ass, face down little nigga."

Malik joined Lars in the full body search were the two took any jewelry, weed and some spending money that was on each. Then, finally, Lars found a pouch hidden in the mid-section of the tatted up young man. Lars snatched it out as he pressed the gun to the back of the head of the nineteen year old who was wrapped up in the nice things but failed to understand the consequences that come when gone about the wrong way.

Lars searched thru the pouch and pulled out a large roll of money that was rubber-banded up. Without looking thru the roll, he calmly picked his head up and turned to Malik who pocketed a couple hundred from the eighteen year old who looked like he was thirty-five. Malik noticed the roll in Lars' hand and a smile came over his face.

"Monopoly huh," Lars said with an air of 'I told ya'.

The young man held down by Lars turned his head to the side so his mouth could escape the floor to speak and he could also get a look at the dark eyes of Lars who stood over with a smirk.

"You mutha-fuckas betta keep those guns close," he spit out as he mustered up all the courage he could. "And don't take those fuckin' masks off or – ."

Lars stopped him quick with movement down toward his face with the gun pressed deep into his cheek. "Or what. What the fuck you going to do cocksucker? Huh? What are you going to do if I put a bullet in your fucking skull?" An incensed Lars rose up and began to deliver a number of powerful blows to the head, the stomach, his legs, the neck and the back. Blow after blow followed with spit and blood flying out the youngster's grill as Lars cursed the very ground that the young man was beaten down on.

Malik stood over and gave a few more kicks then took the butt of the gun and knocked the young man, who was too shook to say anything, out cold. Malik turned and looked on Lars with an amazed expression at the unmerciful beating being given. Lars was punching, kicking, stomping, and coming down in a sledgehammer type of way with the butt of the gun over and over again, non-stop. Malik took notice of the blood in Lars' eyes along with the hate. No one was going to talk or threaten him like that, and the thought of death consumed him to continue his lethal assault. Malik quickly sprung over to Lars, seeing the damage being done and were it was leading to. He grabbed the arm and pulled Lars away from the motionless young man who lay in his own pool of blood on the floor.

Lars wiped the spit from his mouth and the sweat from his brow, "Bitch ass faggot." He delivered one more stomp to the back of the head. "Who's going to have to hide now?"

Malik looked down on the young man whose limp body lay lifeless on the tile floor. He turned slowly to Lars who was about to unleash another blow. "Yo, that's enough kid," Malik stated.

Lars, with a disturbed look, cocked his eyes on to Malik. "What's up with you? You getting Oprah out here?"

Malik and Lars exchanged slight shoves so to move each other, either toward the door or toward the other young man who hadn't tasted a savage beating from Lars yet. Malik grabbed him with both hands and looked him straight into the eyes. "That's enough. We got what we came for. Let's get the fuck out of here," Malik pushed Lars toward the door that sent him falling up against it and off to the side.

Malik slid past a glaring Lars and moved out the door. Lars stood for a brief moment and concentrated his focus on the bodies that were laid out on the floor. He cracked a wicked smile from the corner of his mouth as he placed the gun back into his waistband. With one last look taken, Lars gathered some spit in his mouth and released it out and onto the young laid out fellas. He turned and walked out the door with no care and no remorse. It was just another night in the jungle to him.

The early AM night sparkled with a summer breeze that only the north could feel the sensation that mixed with an artic push. Lars and Malik casually and with no care, leaned up against the front of the falling-apart caravan just outside one of the many Arab markets that littered the northeast side of the city. It was both sad and funny that this neighborhood was close to eighty-five percent black, but non-black peoples owned ninety-five percent of the businesses. Economic control was still in the hands of others after all the civil rights, protests and speeches and after all that, it only led to another form of slavery that had been colored to the population that dominated this land. This distinction always bothered Malik, who questioned this at a young age, and yet it seemed that no one really cared as long as they could get their pork chops for under a dollar, their milk for a dollar and their malt liquor for whatever the market set it at just as long as it was in abundance and it did it's job – keeping the eyes in a fog in an attempt to escape the misery and hopelessness that surrounded.

Malik enjoyed his apple bite by bite, letting each piece digest fully, while Lars gulped down a Heineken beer in a tall, green bottle. They had just completed the job for the night and now they each took in the early morning, 3AM breeze and relaxed with some cash in their pocket.

Lars set what was left of the beer down beside him and started to massage the very knuckles that had beaten a young Blackman to a bloody pulp and left him for dead. He took no pity at what he had done. It came with the game, so he thought. His heart was hardened and his ego was filled with maintaining a reputation on the streets that many heads were aware of.

Malik stopped the apple eating and glanced over at Lars who was making sure that nothing was broken. Malik returned back to his apple, finished it off and thru the core in a bag that laid on the hood. Something was building up inside of him that he had to get off his chest at that moment. "This shit is getting old B," Malik calmly stated in a laid back nature.

Lars refused to respond right away. He just let the words sit there for a moment and linger in space. Not cause he didn't want to hear the statement but because he didn't care. To him this was the shit that makes him and puts him on stage where he can feel some sort of power and if it was getting old, so what. He took his time, being somewhat annoyed at Malik and his constant badgering about how they have been getting paid lately. Malik knew what it really meant to be a gangster and it wasn't staying trapped in one position and it definitely wasn't preying on the poor. That was the mark of real suckers.

Lars continued to rub his knuckles that were now clean of the blood that had smothered over his hands and stained in the creases. "What are you bitchin' about now?"

"I'm sayin this shit we're doing. And that's all it really is. Straight bullshit," Malik said as he raised his long white t-shirt to reveal the gun tucked snug into his waistband. "You know what I'm sayin'? Let's look at what we're really doing out here son. Swiping a few dollars here and there while putting our fuckin' necks on the chopping block. And for what?" Malik looked out at the avenue scenery. "I'm about fed up with this creeping & jacking we've been doin, ya know."

"And. You going to go and look for a nine to five now? Who in the fuck is going to hire your ass?" Lars stated more than asked with a sarcastic chuckle.

"Ain't nothing wrong with a time clock position brother. At least you don't have to keep looking over your shoulder or have one eye open when you rest."

Lars cracked a small, amused smirk as he looked out into the night. "You're fucking around, right? Tell me your just playing cause, I can't see you behind no fuckin' counter talking about 'can I help you mam."

"Look it us star. We're out here knocking off these young heads that are nothing more then pawns, doing the dark side a favor. And you know what I mean by that, and what will happen if they catch us – "

Lars stopped him at the thought of being caught. "If! Mutha-fucka stop"

"They'll either kill us and call it justified, or they'll send our black asses to prison. Now what?"

"Don't be scurred," Lars mocked.

"This is exactly what they want us to do, you better believe. Making them relevant. We're doing their fucking job for them son. And the thing is," said Malik who became more animated and excited as the roll to shape and form with substance, "these kids out here scrambling, are trying to get it like you and me, and then we take it from them."

"You dam right," shot back Lars.

"The cycle continues son," Malik took a pause. "So tell me, what does that make us?"

Lars pulled out a fat roll of money and put it in Malik's face. "Paid nigga!"

"Wake the fuck up son," said Malik as he pushed Lars' hand out of his face. "That makes us blood suckers, since we're following up a wrong with a wrong and doing wrong with it. And you know, it's making me sick. For real. I can feel it."

"Then take a fuckin' aspirin B."

"You take a fuckin' aspirin. This is real shit L."

"Real shit huh? Look nigga, we just came up tonight something lovely and here you are on the soapbox, doing your preaching. What's up with all this?"

"What we get tonight? Five hundred? A thou? Fifteen hundred? What?" Malik lowered the head that he shook in disappointment. "This whole game we run in is set up by them for us, to get us, I'm telling ya B. Shit is wicked."

Lars took a drag on a cigarette that he just lit up and slowly turned to Malik. "Ya know, you're sounding a little bit too much like Malcolm Muhammad Garvey right now," joked Lars with a slight laugh.

"Whatever, I'm talking real talk right now."

Lars wiped the smile off his face and sucked on his teeth as he gave a curious glance from the corner of his eye on to Malik.

Malik realized the conversation was going nowhere but at least he had put his thoughts out there so Lars could have an idea of his direction. However, Lars was not listening to what Malik was speaking. Malik pulled out his do-rag and wrapped it around his tight knitted cornrows that were laid straight to the back. "I saw Divine the other day."

"Yea, what's he up to?" Lars asked with no real care.

"Doing the college thang. He was telling me about the set up out there. Something lovely. Made me want to go and check it out."

Lars rubbed his eyes and then with his mouth wide open, turned and stared at him for a moment. "What the fuck is going on here? You are on that shit tonight. Now it's college?"

"I just see the time that tells me it's time to really do something. And this game, this hustle we're doing, it's a dead end for us."

"What the fuck?! It pays the bills. It puts clothes on our backs. It feeds our stomachs."

"There's other ways of – "

An upset Lars interrupted as he moved off the hood, and took a few steps away from Malik and faced him. "No, there isn't. Not for me. Not out here. This is who I am, right here. I love getting this money, these things, doing these niggas left and right," Lars flashed his chain medallion, "and the hustle, even if it is bullshit small money right now, it's me. So you do what you gotta do. Go to college, pick up a broom, or whatever. But, and don't take this personal, but fuck you B. I can't and I won't leave this."

Lars returned his eyes toward the street and put out his cigarette underneath his foot as he stared out into the night.

A moment of silence was cast as each looked off in opposite directions. Malik sensed the tension that had developed and turned and looked over at Lars, seeing he needed to lighten the situation. "Stop taking everything so personal you fuckin' girly man," Malik said with a smile that broke out on his face.

"Man, fuck you," Lars said with a smile that eked out on his.

"You heading over to mommies?"

"True."

"Handle your business then. I'm out B," Malik extended his hand that was taken by Lars and shook. "Be safe and stay strapped with that hot stuff cuz it's out here, waitin' in the cut."

"And so am I," Lars said as he patted his waist.

"One."

"One baby," Lars shot back with movement made out of the street and on to the sidewalk. He stood and looked around the area then moved his eyes onto Malik. Lars understood at that moment that Malik was in search of something more that would not be found were he was going. Lars didn't desire no hourly pay job, had no patience to wait, and no college could do him any benefit. For him, it was the game that would take him one-way or the other. Now he needed a test. He needed something that would push Malik to see his way. Lars was concerned were Malik was heading and how it could effect his moneymaking ways. But what? What could he use to force Malik's hand? He had to find out if Malik would be willing to go all the way with him in this world that he yearned to conquer. He wanted the fly crib, the stacks of paper, the glittering rides and the diamond crusted bracelets and to do that and obtain that, he knew what it was going to take for him to get that. He had to show Malik that it was in him too.

Malik entered the caravan, started it up, eventually after a couple attempts failed, then pulled off down the avenue. Lars closely watched the caravan disappear into the early morning night. He slowly walked to his late 80's BMW three series car as he counted some money that was in his pocket. He slid into the driver seat and drove off in the opposite direction at a high speed.

Malik and Lars stood in the packed pool room and played against a couple of older men in their forties for some money that laid on the edge of the pool table with a drinking glass on top of the bills. Lars aimed, eyed and sank the eight ball. Malik moved over to the side of the pool table and gathered up the cash. Lars strutted up to Malik's side and the two split up the dough with a small, victorious grin.

Malik and Lars walked thru the south side of the city were groups of people were gathered outside of the various storefronts that were situated on the street. They roamed side by side and shared some small talk about sports, women and music while they greeted and spoke with the many people that they knew who were enjoying the early part of the summer wind blow.

Malik and Lars gathered with a bunch of neighborhood acquaintenances of all ages in the basement of one of the guys who had built a homemade music studio. Malik moved from the couch and into the booth. He put on the headphones, nodded for the person to start the beat, leaned into the microphone and with the nod of his head, let out his vocals that attracted the attention of those who took notice in the rhyme being spit.

Lars stood in the background and took a drink from his bottle of Corona beer as he kept his eyes focused on Malik.

Malik let it out,

"We got Motherly men, fatherly women/Babies with too much, elders with not enough/Romantic fellas/I did good tellers that lust for Stella in a world gone mad and sad/A world in the stone age/Filled with a savage rage."

Malik and Lars stood outside one of the dance clubs that was located downtown on a Friday night that brought a variety of people out to enjoy the taste of liquor and the sight of faces and bodies. Each traded words with various men and women, as they stood side by side. Malik was gifted with the ability to relate with women of any kind. Whether they were gold-diggers, college girls, independent women, older women, thugs, sweet loves, or just those that have been abused in a number of ways. He understood that they needed something more then what was seen and thought of as being a man. To him, man was nothing more then a weak vessel that had succumbed to hoarding God's gifts and submitted to females on all fours. He saw that it was necessary to become more then just that and find the courage to rise up and live. He went thru many women in an effort to show them that something else existed that new how to love correct and firm. Malik and a young lady who wore little make up with a pair of jeans and a comfortable shirt, stood in close contact with each other, sharing some calm and peaceful words with each other. Her well-formed breasts lightly touched Malik's chest that rippled his shirt upon contact. Malik leaned into her ear and spoke of his interest in her, her body and her love that he needed and wanted to be touched with. She had never heard this spoken to her in a state of such bold honesty and with a touch that blew past just sex. It brought a smile to her face to hear the invitation and feel the flirtations.

On the other side, Lars collected some money with pleasure from two young boys who were under the age of fifteen. With no smile, Lars made sure the young eyes took heed in his seriousness when it came to the dollars. The downtown scene was really jumping with traffic on the avenue moving at a snail pace. Malik and Lars took it in and relished the moment being side by side.

Under the lights of a local basketball court in the heart of the city, near downtown, in between the south side and the north, Lars and Malik engaged in a one on one basketball game as night descended on the skyline. The play between the two was extremely physical and filled with an unheard tension. There was something in the air that the two were getting of their chest at that moment in the course of the action and it demanded attention. Malik gave a few elbows. Lars extended a few hard pushes. Malik furiously blocked Lars shot. Lars dug his shoulder in to Malik's mid-section to throw him back and then went into score with no remorse. Each traded eyes but no words. It was clearly heard what was not being spoken. The two young men traded buckets with satisfying looks. A change was to come and each was fighting the other for the direction and the victory in the game.

Late into the night when the rain sprinkled it's drops on the city ground to refresh, Lars and Malik hung out together at a friend's apartment that was on the south side of the city. This was one of many places that Malik let his head dig deep into a pillow and rest his eyes at. The small apartment in a rundown complex that showed the lack of care for housing for the poor in the inner city had only one bedroom and was cluttered with everything from old shoes, dirty clothes, empty containers, music equipment and broken furniture.

Lars and Malik sat on separate, mist-matched chairs that were close to the small television set that had music videos playing on it as it sat on a tall, door-less cabinet. A young lady in a dark-colored t-shirt and jogging pants entered in the front room from the kitchen area with a couple bowls of hot food in her hands. She set the steaming bowls down on the wood table that was placed in between the young men. The thirty-something year old Black woman with long, thin braids and a solid smile that revealed her bright teeth, ushered out a smile to each and asked if they needed anything else where upon she was told that the two were good to go along with appreciations for her help with an emergency ride and some good food. The caravan had broke down again and had left them stranded on the highway after completing a smash and grab job on a suburban liquor store. She leaned down to Malik and in his ear with a sweet and soft voice, let him know that she was about to leave and that he should give her a call so they can do something soon. Malik nodded in agreement as he blew on his lentil soup to cool it off and then received a kiss on his cheek that moved down onto his neck from the young lady with a parting bye. Lars took no notice in the wave of affection being showered on his partner. He was a little too busy with his beer and soup along with the sexy body shaking her ass on the screen.

Lars and Malik continued to eat and enjoy the homemade dish as another music video came over the eighteen-inch screen on the black and white set that exposed a number of black women shaking their rear ends in very little covering.

Lars finished a spoon full of the soup then washed it down with a swig of his beer. Then a thought that he had been rolling over inside his head popped up at that moment. "I've been thinking about what you said the other night."

"When?" Malik asked as he picked his head up from his bowl.

"After that job, in front of the market."

"Aright, yeah, I remember. You thinking about coming to school with me?" Malik asked in a laid back tone as he examined his food.

"Fuck no. But I know a way to get us out of this bullshit hustle we've been doing," Lars plainly stated as he picked his eyes up and looked directly at Malik.

Malik, without raising his head, picked his eyes up from his bowl and met up with Lars' eyes for a brief moment then lowered them back down in between spoonfuls.

He prepared to hear something foolish and clumsy coming out of Lars' mouth. Lars just didn't get it when it came to the fact of how Malik felt about their past activity and the plans he had for the future. Yes, he was a part of it, his hands were dirty from the many days and nights in the mud pit, but there always comes a time to answer for things not corrected. Malik felt he had to check himself and make the proper corrections when it came to this part of his life to better himself. He had to clean his hands and come correct "So what's your plan Lex Luther?"

Lars took his time as he finished a swallow of his beer then lifted his eyes back on to Malik. "We hit Brim."

Malik dropped the spoon in his bowl and fell back in his chair. He exhaled a breath with his eyes that looked away from his childhood boy and up at the ceiling. Did he say what he thought he said? Brim was a mini-major supplier of drugs to the inner city market. He had carved out and leased large territories that he ran and prospered from. The only thing about Brim was he remained in the city. He didn't move away out into the boon-docks. Brim was the type of individual who dared you to cross him, because any act that went against his wishes, justified the penalty to come and he had no problem delivering punishment.

Malik brought his right hand to his face that then caressed his chin with his eyes turning from the ceiling and on to Lars who had been staring at him the whole time, waiting for his response and reading his expression. "What the fuck is wrong with you?" Malik said calm and slowly.

"What the fuck is wrong with me? Nah, what the fuck is wrong with you? You were right about this small money we've been chasing," Lars hollered back as he moved up in chair. "Here's a chance to step up our shit and make a nice come up that can set us up on the top floor. You feel me?"

"Nah, I don't feel you, but I'll tell you this. Hitting Brim is fucking suicide playa, one way or another. I know you love money and want to get out of the nickel and dime hustles, but that right there," Malik shook his head with his eyes looking straight at a frustrated Lars. "That's nothing to play with."

"Whose playing nigga? I'm telling ya, this is the move right here that can change the game for us. We can start doing some of the big things that we've always talked about doing."

"At the same time putting us in a worse position. And Brim," Malik said with a sharp glare in Lars' direction. "That nigga is no front door beat down cat, you hear what I'm saying." Malik moved up in the chair and leaned close in to Lars who had turned his head away from a serious minded Malik. "It means bodies. It means no return. It means no peace. Forget that move son. Leave it alone."

Lars took a deep and let out an exhausted breath as he set the bowl of lentils and rice down on the table and, with hesitation and doubt, nodded his head in acknowledgment toward Malik. Lars might have agreed at this moment, but underneath the gestures, he had found his avenue to reel in Malik and check his heart in the game.

Somewhat relieved but not convinced, Malik resumed eating. He picked his head up and observed another young, sexy lady on the television who was dressed in a thong and bra doing pelvic thrusts that Malik spoke on as if the subject they just spoke about never took place. He had seen enough of this. He thought, when would the real innovators, the ones with videos and music that have something to say be allowed to take center stage? Too much bullshit was floating around these days and it was killing the babies and the art. Malik would hardly listen to the radio, and the television stations that showed videos were even worse. He picked up the remote and began to run thru the channels.

Lars, paying no attention to the television, leaned back in his chair, scratched his nose then rested his head on his hand. All he could think about was his next move and how to pull it off.

Lars stood alone on a dark corner on the south side of the city, underneath a streetlight that illuminated the area were the young man in jean shorts and a tank top thought in silence. He leaned up against the brick wall of an old building and smoked a Newport cigarette. His head was lowered to the ground as the smoke was released out from his mouth and floated away into the muggy night.

In a distance came a Lexus GS300 were the base of the music playing from inside was heard and felt. The booming sound got louder and clearer as the chrome rims arrived at the back of Lars' forest green BMW. The sight of the two vehicles revealed the level of paper accumulation that Lars' eyes took notice in. The doors opened and out stepped a couple of Blackmen, one dark skinned and the other light skinned who was behind the wheel. They took a moment and upon noticing Lars, they alternated looks at each other and cracked a small grin as they made their way toward Lars with a confident swagger. The three young men shared a round of pounds and hugs as 'what up's' were exchanged and tossed back and forth. Crimson, the ball headed dark skinned Blackman who sported some RocaFella jeans and a polo pullover with a platinum chain that swung back and forth with a Jesus piece dangling from it, pulled out a freshly rolled marijuana blunt and lit it up. Todd, with a short s-curl fade that went along with his pretty boy attitude, checked his Blackberry Pearl that relayed a message to him. Dressed in a button down shirt that laid unbuttoned to show off his muscular build in a white wife-beater tank top along with a pair of Gucci sweatpants and a black pair of brand new Air Jordan's, the young man's eyes were glued to his technology toy. Crimson and Todd were known around the city as Brim's main men and top earners. And both of them were familiar with Lars and his reputation. Matter of fact, they had tasted a few ass-whippings from the hands of Lars when they were little boys running around the neighborhood. That was then and now on this night and in this day they were especially interested with Lars' money-hungry hustling ways that had kept him an independent on the street scene. They were also aware of Malik.

They smelled an opening and the possibility of the earning potential someone like Lars could bring to Brim's operation, but also to their pockets since he would be under them.

All Lars could think when he took a look at the twenty-something year old men was billboard city straight out of these rap music magazines. These mutha-fuckas may have looked the part but down deep, Lars knew they didn't possess one ounce of unmerciful heart that he had. To him, they were nothing more then 'Hollywood' ass niggas.

Crimson, standing on one side of Lars, blew the weed smoke out into the night and casually, with an air of curiosity, looked over on to Lars. "Watcha doing out here Lars? Thought you weren't working like that. Didn't you say that you don't sell rocks?"

Crimson shifted his eyes to his partner Todd who stood on the other side of Lars and both the young men cracked a cock-eyed grin that revealed the gold tooth in Crimson's mouth. Crimson offered the blunt to Lars who put out the cigarette on the sidewalk then reached and took the offered blunt in hand, followed by the preparation to take a drag on it.

"What the fuck does it look like niggas? I'm just chilling. Do I have to be slinging that to be out here?"

Lars took a drag on the blunt and held it in as he passed it to Todd who had finished with his texting business on his brand new device and attached it back to his hip. He took the blunt and just as he was about to bring it to his mouth, the 50 Cent 'Get Money' ring-tone went off again. "Dam," Todd blurted out. He took a quick look down on his hip at the larger than normal screen for a cell phone, then turned his attention on to Lars with ease. "Chilling huh? Looks like someone out here is a little indecisive and doesn't know how to really get it," commented Todd as he shot a glance toward his partner.

Lars took his eyes off the broken concrete and dived straight into Todd's low lids that covered his pupils that were facing out into the night of the street. "What is it?" Asked Todd who turned his head and looked at Lars. "No heart to really be in the game?"

Lars flipped-flopped his glances from one young man to the other that stood at his sides. "Why are you all fucking with me tonight? I'm really not in the mood for you mutha-fuckas. Don't you two got to go and jack each other off?"

Crimson bent over slightly and looked at Todd. "He got jokes."

"I'll tell ya what you need to do," Todd announced as he took a drag on the one-quarter length blunt. "You need to kick that bitch ass nigga you run and rob pennies with to the curb and get with some real players and make some long paper." Todd, with a straight face, pulled out a large roll of rolled money rubber-banded up and glared at Lars with it in hand. "You know what I'm sayin?"

"So is that what I need to do?" Lars questioned with sarcasm as he took the blunt from Todd's grasp. He was impressed but that was not going to be shown on this night and especially to these two jokers.

"Black, we're only concerned about you out here. You've been in this hustle awhile. Longer then a lot of us. And what do you got to show for it? Nothing but a pussy on your team who is causing you to fall from the block hierarchy. Time is a tickin dog." Crimson said with a touch of urgency.

Lars blew the weed smoke out and passed what was left of the blunt. Both Crimson and Todd rejected it so he tossed it into the street. "I'm falling of the hierarchy huh?" Questioned an amused Lars with a slight grin cocked from the corner of his mouth.

"No doubt dog, take a look around. What the fuck do ya see? Where's the real money at?" Crimson quizzed. He then moved up close to Lars and placed his arm around his neck as he leaned his head toward Lars. "Out here, in this, we can never let another booty-ass nigga dictate what we are going to do and how. Otherwise, in the end, you'll be like these fiends, on the block and in panties – "

Todd moved up close to Lars' ear, "And your boy will be driving luxury style. You hear what we're saying?"

A silent Lars kept focused on the cracks in the sidewalk with his head lowered. Over and over, he had asked himself the same question regarding him and Malik. 'Is he holding me back?'

Crimson and Todd picked up their heads and met eyes that revealed a sinister objective. They knew what it meant to get Lars to play on their team. He was an asset worth recruiting. And to do this, they had to separate him from Malik cause they were well aware that he was not open to playing with them and for them.

"We can see you're hurtin' playa. So you better get your shit right or else," Todd said then backed away from Lars and unhooked his Blackberry from his hip.

"The way you're going, you might be working for him right now and you just don't know," Crimson said as he stepped forward toward the Lexus and motioned with his head to Todd that it was time to leave.

"So the question is, are you a player or a playa?" Todd quizzed with a sly accent to illustrate motivation. He moved away as he began to push buttons on the over-sized keypad and joined Crimson in the walk to their ride. "When you find out, you know my number."

The two well-shaven young men got in their ride and turned their faces to Lars who glared at them. At the same time both Crimson and Todd broke out in laughter. Crimson started the luxury ride with Jay-Z booming from the custom stereo and zoomed off down the dark block.

Lars stood still up against the wall with the bottom of one of his feet posted up against the brick. He turned from the direction that the Lexus disappeared to and up into the black sky. He licked his lips, took a deep breath then let his head fall to the ground. Who in the fuck did these g-money kids think they were? How dare they talk to him like that? Lars was incensed with the disrespect that was thrown at him. Then it came to him, 'these were the pillow-heads that will be my test'. It all was so clear to him at that moment.

On the fringe, just outside the downtown area, existed an area know as the 'Banks'. A place were immigrants from Africa resided in tall tower buildings that stood in various areas along with café's, small shops, and various bars and clubs all along the main street that was full of activity on this night.

Malik and Divine, a young Blackman in his twenties with a burly nature that some would say was fat and sloppy but fit him just perfect, dressed in a pair of old faded dark blue jeans with a no-brand t-shirt, moved out of the grocery store. Malik exchanged handshakes and greetings with a couple older men who only wanted everybody around to see that they knew Malik. The two confident and calm young men shared some quick, back and forth words that were thrown with precision and went fully understood by each.

Just as they were parting ways, Lars, in his car, drove up and viewed Malik and Divine with a questioning look about the nature of their conversation. Divine and Lars really never got along and always stayed at an arms length from each other with little acknowledgment given in both directions. Lars saw Divine as too square and too abstract to deal with. Divine on the other hand saw that Lars was too much in the grip of money and only cared for the angle he could work to get what he desired.

Divine and Malik ended the brotherly words and came to grip with their hands that pulled them close in contact were they traded a meaningful hug that merged the two into one. Divine turned and headed off down the sidewalk but before he moved to far away, his eyes caught the site of a suspecting Lars who had just exited his ride and gave a 'what up' with a small head nod that had the too cool to show any love connotation attached to it. Divine made his way down the block, thru the sea of people and garbage that surrounded and filled the area. Bit by bit and step-by-step, his firm figure moved out of view.

Malik fell back and stood up against the grocery that he just exited. He observed Lars approaching him from the street were he parked his car and extended his hand that Lars took with his right hand. He pulled him close and gave a deep hug that was loosely and with no real care returned by Lars. Something was on his mind and exchanging a hug was not it. Malik then noticed a SUV drive by down the block that honked. He raised his right fist to acknowledge the moving vehicle. Lars stepped to the side of Malik and gave a look both ways down the street then on to the people that gathered and moved about to sell tapes, black market items, and ask for change or a dollar to get some food, that was said, but the truth was to buy a bottle of beer or a pint of rum. Others just lurked for easy prey that was in abundance in the Banks.

Even around the madness, filth and helplessness, Malik was able to relax back as he finished his juice. Lars turned his attention on to Malik.

"I saw Brim's boys last night," Lars said plainly, looking for reaction as his eyes turned away from Malik.

"Who that? Crimson and Todd, them funny kids?"

"Funny? Those kids are rolling fiesta style. Lexus, chains, stylish garments, new Jordan's, the whole shit."

Malik placed his eyes with out moving his head on to Lars. "Aren't they like Brim's top-dollar boys."

"Yep."

"Then I see why. That man has had a grip on the blocks for years now."

"And look it us," Lars said with disgust.

"Ahh, come on son. Don't start."

"Yea, I'm going to start, cause what I saw last night were a bunch of floss heads making major chips out here when they don't got one grain of what I have," Lars said with frustration as his eyes canvassed Malik.

"We're doing aright."

"Is that all you want to do, is aright?"

"It's better then being trapped behind bars or laying six feet under. Patience baby boy, patience."

Lars rose up from the grocery store's glass window that advertised accepting food stamps, walked a few steps away and then slowly turned and looked at a calm and relaxed Malik with pure anger in his eyes. He was tired of Malik's half-stepping. He wanted it all and he did not want to be held back any more. A choice was going to have to be made. "Fuck patience! See, that's one thing I noticed about them kids. They have no fear. Not about prison, these marks or death. They put it all on the line and they walk in this hell with their balls swinging."

Malik took a moment and sharpened his eyes that beamed right at Lars. He sensed the displeasure in Lars and understood were he was heading. "You call that walking in hell with balls swinging?" Malik took a moment and glared at Lars. "You aright B?"

"Naah, I'm not aright. I'm fucked up right now. Some things ain't sitting pretty and lotta the shit they said was . . ." An emotional Lars caught himself from going any further. He backed up a couple steps and wiped the saliva that had escaped out his mouth.

Malik showed no response to what he just learned and observed from Lars. He knew it was coming to this. It was just a matter of how far it would be taken. "So watcha saying L?"

"I'm saying, where's your heart at nigga?" Lars started to walk off toward his car. A beggar decided not to ask a furious Lars for any change when he saw the fury in his eyes. The tattered old man quickly made his way from Lars and out of his sight.

Malik, still up against the wall and with a comforting expression, followed Lars with his eyes. "What are you getting all upset about?"

Lars continued to move off toward the car, "I'm tired of mutha fuckas stopping my groove. You hear what I'm saying?"

Malik leaned down and placed the bottle of juice down on the sidewalk by his side then stood back up and gave a look down the busy street. "So you out?"

Lars opened his car door then turned his ambitious eyes toward Malik whose own moved up with his were they locked on to each other for a moment. "Yea, I'm out. I gotta handle a few things."

"Be safe baby boy."

Nothing was returned. Lars got inside his car that had some trouble getting started, but eventually turned over and he pulled off down the block in a rush.

Malik moved off the window and observed Lars drive off. A feeling of concern overcame him. Not only for himself, but also for Lars. He realized this was a decision that Lars must make. As for Malik, he'd be there until the cord was severed.

It was 3AM in an abandoned parking lot in an isolated section of the city that was filled with condemned buildings, railroad tracks and old bars that rarely did business when not catering to the poor people who spent whatever was left over after the bills took most of the week's earnings.

In the dark parking lot sat a gray Ford Taurus with it's motor off. Through the window sat a dark figure silhouette that lifted an arm to check his wristwatch. Lars' BMW pulled in slowly and came to a stop right next to the spotless car. Lars exited his ride, looked around the place as he made his way toward the vehicle and got inside. The dome light illuminated Crimson's face sitting in the driver seat with a grin. The two sat in the dark interior for a moment and held a conversation in the hushed darkness. Lars had made the decision and had chosen the path to take. This was an opportunity that he could not resist and it was time to move up in the game. All that could be distinguished thru the dark windows was burning cigarette ashes when they were inhaled.

The brief conversation came to an end. Handshakes were exchanged then Lars exited the vehicle that pulled off and out of the parking lot, leaving Lars standing at his car.

"Make this happen. Make this happen," Lars said as he flicked his cigarette to the ground and then hopped into his ride that he had left running and drove away thru a back alley.

Roberta Hammond, a nineteen-year old, caramel-skinned beauty, rested her well-formed head on the hairless chest of Malik in Roberta's parents home. The movie 'Blow' played on the television that the embraced couple enjoyed viewing as they relaxed with each other. Roberta took her delicate and gentle hand that went along with her soft light-brown skin and relaxed, dark long hair that illuminated her green eyes that were real, and massaged a scar on Malik's bicep. She moved her full lips up to Malik's and the two begin to feel each other' mouth, inside and out. Malik wrapped his arms around her physically fit body and pulled her firm and fit figure close to him. The kiss continued with no break and then the cell phone, with a distinctive Darth Vader tone, went off. Malik opened his eyes, aware of what that tone meant – it was Lars. Roberta didn't want him to answer it as she wrapped her biceps and curled her strong thighs around him to hold in place. Malik broke the kiss and gave her a look that demanded a release.

Malik moved over to the bookshelf that was littered with all types of African-American history, literature and biography books. Everything from W.E.B. DuBois to the Civil Rights Movement to Uncle Tom's Cabin to Nat Turner.

Malik picked up the cell and pushed the button to answer. "Yea." Malik said with a touch of disappointment as he adjusted the discomfort in his jeans that revealed his aroused nature from the feminine touch of Roberta. He then listened to the voice of Lars. "What's the deal?" Asked Malik who turned and headed out of the room. Roberta watched him closely move out of sight then laid back in the couch with a disappointed yet concerned look.

Malik took a seat on the corner of Roberta's bed in her bedroom. "Well right now I'm with this sweet little honey dip. You aright?" Malik listened to what Lars needed from him. "What?" Malik needed more information so Lars went into an explanation that would satisfy Malik. "Tonight?" Malik questioned as he sensed something wasn't right but this was his boy of too long. It was loyalty, it was friendship, and it was honor. The kind of honor that was hard to find when it came to Blackmen in the city. "Aright, aright. Where?" Down deep Malik felt the cord being yanked on. This could be the moment. This could be the door that I step into that I face a bullet cause of him. He kept on telling himself to do it right, cover all your bases, and make sure everything was known.

But down deep, nobody could be prepared for these types of moments, only aware. "I'll be there," confirmed Malik as he recalled the words that Lars spoke on the Banks. Of stopping his groove, his heart and Brim's boys making sense. "One." Malik pushed the button that hung up the cell and he threw it on the dresser. He fell back into Roberta's bed and stared up at the ceiling. He knew that all friendships go thru periods of challenge and adjustment. It was necessary to find out if friends were family or if friends were enemies. A change was upon Malik who was coming up on twenty-five years living and what he had been doing was going against the nature of his true self that had been kept submerged and now it was coming to the surface to take over. Would Lars walk the same path as he was prepared to do? How deep was their bond? Would Lars be there for him just as Malik was going to be there? As a flood of questions, answers and thoughts flew threw his mind, Roberta stood at the door and observed him for a quiet moment. She could sense that Malik had a ton of weight on his shoulders. How could she be of help? Malik felt a pair of soft eyes on him. He picked his head up just slightly and noticed the lovely sight looking on him from the entryway.

Roberta began to slowly move toward the bed. "I'm getting kind of lonely out there."

Malik reached his hand out toward her that was taken by Roberta. She moved gently and sensuously on top of him with their bodies barely touching each other as they looked into each other's alive eyes. No words, only a deep feeling of respect for each that brought their faces together slowly to feel each other's lips.

The night was lit up when the ashy flame from the cigarette burned orange when a drag was taken in deep. Malik pulled up in his caravan and let the brakes squeak to a stop as he parked behind Lars who sat on the trunk of the battered BMW. Malik stepped out of his vehicle and met up with and took a seat next to Lars who puffed away on the cigarette in the middle of the parked vehicles. Lars, with a small duffel bag draped around his shoulder, exchanged hands with Malik.

"Talk to me L," Malik demanded as he looked around the familiar neighborhood.

"I just need for you to watch my back in here," Lars said as he put out his cigarette. "One of these kids in here owes me some dough, and I intend to collect tonight. Can you do that?"

"Aright now, don't go getting crazy in there. Let's get in, get it, and get out."

"That's all I want," Lars confirmed with a slight grin.

Lars and Malik hopped off the trunk and began to walk to the desired house that was a few houses down from were they parked.

The two young men arrived at the two-story house and made their way around the large, fenced in place and to the backdoor. Lars gave a couple of hard and firm pounds then looked around the neighborhood of a quiet area in the city, or at least on this night. As he turned back, he caught the eyes of Malik, which were focused on him, and broke out an uncomfortable smile then faced back toward the door. It was at that moment that Malik sensed something, a feeling that gave him a brief chill.

The door opened to a relaxed Crimson, standing, who smiled at the site of Lars. The young man with a red Iverson jersey on allowed the two to enter the slanted, screened in porch. Crimson stopped them before they could go two steps more and patted both of them down on the porch way. He frisked Lars up and down and found nothing but failed to look inside the duffel bag. Crimson moved over to Malik as Lars gave him a few teasing words on his frisking technique. As he felt Malik's hip, he came across his 9mm pistol. Crimson let it be known that no guns were allowed inside. Lars cracked a small grin to ease the situation as Malik gave up the pistol to Crimson who promised to return it when their business was finished. Crimson motioned with his head to follow and led them thru the barely furnished house and upstairs. As they moved up the stairs, Malik took a glance back at Lars and caught a glimpse of him placing something from the duffel bag in his back area. Malik turned back around and thought about what he was walking into as the three arrived into a main room that had only couches, chairs and a couple tables.

Brim, an older Blackman in his mid forties with short hair that was all the same length and lined up perfectly all the way around, sat in the main chair draped in jewelry and an expensive suit. His eyes stay concealed behind the dark glasses he wore as he sat comfortably and confidently. He had known Lars every since he was a little boy terrorizing the neighborhood. Brim gave him a few jobs here and there that Lars executed to perfection. Todd stood behind his chair in a blue and white Addidas jogging suit with arms crossed.

Malik stepped into the room and immediately recognized the other two faces that were gathered along with Crimson. Malik's worst thoughts had come to fruition and he knew what he was in the middle of. He had some notion when that call came over the cell and the way of urgency that Lars had in his voice box, but this was the bad news he thought possible. Lars had put him a tight situation that he had to maneuver calmly in. Malik had walked into the lion's den and here he was playing the part of Daniel. Malik shot a look toward Lars that went unnoticed. How is he going to play this? His eyes quickly pin pointed the guns that were holstered on both Todd and Crimson.

Lars and Malik greeted each one with brief introductions made by Crimson followed by some small talk then each took a seat and made them selves comfortable. Malik knew that at any moment, anything could pop off and he sensed that it most likely was going to.

Crimson remained standing to the side of Lars as he rubbed his hands together in excitement and anticipation. "Let's make some real money now playa." He gave a couple of pats to the back of Lars then picked his head up from him and flashed a grin.

Todd continued to stand behind Brim with no expression, stone faced, as his concentration was focused on the two sitting men but mainly in Malik's direction. "Did you bring – " Lars, who was discomforted and needed to use the bathroom and quick, cut off Todd quickly.

Malik remained calm and looked around the place and the faces with out being detected. Lars moved up in his seat. "Hold up. First, I have to use yawls bathroom. I've been holding this piss for the longest," Lars squirmed around. "Where's the spot I can use?"

Todd looked down at Brim who directed his look toward Crimson who returned the look to Brim and then looked at Lars who returned the look to Brim, Crimson and Todd while Malik took a casual glance toward Lars. Malik sensed that the awkward moment smelled of unusual business and by the look on their faces, they were alert to it, so he thought.

"Their clean," Crimson chimed in then Brim slowly nodded that allowed Crimson to point in the direction of the bathroom.

Lars moved off into the small washroom a few paces down the hall and closed the door.

Malik remained sitting back calm. Lars had placed him in a deadly spot without any word of preparation or notice. This was truly the oven with no hand of honor present. He could tell by the look in these men's eyes that they would have no problem putting two in his head and burying him out in Whiteville. He observed the magazines that were spread out on the center table. He picked one up and began to flip thru it.

Crimson was ushered over to Brim as Todd leaned down and the three held a brief and hushed conversation. With an agreement made, Crimson returned close to Malik and away from Brim as he kept an eye on the bathroom while he moved slowly and cautiously around the room. Brim backed up in the seat and pulled out a cigar that he moistened then searched for a light.

Todd remained standing behind Brim with the gun swinging back and forth from under the jogging suit jacket inside.

Brim leaned forward toward Crimson who lit the cigar for him. "You're boy better not be playing with my time," warned Brim.

"Then he would be playing with mine," shot back Malik with a casual tone.

Brim removed the glasses and locked eyes with Malik for a moment. The big-time, street supplier saw the realness in the eyes that bought him a feeling of comfort. That was why Lars needed Malik with him. Anybody else and it would have been a gunfight the moment the bathroom was brought up. Not with Malik, cool as a cucumber. He leaned back in his chair, placed the glasses back on, and puffed away on his cigar. "The only reason I allowed to meet with you two is cause Crimson vouched for that nigga in there," Brim explained as he exhaled the smoke. "So, if any thing goes wrong, he'll be the one that will deal with you. I don't give a fuck about you, just so ya know."

Malik nodded that he understood the consequences, but down deep all he could think of was Lars and what was he doing and what he was going to do. He flipped thru the pages of the Source magazine and checked out a couple fine ladies who showed off some clothing attire. "Ladies look so ugly in this type of get up," Malik commented as he showed the go-go girl outfit to Crimson.

"I'll take it though," said Crimson with a sly smile, admiring the girls figure.

As Malik continued to flip from one page to the next, Lars exited the bathroom with wet hands that he held out, dripping water that fell to the floor.

"What the fuck! Y'all don't got no hand towels or anything."

Lars began to dry them off on his oversized, gray sweatshirt. As he rubbed them on his jeans and moved them toward his back to finish the drying session, he reached smoothly into the back of his baggy pants and pulled out a chrome forty-five. He whipped it out with silent ease and aimed it sideways.

Before Crimson could react, he was hit with two shots to the chest that threw him on his back, over the couch and on to the floor. He took his last breath with his eyes wide open.

As Crimson was getting laid out, Malik, with the speed of a ninja, dove over the couch for cover and got down low. His gun had been given over to another, which brought a sense of comfort in the frisk. Malik took a look at the body near by and the gun that laid close by.

Lars, firing non-stop, stepped into the middle of the room. Todd yanked his gun out of his holster and got a handle on it quickly as he moved forward. His aim was terrible. The two shots he was able to get off missed Lars and lodged into the wall. Lars cracked a grin and fired two shots that hit Todd in the chest and the neck, slamming him to the wall.

The light-skinned young man slowly dropped to a sitting position. Inch by inch, he slumped over and died as the blood leaked out of his neck.

Brim remained sitting as his two gunmen were lying in their own blood. He knew that all he could do is hold on to his honor since he wasn't holding no steel. Plus, this kid better know who he was messing with and who had his back. But this was Lars, he was no kid and he didn't care who had his back or who he was messing with.

Malik, who had finally got the gun in hand, picked his head up and looked at the bodies on the floor. "Yo Lars!"

Lars continued to grin at Brim as he lowered the shiny piece of steel to his side and moved toward the older man. He placed the gun to the temple and grabbed him by his silk tie. "Now what nigga!? Whose the major mutha-fucking man now?"

"Lars!" Malik stood up and faced a crazed Lars who had nothing but blood in his eyes like he did when he beat that street dealer down.

"What!?" Lars yelled back with irritation.

"What the fuck?

"What the fuck. You see what I just did nigga? Two down," Lars said as he turned back to Brim and grabbed him furiously by the chin. "And one to go. He was easier then a front door beat down. Now, were is it?"

"You just killed yourself boy," Brim said calmly, looking into Lars' wide opened eyes.

Lars wasted no time and delivered a solid shot to the side of Brim's head that knocked him out of the chair and on to the floor, next to Todd's dead body. Lars rushed over to him, picked him up, and slammed him up against the red, blood stained wall. "I'm going to ask you one more time. And if I don't get the answer I'm looking for, you're god dam dome is going to be on that wall along with that niggas'. Now, were?"

Brim took a moment and moistened his lips. His eyes darted around the room, contemplating the choices to be made, then focused back on to Lars and then toward the gun and back on to Lars' eyes that were glaring in a flame of pure hatred at him. "The floor in the back of the closet in that bedroom," Brim said with a head nod to illustrate the direction.

"Good boy," Lars uttered, breaking out a smile as he sent a couple of light slaps to the face of Brim. Lars turned to Malik who remained standing and watching him do his thing with no honor in a disappointing amazement. After everything, this was how it was going to go down between them. Played and betrayed in an egotistical way for the lust to obtain a sense of power that was far from real at the expense of their friendship. Malik kept his eyes focused on the thirsty young man who he considered more family then friend. Lars noticed Malik wasn't doing anything. "What the fuck?! You standing around, looking like decoration! Bag that shit!"

"So this is you huh?"

"Mutha fucka, we don't have time for a sermon."

"You should have listened to your boy," Brim chimed in.

"Shut the fuck up bitch!" Lars cracked Brim in the face with the butt of the gun that knocked him to the floor and opened him up. Lars turned his head and observed Malik wiping his prints off the pistol and then dropped the gun and moved to the stairway that led downstairs. "Were you going nigga!?"

Malik stopped with his back toward Lars for a quiet moment at the top of the stairs. With nothing said, he then walked out of the room, down the stairs and toward the back door as Lars continued to stand and alternate looks at Brim and in Malik's direction.

"Aright, run the fuck away. Bitch ass coward. I don't need you nigga. I don't need your scary ass! I'll do this by myself!" Lars turned back to a bleeding Brim who sat on the floor in pain.

Malik stepped out the back door, hopped over a fence and nonchalantly walked down the alleyway. A few steps and he heard the gun go POP, POP on his way toward his vehicle.

Malik sat on top of a picnic table that was near a local park basketball court on the south side of the city. He ate a green apple and watched a father and his son play basketball on the court that was empty except for the two, on this evening under the lights. The child took a fall, going after the ball, and the father urged him to be strong, get up and keep playing. Malik observed a sight that was rare out here in this day. He was overcome by a grand feeling of viewing a black father who showed his son how to be strong and fight and overcome the pain and the feeling of giving up.

Lars drove up in his brand new black late-model seven series BMW that was kitted up with chrome wheels and dark window tint. Lars parked crooked which took up two spots and exited the ride cool, calm and slowly made his way to where Malik was seated.

Lars hopped up on the picnic table and settled down next to Malik. He flicked his lighter up to a cigarette and placed it in his mouth were he took a drag on it, exhaling the smoke. The two quietly paid attention to the father and son.

"That must be nice," said Lars with a touch of jealousy as he broke the air of silence.

"That's on us with the choices we make for our seeds."

Silence, with a questioning tension that filled the air, settled in for a moment. Lars dropped his head, continuing to smoke on his cigarette. "You cool?"

Malik turned his head toward Lars, "Oh no doubt. I see you handled your business," said Malik as he gestured with his eyes in the direction of the shiny, black 745.

Lars broke out in a smile that showed satisfaction with his recent purchase. "You like that?"

"It's nice."

"Well, ya know, half of this is yours."

"That's aright. You did all the work."

"Can't argue with you there."

"So answer me one thing."

"What's that?" Lars looked up and engaged in an unsmiling eye contact with Malik for a brief period.

"Did you buy that or are you leasing?"

Malik let out a comforting smile that Lars returned. "Lease, you know how I do."

"Smart."

The two young men, one in jogging pants and the other in designer jeans, lowered their eyes to the ground.

"You still planning to head out to college?" Lars asked.

"You know it. I leave tomorrow morning."

"Cool, cool. Handle your business out there," Lars jumped off the picnic table and then stood and looked at the father and son playing with each other. "I better get out of here. I got a lot of things to take care of."

"I know you do. Brim's peoples are going to come hard."

"Ohh, I won't have to worry about them," said Lars with a wicked smile as his head turned and gazed toward the vehicle. "And either will you."

Malik rose up and stepped down off the picnic table. He moved in front of Lars whose eyes continue to dart to all sides around him. "You take care of yourself."

"You do the same B."

Malik and Lars extended and shared a firm handshake with eye contact then moved into each other's arms to embrace.

They broke apart and took a moment to look on one another as if to say with their eyes that this will be the last time we will look at each other in this state of caring and friendship. Each realized were the other was heading and it was in opposite directions. Lars turned with no care and walked with a cocky air away toward his vehicle. He was the king of the streets now. A humble Malik watched him move away and enter into his ride that pulled off and vanished down the block. He thought it is what it is, so be it and began to walk away from the court and across the grassy football field.

Malik gathered on a south side street corner that was hopping with activity as the night prepared to ascend on the city. He stood with a group of young men he went to high school with that were in all shapes, shades, styles and sounds. They talked with each other about anything and everything as young ladies passed by, drinks were consumed and weed was smoked. Malik stood next to Divine with crossed arms and two lovely dark-skinned women who showed off their minds and bodies that were too attractive.

As the fun continued on the block, Lars slowly rolled by in a black Mercedes CLK430 and sharpened his glare that spotted Malik and the group on the corner. Malik saw who was at the wheel of the shinny car that passed thru with windows down and another Blackman sitting in the passenger seat, bouncing his head to the beat with a scowl wrinkled on his face.

It was at that moment where everything seemed to slow down and all that existed in space was Malik and Lars. Their eyes locked hard on to one another for a moment that revealed the separating bond that had developed and was expressed in the nature of the glare. The true caring was gone and the connection had taken another form.

As one stood still on the cracked sidewalk and followed with the turning of his head, the other floated by on his thousand dollar wheels while keeping his eyes laced on the subject of interest. Far enough by in the opposite direction of each, eye contact was broke. Malik turned back to the group and the ladies. Lars turned his head to the front and drove off down the avenue with his boy. Malik and Divine continued to socialize, laugh and enjoy their time amongst the gathering of bodies. The choice had been made and the stage had been set.

CHAPTER TWO

One plus One equals two which will then answer the question 'Who'.

A Couple of Years Later . . .

THE RUNDOWN MOVIE theatre located in the heart of downtown was full with activity. 'ColoRain', a horror/slasher picture about a group of rap kids getting hacked up in the wilderness, sat on the marquee in big, black letters that was illuminated by powerful lights. Crowds of people, young and old, but mainly Black and Hispanic, since this part of the downtown area had been reduced to XXX shops, low-life bars and dirty streets that attracted a hostile, young element who searched for the white lady with a large rock on her finger as she sat behind the wheel of a luxury European vehicle. How dare she? She should know better, and because she failed to, she must be taught a lesson. That's how things rolled and it was getting worse with each President's speech that was made to numb so to overlook the real cause of the problem along with the solution needed, and guns, a lot of guns that had become a natural part of the wardrobe.

At the entrance of the six-screen theatre complex, a number of large congregations of young rowdy people smoked, drank, talked shit in various degrees with each other and prepared to head into the next showing of the movie.

A full house sat inside the two hundred plus seat auditorium and took in the visual that played on the large screen. A chatter of voices filled the air, either complimenting or condemning the actions while others messed around with each other with little interest in the movie.

Either way, it was pure chaos that left the movie secondary in attraction with all types of commotion and distractions taking front stage.

A few rows from the back of the place, in the middle of House number three, sat Malik and Divine who shared a tub of popcorn and each drank a bottle of water. In a relaxed position, the two young men, still looking fresh in their twenties, blocked out the extracurricular activity that surrounded them in all directions and focused their attention on the movie screen. Not much had changed physically but what went unseen was the experience that had been gained in the passing of time and the recognizing of right from wrong that led to a maturing nature.

The scene flashed up on the screen when one of the characters in the middle of the wilderness that is cast in pure darkness has an idea about what is going on but instead of turning around, he continues to move thru in the woods in search of a young woman who has just disappeared.

"Ahhh, fuck that hoe and her melon head," a young voice close to the front yelled out that was loud and obnoxious with no care of who was around. "Get the fuck outta there nigga!" He threw some popcorn at the screen and continued to shout. "This is some bullshit! He needs his dumb ass murked!"

"Yo dog, eeaasssyyy. It's just . . ." His partner spoke up with a twinge of agitation but at the same time being intimidated by the uncontrolled force of nature that was his partner to the side. These young voices knew nothing of restraint and respect. Everything was attack or be attacked.

"What? Fuck these niggas. I'll say what the fuck I want to say."

"Fuck you nigga!" Said a low and distinctly older voice that had heard the words of disrespect from a few rows back to the left that caused a few other heads to turn in both curiosity and awareness at the coming confrontation.

"Whose the mutha fucka that said that?" The young man who couldn't be more then twenty-years old demanded with an unbridled air of arrogance. He stood up, turned and scanned the audience for the face to reveal himself.

"You ain't gotta look far faggot," said the older man with a perm. He moved up in his seat and raised his head up with a glare thru his bloodshot red eyes that stayed stuck on the young voice.

Malik and Divine continued to make an effort to watch the movie as the commotion carried on in an aggressive and boasting nature, but their eyes were well aware of the situation and where it was heading.

"Aright nigga. I'm a remember you," said the young voice as he backed down an inch to catch his breath and let his anger simmer for a minute.

The older man in his early thirties sucked his teeth. "Remember it then little nigga! You ain't going to do nothing mutha fucka, but bump your gums, sit your ass down, and take it."

"Aright nigga, aright," said the short and stocky body with a big head who returned to his seat and looked up toward the screen. The movie was of no interest to him. All that was constantly building in him was anger and hate that was stroking his courage to take further action.

Silence and calm reigned over the place temporarily with heads turned up at the screen. Each hoping that the words would end there and calm would be sustained. Somehow the heated exchange had quieted all the other non-sense that was taking place before.

A cold breeze had swooped in and brought a violent chill to every one in attendance. Only the aware could feel it's meaning. It was just a matter of being detected so to move properly.

Malik and Divine were about to drop some popcorn in their mouths when their ears heard the sound of a set of clicks that a latch on a piece of steel makes when pulled back to put one in the chamber, one following after another. They both turned to each other and shared a knowing look with their eyes that communicated the intensity of the spilled emotions. They set their tub of popcorn down, finished their water, rose up smoothly and made their way toward the exit. As they advanced up the aisle, Malik spotted a group of gorgeous young girls from around the way who were engrossed into the urban horror picture. Malik took a few steps back and moved to his right side where he then kneeled next to the young lady who sat in the aisle seat, chewing on some gum. He leaned into her delicate ear that smelled sweet with a touch of ivory.

"Hey sweetness. How about you lovelies join me and my brother outside?"

The girl was at first a little shook at the abrupt advance out of nowhere and then taken back as if to say, 'who in the fuck is this and why is he bothering me', but quickly she then got a handle on the situation and took a lick of her lips to intensify the glistening effect of the applied lip balm. "What, what for? We're watching this movie."

"Not for long. You hear those sounds? Trouble is a coming love, ya hear."

The jean-wearing girl rolled her eyes with a sexy appeal that Malik observed. She turned her head away from him that swung her long earrings into her face and proceeded to watch the movie. "Now why would we go out and stand with you and your boy and miss the ending to this? Please, you'll have to come with something better player," said the young lady with a sarcastic tone. Her girlfriend's heads aimed and smirked at Malik as they overheard the exchange.

"Is that all you see?" Questioned Malik.

The group of girls each took a closer look, with a crazy expression, at the ball cap fitted snug over the do-rag wearing young man in baggy jeans and a dark colored hoody. Malik looked at the 'love-me' ladies who were high on their own shit. He thought Oprah, Tyra and Halle had brought about what is killing us as a whole along with these fucking Romeos who knew nothing about real love.

She shook her head in a way that communicated her frustration at the question posed and the intrusion made as the other ladies rolled their eyes and turned their heads back to the screen. "What I see is you interrupting my movie-watching. Now, please, leave me alone," said with a serious voice that was turning unpleasant and irritated.

"Come on, we won't bite you. We only want to love you."

"Nigga please," said the young lady with a laugh.

The wrathful voices began to go at it again with violent intentions traded back and forth in a state of disrespect that had no care attached.

The girl ignored the commotion that surrounded her and focused on the screen ahead of her, attempting to get her message across with a few non-verbals. "Check with me after, maybe then I might let you love me."

Malik pushed up off his knee and came to a standing position over the young lady who ignored his presence that just stood for a moment and stared down at the girl who definitely was feeling herself. "If that's how you want it baby girl." Malik headed off and left the group of ladies in their seats among the threatening voices that barked out at each other in an array of threats and insults. Malik joined with a standing and observing Divine at the exit and they left out of the rowdy and commotion filled auditorium.

The young woman turned her head toward the exit but Malik was gone. She gave a moment to think of what was expressed and how he expressed it. What did he mean by all he wanted to do was love me? Did he want to just have sex or was there something more he was talking about? To her, it seemed every man was searching for a new way to get into a women's pants. But something about Malik had given her a sense of caring in a real fashion. She ignored the possibilities that existed. To her, he was just another dog hunting for a fuck. The urge to get up and go find him was submerged underneath the cover of ice. Then she let out a small breath and resumed watching the movie that her eyes had trouble staying on as they darted toward the area of the place were the hateful voices were coming from. The verbal attacks grew louder and louder with more intention in them that made the place become uneasy.

Outside the theatre, across the street, Malik and Divine leaned up against the old, rusty caravan that was still doing its thing on the road. They greeted and exchanged handshakes with a variety of people that passed by. Malik and Divine had garnered much respect amongst the city by young and old. They each had a reputation that what they spoke, they carried out and lived. Instead of letting their word loose to float around without substance, these two carried it with much honor, much weight and much value.

"What was shorty talking about?" Asked Divine.

"Nothing. Nose up and ears closed, encased in ice."

"Word. Dam, hunny was nice too. Fog so fuckin' thick out here, mommies just letting the cream pass on by cause he don't have a beamer, ice or got that name ya know."

"No doubt. The thing, though, is to measure these chickens out here so you don't get caught up in their punishment."

"I heard that," replied Divine who took a few seconds to see if he knew an old man who walked across the street. "Kids in there are wildin' out tonight."

"Too much pork, malt liquor and Springer," added Malik.

"Stranded and scared."

As the two took a moment and looked down the downtown avenue, gunshots erupted from inside the theatre.

Inside, the short and stocky young man stood with his back to the screen and held his Glock pistol out that fired in the direction of his older adversary with a bad aim. People ducked, screamed and yelled as they fled uncontrollably out the two exit doors at the rear and the one exit door at the bottom of the theatre, near the screen. Young people covered their heads, dodged and ran to avoid the steam of bullets that had been let loose by the young hand. The young lady who Malik had approached, hopped over a young couple that laid in fear on the floor. Just as she was some steps from the exit, a bullet hit her in the back that threw her to the ground, face first. She was spread out on her stomach as she gasped for breath but eventually it would run out. She died with her head on a dirty floor that was ignored and stepped over. More young feet trampled over her dead body to escape the bullets that were let loose by the out of control youngster who was filled with hate, distrust and confusion.

The older man who had took cover behind the seats, pulled out his two-toned black and chrome 9mm Ruger with a full ten shots in the clip and let loose with a fury, one after another. As he moved toward the exit, the bearded man stopped and let out a few more bullets. But this time they didn't miss. They hit their intended mark in the chest, stomach and shoulder area and threw it's victim back over the seat were he laid in his own pool of his own blood.

The older man quickly tucked the warm steeled Ruger back into his jacket pocket and made his way out of the theatre, merging into what was left of the crowd of people scattering out of the exits and escaped out the door. The place that was filled with jokes and come-ons earlier had become a madhouse of disorder littered with young, dead, black bodies.

Outside the theatre, bodies dispersed in all directions that held up the on-coming traffic in the streets. Yells and screams filled the air. Vehicles began to pull out and drive off in a hurried rush. Police arrived in mass as they surrounded the theatre with guns drawn. Inside the lobby sat a few of the wounded that were bleeding, crying and screaming out in pain. In the auditorium, the young lady's body laid on the floor with a bullet to the back. A number of rows down, near the screen, laid in between the row of seats was the short and stocky, loudmouth young man who was barely twenty-years old.

In the parking lot across from the theatre, Malik and Divine observed the chaos flood out to the streets with a knowing concern. A police officer walked by and told the two with a stern voice that they should leave the area. The calm and steady young men moved toward the doors of the vehicle and opened them up. Just as Malik was about to get in, he turned his head toward the theatre entrance and searched the area for a specific face that he hadn't seen come out.

Here was Malik Joseph, also known as Leek. This young Blackman was a born leader with the gift, and the strength, to do what was necessary, when it was necessary. He was the only child to an alcoholic mother and an unknown father. Malik was birthed in the city, lived in the city and when his mom moved out of the city to take a good paying job, he remained in the city. He moved about constantly, from open bed to open bed that was always offered by the many he befriended and became close with. He graduated from high school, ran and hustled on the streets, and loved many women but thru this all he had no children. Malik cared very little about popularity. He instead chose loyalty that he carried with him in high regard. After the drama with Lars, Malik joined Divine up at college where he went to classes, joined a few organizations and took in the college life. But all the one-sided books, various rules and uninspiring teachers possessed a lack of stimulation for him which brought Malik back to the city and to his brothers that he grew up with. So here he was. Not a month back, and right into the mix, ducking bullets. He had no plans to go back to what he used to do with Lars. That was not on the docket. He was looking for a job and hustling wise in a more productive manner to make ends meet. He would rent out hotel rooms and hold crap games. He would trade dollars for food stamps and back for dollars. He would sell incense, body oils, and bootleg movies for good prices. And he would steer customers for small businesses and collect a finder's fee.

Back out on the ave, in the midst of the chaos, Malik lowered his head when there was no sight of the beautiful young girl who had to be in her late teens to early 20's. He thought she probably had a few bad experiences with boys that had led her to distrust all male gender. Or maybe the television, radio, and magazines had painted a picture for her that if they didn't look a certain way, then they weren't worth the time. Did she realize what she was truly passing over? More importantly, did she care? Either way or whatever way, it had led to her death. She refused his words and hand of real love that was not a feeling, it was a process, and instead of taking his hand, she kept her eyes looking away from whom he was and what he had to offer. Malik hopped into the same caravan that he and Lars use to travel from one robbery to the next in on many a night. That was the past and this was the now, and Malik was overcome by a feeling of pure anger with a touch of disappointment over another night and another dead Black body. Too many were drawn into the destructive emotions that had been laid thru slavery, he thought as he climbed into the driver seat, turned the key and pulled out and drove away from the blue lights, sirens, ambulances, cries and tears.

The caravan motored the best it could down the city street that displayed a number of homeless people that shared a drink from bottles of wine while others searched for food and a place to sleep. The van traveled a few more blocks and came upon a couple of drug fiends who flagged down a vehicle, in search of that hit to send them off into temporary ecstasy.

Malik's eyes scanned the whole area and took in each sight as the van rolled up on a group of young kids who made hand-to-hand sales to customers that surrounded them with money in hand.

Malik moistened his well-formed lips and turned his baby black skinned face to share a knowing look of displeasure with Divine at what their eyes witnessed. The tape in the radio was having some trouble playing. Divine moved up and ejected the tape out, checked it and popped it back in. It played fine so Divine turned up the volume to let one of his people's tracks bump. Both bobbed their head in unison to the rhyme that was spit.

> 'Yo, he came by himself to free a nigga from hell/Now we killing ourselves and feeling themselves/Play ball with the cards that a nigga was dealt/Cause it's all Back 2 God off this miserable hell'.

"How's your son doing?" Asked Malik.
"That boy is growing fast and, whoa, can he eat."
"Just like his father."
Malik and Divine faced each other and smiled knowingly in agreement as they bobbed their head to the rhyme that moved the beat forward.

Divine looked out the passenger side window at the mess they were driving thru and thought of a way to end what he observed and instead see children play free and adults caring with real care. "Ya know, there comes a time when enough is enough," Divine spoke as he turned his eyes that met up with Malik's. He knew exactly what he was referring too.

Divine aka Clyde Alverson was the quiet, laid-back, strong one. He was the type of leader who preferred to play from the back room and calmly make his moves at the proper moment. He was never one for giving in to emotions and was always available for a friendly hand or an energetic conversation. He was the type that would rather play chess then go out to the clubs. And grimmy cats were well advised to not even try to run any bullshit on him cause it would be detected quick, and no one wanted Divine for an enemy. He was raised by a single mother in the heart of the city along with a younger brother. Divine's father lived out of state who, as he grew older, he hardly saw. Him and Malik were real close but him and Lars despised each other. Divine knew what powered Lars and it had nothing to do with life. Divine loved school, loved learning, loved good and caring teachers, which were few if any in the city, and loved the Black woman. A couple teachers pushed him along thru high school and off to college. It was at that time he had a son by his high school sweetheart. Then that sweetheart turned to heartburn and eventually the two went in separate directions. In college, he found himself financially pressed to care for his son and when financial aid started pulling money from him and asking for more, he decided to head back home. Once back in the concrete jungle, Divine worked job to job and stayed taking care of his son the best he could under the circumstances. It was about keeping his head above the rising water that was flooding the city and Divine loved his people way too much to turn and run.

Back inside the vehicle that rolled down the sweaty block, Divine wiped the perspiration from his brow with a small hand towel. "I'll tell you this, going thru hell with her has brought an understanding of our fathers and their acts that have to be acknowledged," added Divine, still with a serious tone.

"That's what makes us stronger son – that understanding of knowledge," answered back Malik.

Each took a moment and listened to the verse spit by another one of their brothers, Rassa.

'VS they lovin you/hugs and kisses back/and no nigga gets on the top with out that/no gold and platinum plaques/no cabbage patch/no macks in the back of the ac/none of that'.

"This piece right here is blazing. Did Rass produce this military beat?" Asked Malik thru the music.

Divine nodded as he turned up the volume all the way. They moved thru the streets were they passed an around-the-way eatery place located in the uptown area of the city.

In the quarter filled setting were workers served the customers and the customers consumed in a peaceful setting. Various plates of tasty health food were prepared from bean soup to fried tofu to fish dishes. Black, white, Asian and Mexican were all seen and all comfortably seated around, enjoying the relaxed atmosphere.

Seven, a clean-cut bald Blackman who despised jewelry, sat at his table with the love of his love, Tanisha, a twenty-something year old Black woman who wore a full length spring dress that revealed her toned biceps to show how she worked out. The twenty-something year old, well-dressed Blackman took a drink of his water as a waitress passed by, attempting to keep her eyes off him who was in the middle of a conversation with Tanisha about a movie they had just saw.

"Well, at least she did rejoin with her man. That was love," said Tanisha with a sweet and honest voice that was at the right volume.

"True, true, but her ways and acts were funny style. I mean, enough of these contradictory and mixed up messages like so many black movies out here. She came like she knew but didn't. And that reject the pussy thing was rejection of true woman hood."

Tanisha agreed with a humble smile that revealed her perfectly framed white teeth as the waiter arrived with their plates of food that were set down on the small table. The couple took bites from their plates that were enjoyed followed by pleasurable smiles. This is what Seven saw as life being lived. Forget all the other extra stuff that was force fed to the youth. Here he was with somebody he cared for and who cared for him and so they were able to sit, speak and relate in a state of freedom, working and growing together so to make it thru anything that confronted.

Seven was the perfect number so it was the perfect name for him self. His mother and father named him Stephen Briggs. The name Seven just came from the neighborhood that saw the perfected sense he possessed. He was looked on as the business mind of the group. Intelligent, good with numbers, sociable, professional and completely devoted to Tanisha. The two had been together since their sophomore year in high school. Seven grew up in a shattered household were he saw his mother and father divorce at the age of seven then was pulled in both directions in a nasty custody battle. He would eventually live with his mother but would spend quality time with his father. This situation led him to see the importance in the decisions that are to be made and how they affect those around you since he was aware of how he was affected by having a part-time father and a spiteful mother. A good student who graduated in the top half of his high school class, his devotion lay with Malik and Divine whom he was tight with all thru junior high and into high school. After four years of high school, he moved out of his mom's, got a place of his own and found a full time job at a financial institution in the city that he's been at ever since. At the same time, the young man worked toward finishing his degree in business at night school. He rarely spoke with his parents and had very little to do with them due to their inability to face how their conduct effected Seven. His time had been devoted to his girl, his brothers and his part to play.

Seven and Tanisha took forkfuls of their vegetable dishes with rice and bread. Tanisha reached over with her hand and placed it on top of his lovingly, followed by a pure look of love that radiated her brown skin. She really did enjoy Seven's company, his attitude and what he brought to the table that pushed her to be a better human being. This appreciation allowed him to feel the care of her hand that allowed a mutual affection to grow and become something that could stand the test of time. Seven took some of his food into his fork with a steady hand that moved with grace and offered it to Tanisha. "Taste some of this."

"Aright," said Tanisha as she brushed a piece of her hair from her eye and opened her mouth. Seven gently placed the food in her mouth that she consumed. She liked that brought a pleasing expression with a glowing smile. "That is good. Here, try this."

"Come with it."

Tanisha returned the favor that Seven accepted willingly and swallowed. Seven nodded with approval as he wiped the corner of his mouth. "Good choice."

The under six foot couple leaned over toward each other and merged their lips together for a brief kiss that captured the bond that they had developed with each other.

Back out on the city street, Malik rolled out of the dirt, gloom and filth of the inner city that had built up over years of neglect, plastic words and failed programs, and into the clean and orderly area were large and luxurious homes surrounded a couple of lakes. Malik arrived at a particular home where he stopped at the front gate of a large white and light brownish house that was big and gorgeous. He parked the caravan that sat and idled for a moment and moved toward the radio to turn down the volume.

Divine opened the door and with one leg out, came to a stop as he noticed Malik remain sitting in the driver seat in observation mode. Malik glanced over, knowing what caused the pause, at a staring Divine. "Don't be in there all night son."

"You're coming in, right?"

Malik shook his head and faced toward the front windshield that he gazed out of with a serious, low-eyed expression on the five foot eleven inch, one hundred and ninety pound thin frame that was solid muscle. Divine pulled his leg back into the vehicle and with an air of disappointment, laid back in the passenger seat with the door still opened. "What's the deal?"

"Doing the knowledge. Look it were this kid lives. His parents. His up bringing. What surrounds him and influences him. He just has a way to go before, you know. Special attention son, you know that. And right now, he's a real danger."

"You are bugging out B. You can't penalize or pigeon hole the star cause of his parents or were he lives. That's fucked . . ."

"I'm not penalizing the kid. I'm just being delicate and slow with him, that's it."

"Delicate? Aright Dr. Phil."

"Yea, you know what I'm sayin'," shot back Malik

"Yeah, whatever cornball Calvin," said Divine who then stepped out of the ride, entered the front gate and approached the front door. He thought Malik had a point and he understood his reason for keeping a few steps away but he knew Benji. He was truthful, real, grounded in doing what was right. He might not have had the street knowledge and wisdom that him and others had or the lessons that came with it, but Benji was just as committed and dedicated to improving what was seen day in and day out. And Divine knew that he was willing to put it all out there on the line when it came down to it.

Malik, with a slight smile on his mug cause of the cornball Calvin remark, remained in the caravan at the wheel and looked around the neighborhood. He turned his head and observed Divine who disappeared inside.

Benji was a frail looking young Blackman with short hair that was the same length and a thin mustache on his baby face that was barely visible. He stood in his bedroom and finished getting ready for the evenings activities. He washed his face, brushed his teeth and then applied some wave cream in his wavy hair that had begun to form little waves while in his own adjacent bathroom that was furnished with a large tub. He took a look at himself in the mirror then moved into his bedroom were he finished getting dressed among the pictures of Huey P. Newton, Malcolm X, Anwar Sadat, Che Guevera and other political figures. He danced, badly and off beat, as he slipped on a pair of Nautica jeans to B.I.G.'s 'One More Chance'. He threw on a white t-shirt followed by a gray button down shirt then moved about his large room and straightened it up as he finished his preparation. He threw some dirty clothes into his hamper then skipped across the room were he stubbed his big toe on his bedpost. He fell on to his bed as he let out a sound of intense pain as he buried his face in his pillow.

Benji, or Benjamin Makkir, was a gentle soul who only saw the possibility and potential of doing rather then complaining. Benji or B, as everyone else called him, was a sweet looking young man who looked more like he was a freshman in high school then a college graduate. He was the political mind of the group who knew how to use the angles, the laws and the words to accomplish goals. His father, Roger, was a state legislator with some political clout and his mother Liasa was known through out the community. Benji's contacts and resources were many and they were scattered all over the city landscape. There were a few things about Benji that put him alone when it came to him and his brothers. One, he was virgin. Two, he didn't drink or smoke. And three, he hardly argued or cursed. His demeanor was low key yet with a steadfast determination to succeed and achieve. His parents had been together forever and raised him up to help the poor and needy by becoming that instrument that worked for change. But as some took that to join some organization that supported a propped-up position or cause with words or gave to a charity as a show to the world, Benji had decided to be out in the public and be one instead of taking pity on one and looking down. He attended a different high school then the rest of the others, but him and Divine grew up together and played at the same park that Benji would travel too. He was always around the so-called hood, even though he was looked at as the nerd of the neighborhood. He was the odd ball, the type who never had a girlfriend. Whose total focus was on his career, his books, and his plans. He would rather read the book then go see the movie. But his ability to relate to all was actually his strength in the streets despite his limited street-cred. He excelled in high school along with Divine, went off to a prestigious college and graduated in four quick years. He then followed that up with law school, internships and traveling that increased his knowledge of the political arena. His father had big plans for this young man. The only thing was Benji had some plans of his own to execute.

With the pain subsiding, Benji rose slowly from the bed and limped out the room and down the hall, arriving at his father's closed den door. Benji gave a couple knocks then, with no hesitation, opened the door and entered into the large room, decorated with Black history photos, sculptures and books.

Roger Makkir sat comfortably at his huge desk and spoke on the phone in a calm and likable manner.

Benji moved thru the room and grabbed a seat in one of two chairs that were situated in front of the oversized marble desk. He looked up at his father as their eyes met up with each other briefly as Roger continued to speak into the phone.

After hearing what he needed to hear, Roger leaned over his desk and hung up the phone. "Well, it's all set up for you."

"He offered the position?" Benji asked with an air of excitement.

"For the moment. He first wants to see how you do in an internship-type capacity."

Benji was making the rounds in a search of the right appointment in the political arena that could be of some positive use, which he was finding hard to locate. But he came across a councilman in the city who he related with and noticed the sincerity and commitment he possessed.

Benji fell back in his chair and let out a frustrated and tired breath. "Another internship? What's up with that Dad? I'm so fed up with all this interning. It's time to get serious here, don't you think?"

"This is the district that you wanted to be involved with, right?" Asked Roger as he removed his eyeglasses. "And this is the councilman you want?"

"Yeah but . . ."

"Then this is more then just an internship son."

"Yeah, I know," said a relaxed yet energized Benji who rubbed his toe. "Well, when do I start?"

"Next month."

"How come so long off?"

Roger fell back into his seat and remained looking on Benji for a brief moment. "You young people today. You are becoming tougher and tougher to please, I'd tell ya."

"It's our time old man or don't you know," said Benji with a smile.

"Then is it time to get out and get your own place?"

Benji rose from the chair and moved toward the closed door with a chuckle. Him and his father always had fun with each other by giving the other a hard time, one way or another. "You're the big time poly here. When you going to retire down south with mom and give me the house?" Asked Benji who turned around and looked at

Roger who searched thru his desk then stopped and met up with Benji's eyes when he heard that word 'give'.

"See, there you go again with that word – give."

Benji cracked a smile and turned his body back toward the door that was opened. He moved out of the room and toward the downstairs area where the smooth and comforting voice of Liasa could be heard.

Benji's mother, Liasa Makkir, stood in the kitchen over a hot plate of casserole that she had just finished preparing. Liasa was a magnificently, beautiful light-skinned woman who looked much younger than the forty plus years she was. She took a spoon full of the pasta, vegetables and sauce dish and turned to Divine and offered it, which was taken eagerly and without pause. Divine hardly ever turned down good food and this wasn't going to be one of those rare times. He savored the taste with his eyes closed for a moment to concentrate on the tangy but delicate pieces of vegetables and spicy sauce. He nodded in an appreciating approval.

Benji entered into the large kitchen and observed the taste-test session that was in effect. "How is it?" Asked Benji as he dipped his finger in the sauce and then placed it in his mouth.

Divine moved away from Liasa and her hot plate of food and exchanged a handshake and a hug with the five foot eight Benji. "Scrumptious. Whoa, can your moms cook."

"Well, thank you Divine," said Liasa with a humble tone that included a sweet smile.

Divine stepped back over to the pan and took another taste. Liasa saw that if she failed to step in, Divine would finish the whole dish off. Liasa gently took the spoon from Divine and placed a covering over it. "Now it's ready for the women at the UWAD meeting tomorrow," informed Liasa who organized and led the various community action committees in the city. This specific meeting was for the United Women Against Disrespect that was formed as a way of teaching younger women how to carry themselves as well as listening to them and the obstacles they face each day.

"You ready?" Asked Benji as he observed Divine stare at the dish being put up and away, out of his reach.

"The question is are you ready? You got Leek out there waiting in the ride. You know he's going to Fred Sanford it," replied Divine who then turned back to Liasa and her food. "Can I take some of that to go?"

"Sorry Divine. This is strictly for the ladies. None of my men are touching this, so feel special."

"Aright, aright. Yo, matter of fact, I need to speak with you about the community newspaper. We definitely need some young voices in there that'll reflect the youth in the city. It has none or those that reflect that mind state at least."

"Okay, I have to say that I agree and I'll bring that up with them at the meeting. Come by some time next week. My door is always open to you."

"Aright," said Divine as he followed Benji to the door.

"What are you boys, excuse me, young men going to do tonight?"

"Just hang out with some friends," answered Benji who moved over to Liasa and gave her a kiss on the cheek. Divine observed the affectionate act of mother and son. As Benji backed up and reached for the doorknob, Divine moved to Liasa and planted a soft kiss on her cheek that brought a smile to her face.

"Say bra, don't be kissing on my moms," joked Benji.

"Look, he's jealous," said Divine to Liasa with a laugh.

"Be careful out there fellas."

Benji and Divine acknowledged her concern as they moved out the door and down the long winding sidewalk that led to the front gate. Liasa stood at the doorway and watched the young men shove, laugh and play with each other on their way to the ride. To her, they have always been the two little boys who played a variety of games together when they were younger. A warm feeling overcame her as the two entered the caravan as Liasa, with a smile, closed the front door.

Benji climbed into the backseat as Malik finally got the vehicle to start and slid the side door shut on the caravan. Divine got in, closed the door and gave a low-eyed look toward Malik who took notice and knew what it meant.

"Peace Leek," said Benji with excitement laced.

"What's going on with you baby boy?" Questioned Malik as he pulled out while he looked in his rear-view mirror and caught Benji's sight.

"Staying good out here. What's been up with your self? I haven't seen you in awhile."

"Working to live like you are. Look it this shit."

"Right, right. Were are we headed too for the night?"

Divine played around with the tape player as he attempted to rewind the tape. "Freddie's. Some of our brothers are over there."

"That sounds like a plan," returned Benji.

"You up to going into the wild part of the city?" Asked Malik with a touch of sarcasm.

"Come on now Black," Benji answered back with a small smile.

Divine blew in to his cupped hands that were closed around his mouth and took a whiff of his breath. "That taste is going to be with me all thru the night."

"What's that?" A curious Malik asked.

"B's moms made a banging casserole dish that she let me get a taste of," stated Divine who turned his head toward a curious Malik and paused for a moment. "While you sat in the ride."

Malik met up with Divine's brown eyes that they locked on to. Malik let the words evaporate and slowly and confidently turned his head to face forward. Divine finally found the part of the tape he was searching for. He pushed play and turned up the volume that got all three to start moving to the beat and the words. Even though Benji and Malik were of the same age, Benji always felt that he was the younger brother when it came to their relationship. To Benji, Malik was influential, intimidating and dominating. His presence was demanding and overshadowed any senators, congressmen or mayors he had come in contact with. You had to respect Malik cause if you didn't respect him, you didn't respect yourself.

The caravan drove out of the nice, clean, quiet part of the city, rounded a curve, passed a stoplight and arrived right back in the mess and filth that filled the streets, storefronts and sidewalks of the inner city and concealed the unknown beauty and potential that existed.

Malik navigated his rusty but trusty caravan down the dark residential street on the south side very slowly as they each kept their eyes open for a parking space. Divine's pupils caught one in his sight and he made a gesture with his index finger that caused Malik to pull in, back up to get lined up then he moved forward to settle the wheels in place.

Benji, Divine with Malik made their way out of the ride and strolled to the front door of the desired house of a high school friend who Malik had been staying with.

"Kids just started blazing like that?" Inquired Benji as he moved thru the street with his hands in his pockets.

Malik picked his head up and looked straight at Divine then on to Benji. "That's how things go down out here were everything isn't all nice and neat."

"I'm just saying," said an intimidated Benji.

"Son held out his hand for these lovelies to come and walk with us," chimed in Divine.

"Yea, they come?"

Divine shook his head as he stepped up on to the sidewalk. "Too big in the head."

"They end up getting caught up?"

"She did," said Malik who glared at Benji. He realized and saw at that moment the feeling of disappointment and hurt that Malik felt by not being heard.

The three men arrived at the front door. Music and voices could be heard coming out from inside the two-bedroom, one level house. With no knock, Malik moved thru the front door and into the gathering of people.

Malik, Divine and Benji walked into the main room and moved thru the crowded place that was jumping with action. Each exchanged handshakes, pounds, and hugs and words that showed love that greeted the many young faces in attendance. All types of activities took place in all areas of the recently purchased home. Most drank a variety of drinks that were offered. Others filled, rolled and smoked weed blunts along with the numerous cigarettes that hung from many mouths. Each socialized in various sections, ate what food was left, showed off some dance moves, watched the sport highlights on the television and gambled, either at the card game table in the kitchen or the large dice game that roared in the dining room.

As Malik, Divine and Benji moved toward a specific area of the place, an attractive young woman in her early twenties pushed into Malik's arms and planted a kiss with her luscious lips on his neck. Divine and Benji stepped back and crunched their face up as they stared at an overcome Malik by the affection. Cherise was a simple yet easily influenced young lady who loved nice things and powerful men. Malik may not have had the money but she was drawn to the way he carried himself and the power he presented. She wanted Malik all to herself and she made it known to any female at any time about her intentions and his availability.

Malik calmed down her advances that Divine and Benji were having fun with at his expense, and moved off toward the dice game with Divine and Benji who walked ahead with smiles that remained on their face. They were aware that Malik had his hands full with that dime piece whose body was straight out of the many music videos that littered the tube.

The dice game was in full session with Rassa, DJ, Lite, J-Rob, Freddie, Lars and three of his boys who stood, kneeled or sat in the circle with a mountain of money sitting in the middle and other bills on top of other bills off to the side of the players. Some yelled in excitement for their point, others focused on the dice and the hand movement and some stood and counted their money to find out were they stood.

Malik, Divine and Benji arrived at the game and observed who was winning, who was loosing and who was just having fun. Rassa, a tall six foot five Blackman with a tight fade and athletic geared up from top to bottom, had just lost the dice. As he let out his frustration, he spotted his brothers and moved off toward Malik, Divine and Benji. Taking notice of the new arrival were DJ, Lite, J-Rob, and Freddie who joined Rassa. The group of young men showed love to each other in a variety of ways that reflected the close nature between them. This was something more then just a good neighborhood friendship.

Lars picked his head up from the floor and looked on them all sharing words and smiles with each other that caused him to become incensed that the game was being held up. "What the fuck is this?!" Lars gestured wildly to resume the game that went unheard. He was well aware of the change that had occurred between them. Malik had grown socially while Lars had grown materially.

There was something more important then a dice game to Rassa. Given the name of LaMont Wallace when he was birthed, he was better known as Rassa around the way. Rassa was the lyrical tongue, one-line operator, all-day negotiator, smooth-things-over navigator of the group. He was the one called when the party got dull or the microphone went cold. Rassa lived with his parents who were still together after twenty-something years. His father had been at the same construction job for almost two decades and his mother was strictly a homebody who enjoyed keeping her home in tact. Rassa was never that much into the books, the labels or a menial job. He was more about the relationships and the social aspect that school and the streets offered. His teachers in high school loved him due to his open and free nature that he fully expressed in a respectful nature. Rassa could cool a chaotic situation in the lunchroom out by just getting his hands on a mic. He graduated high school and thought about going to college to learn a trade, which were his parent's hopes. But he had different plans and that involved hip-hop – his instrument of self-expression and artistic creation. This was his way to show love to the world and to tell his story. To Rassa, hip-hop was much more then spitting a bunch of words that demeaned, talked shit or bragged and boasted. That was rapping and almost anybody can do that and did. It was the transfer of ideas and the willingness to teach with a beat, all created from the mind and the hands to instill a sense of right and wrong, good and bad, what works and what doesn't. And Rassa saw that in this day hip-hop was being destroyed and turned into something it was not. This dream of his caused some hard feelings between him and his parents who felt he was puffing on a pipe dream. But not Rassa, he understood it took patience, time and commitment and his brothers had his back just like he had theirs.

Next was DJ aka DeLonte Jenkins. The kind of young man in his twenties who had a natural gift that he embraced fully and practiced any chance he got. But unlike most, DJ saw it, understood it and made it work. His gift was the ability to see the potential in whatever position was taken, and to prosper from it, one way or another. DJ was someone who you better know your shit around otherwise you will get stung. He was looked up to as the dealmaker. When money had to be made or a place had to be found or somebody had something of value for sale, this was the one to send in. He could talk, pitch and literally play with the best of them and get the best price. DJ's childhood was nothing pretty. His father was killed in a robbery at a gambling spot and his mother was killing herself as she held down a full time job at a nursing home were she put in some torturous hours. DJ was blessed with handsome, good looks, a swift tongue and knowledge of how to make the bed rock and legs shake. This all attracted the numerous faces of the opposite sex to him, and they really loved him that was shown in a number of ways. One in particular, Aiesha, had been on again, off again. She gave birth to his two children, a boy named Hamin and a girl name Leigha. But before his children came into the world, DJ headed up to college with Divine after he graduated from high school, which became his moneymaking playground. At college, the game was wide open for him. With rich white boys, let-loose white girls and Africans coming over with full pockets along side Asians who just wanted to be down, he had found his bank to draw from. It was like putting Clinton in the bunny ranch – it was on. However, and soon, the authorities came a knocking which chased DJ back home to the city and the familiar streets. And this was where he spent his time, on the block, hustling, making moves, cultivating angles, and becoming wise to the many rackets that canvassed the city. This was how DJ saw himself taking care of his responsibilities and taking care of his part in the whole.

And then there was Lite who was given the name Twan Jones. A firecracker, a spark plug, a six-pack of dynamite that only needed to be lit. He was fire and ice wrapped up in a tight coil. The youngest of the group, a little over a year back of the rest, was taken in and looked after with extreme care. Lite was the most hardheaded, hot-tempered, short-wired, quick to knock the teeth out burst of energy they had. In other words, when diplomacy failed – here came the Lite. Lite's mother and father were killed when he was a child of eight years old. How they were killed was still under question. The cops reported that a couple robbery suspects gunned them down. However, others have reported that there was a gunfight between the cops and a group of young militants that Lite's parents happened to get caught in the crossfire of. The so-called robbery suspects were never caught and the cops just received a paid leave. Meanwhile, Lite lost everything in his life. He moved in with his grandma who was too old to give the necessary discipline or teaching that Lite required. If it wasn't for a couple of his brothers, Tajaa and Malik, Lite would never of graduated or stayed alive. Lite was constantly fighting, arguing and getting kicked out of classes. Teachers only saw an undisciplined child who had no remorse. They failed to understand what lay underneath and what was missing. There was no late night kisses from a mother. There were no constructive words from a strong father. There was no family structure to show order. Lite was the product of what raised him. And because of Tajaa and Malik and their strong hand, caring words, and understanding motions, Lite graduated high school but that would be enough schooling for him. Instead, he got serious with Tajaa and spent the majority of time learning, listening and watching out in the streets. Beside temp positions here and there that fit into his schedule, it was more important to be out in the streets and hold down the blocks in a variety of strong-arm ways for his brothers. That's all that mattered to him – his brothers who were there for him.

The young men finished with their greetings and broke up the gathering of smiles, jokes and gestures and moved back over to the dice game circle. The three of them resumed action with a still agitated Lars and his boys who were dressed in all black with long platinum chains, Rolexes and diamond rings. They loved flossing, especially Lars.

Before Rassa headed back into the circle, he took out a small book on food and health that was tucked away in the pouch of his Detroit Piston hoody and handed it over to Benji. The non-threatening, brown-skinned young man took the book in hand, followed by a nod of appreciation and then made his way over to a chair in the main room, near the television and started to take the time to learn what the book had to offer.

Divine stood to the side of the dice game and held a conversation with the young homeowner named Freddie as he took glances at the dice that were rolled. Freddie, a thin, half black, half Asian twenty-four year old man, gave a gesture with his finger in the direction of the phone that was in the hands of a thick-thieghed and big-breasted ebony skinned woman who was a little unhappy with the other line she was talking to. Divine casually strolled to where the phone was being used and began to play around in a flirting fashion with the sour-faced woman, attempting to make her smile.

She hung up the phone then turned to and made a snarl toward Divine. She stomped off and left Divine standing alone. The messy dressed Divine in wrinkled jeans, an untucked old t-shirt and a pair of outdated running shoes, shrugged his shoulder with no-care as if to say 'she digs me' and picked up the phone and dialed a number. As he waited for the other line to be picked up, he grabbed a loaf of bread near by and read the ingredients to himself.

"Di-glycerides. Come on B, keep it righteous," sang Divine slowly as the ring was answered. "Peace old man."

On the other end of the line was Pops who was enjoying the quiet evening relaxing back in his small apartment with the television on, the music playing on the radio and resting with his baby girl who was curled up on his chest. He cocked his head to hold the phone to his ear. "Peace. Old man? You know I'll still hold you up for twelve rounds," snapped Pops with a playful twinge.

Pops listened to Divine as he caressed the back of his peaceful daughter whose tiny body snuggled on her father's oversized chest.

"Yeah, I hear you talking. What's going on with you tonight?"

Pops squirted some of his daughter's juice from her bottle into his mouth as he paid attention to every word Divine spoke thru the phone.

"Just my daughter and self maintaining together. Doing the knowledge to happenings on water and land."

Pops gazed down on his beautiful girl who clutched to her fathers body.

Pops, known also as Ranell Watson, was the elder statesman of the group. He was referred to as Pops cause to Malik, Divine, Tajaa, DJ, Born, and Lite, he was the father figure they looked too that they never had in their lives. He was their voice to the elders who were unable to see.

A large man of 6 foot 4 and over two hundred pounds that was in good shape with agile quickness and equipped with heavy hands. Pops had seen and lived thru all types of situations that allowed him to relate to the younger generation in the city streets. Pops was able to relate cause there was no condemning with a closed mind, instead only understanding. He was birthed in the fifties, watched with amaze at the Nation of Islam and the Black Panthers in the sixties, ran the streets during the peace movements of the seventies and decided it was time to work when crack hit in the eighties. Pops had seen it all, so he thought. Pops was big into the gangs when he was a youth and he had to find out the hard way when he was shot and his close friend laid beside him with his brains hanging out the back of his head. He picked himself up, patched up the wounds and scars and started to do something with himself. Pops put him self thru school were he graduated from college with a degree in education. Soon he found himself a teaching position that opened up in the city. Year after year, Pops' service, commitment and loyalty to the children in the city became a tower of strength that helped a helping body. This was how he came into contact with Malik, Divine and the rest of the bunch. He developed a special bond with each thru seeing what they were about and were they were headed. Pops remained a rock for the group that they could count on and was a fountain of wisdom. His counseling and advice, not to mention the various contacts he had at his disposal, were in invaluable.

Pops nodded with a smile as the conversation on the phone came to a close. Divine had only called to see how Pops was doing, nothing else. It was just the thought of making sure he was good on this night and in that moment that mattered. The big guy hung up the phone and relaxed back in the worn out couch as the news reported on the war that continued to wage overseas. He closed his eyes, laid his head back and enjoyed the moment with his daughter. Rest was his for the moment.

Back at the party house that had increased in faces, traffic and activity, in entered Tajaa who moved thru the place like a king of kings. With his head up, his body firm, and his expression stoic, Tajaa exchanged handshakes and hugs to all that stepped forward. Humble and reserved, with a warm smile and a real handshake, he headed toward the back of the house were the dice game roared. The well-sculpted Blackman with circular cornrows, a full beard and no jewelry of any type, stepped into the room and was quickly noticed by his brothers. DJ, Lite, J-Rob, Rassa, Benji and Malik extended their hands that were gripped firmly and then pulled into his large arms that stretched the t-shirt he wore. Tajaa cracked a smile and stood with Malik as the others returned to the dice game after a brief word or two. DJ handed a few twenty-dollar bills to Tajaa, with no words on the reason. He took with a nod and stuffed the bills in his jogging pants pocket with out even looking at it.

Malik and Tajaa remained to the side of the game and looked on, just at that moment, Divine entered in and exchanged an enthusiastic hug with the large, well taken care of young man. Tajaa and Divine settle down their playful enjoyment of each other and joined Malik near the group of players who let their emotions be expressed at each toss of the ivory.

"You get that job son?" Asked Tajaa of Malik with a low tone.

"No word yet, these mutha-fuckas be half stepping in shit, ya know. But if they don't call on Monday, I'll get in touch with them and see what the deal is," said Malik with his back faced toward the dice game and full attention given toward Tajaa and Divine.

"Make'em, that's what you have to do sometimes out here."

"Definitely, otherwise it's stagnation alley, and they keep smiling."

Tajaa gave a nudge with his elbow that tipped Divine over a step. "I heard Pops looked out."

"True, true. Hooked me up with a coaching job at the Rec center," answered Divine with a small smile that he attempted to hold back as he returned the nudge that didn't budge the larger Tajaa.

"That's what it's about right there," said Tajaa who was overcome with a grand feeling of honor in being a part of these young men who looked out for each other in more ways then one. Tajaa knew this was the way it could be and should be for many if the pettiness was left alone and the realization of what really mattered came into focus.

To his brothers, Tajaa was Mount Everest. He was the shining reflection of pure power, strength and courage. Named Tory Linox at birth, Tajaa or Taj was a very sociable and likable young man who knew when it was time to test minds, love bodies and smash arms. Tajaa was well versed in martial arts and had learned all about firearms and nature survival. Not only could he survive in the urban jungle, he could also sustain himself in the forest, the desert and on sea. Tajaa had an older brother who had ventured into motion-stopping activities to satisfy his wanting desires. The brothers where abandoned by their strung-out mother and their father, who went to prison for life on account of a double-murder. So him and his brother raised themselves until his older sibling followed his father's footsteps and got locked up. He was a petty crook with a strong habit and lost emotions that led to unstable chances taken. Tajaa resisted the temptation with the strong hand of Pops and brothers like Malik and Divine. He slept many nights at Pops' place that allowed him to graduate from high school. What was seen in these days was the military general of the group. When an out of hand problem had to be handled, this is the one who was sent. Tajaa remained in the city after high school and worked various odd jobs to put a roof over his head while at the same time doing favors for those in need that earned many stripes. He attempted to enroll in a technical trade school that specialized in radio broadcasting, but when the only money he could receive was a 28% adjustable interest rate loan that still wouldn't cover the full amount, he decided to remain debt free and teach himself. Tajaa, along with Lite who he trained with and taught the many techniques he had acquired, patrolled the city, laid low and kept to himself until needed by those who had the same objective as he.

Tajaa took his eyes off of Malik and Divine and turned them on to Lars who roared with excitement at just winning the pot of wrinkled bills. He was familiar with the boasting, money-counting young man and held little love for the way he carried himself. "Yo, speaking of basketball. Born hit me up the other day," broke out Tajaa who turned to the calm duo of Malik and Divine. "He told me to tell you two that yall have to get a reliable phone number."

"What's up with the master baller?" Asked Divine who thought about the last time they got up with Born.

"He's getting ready for his final season."

"Is he going top five?"

"I'll tell you something," said Malik as he scratched his cheek and glanced at a young Puerto Rican mommy dip that caught his eye. "I've seen the star do some things out on the court that show and prove his ability and potential that has no limit. It all comes down to a matter of accepting, recognizing and controlling the stage that can be his."

"He's also wise to get his degree," added Tajaa who exchanged hands in agreement with each.

In the circle, Rassa just hit his point and rose in excitement and collected his money from the center. An aggravated Lite gave him a playful shove to calm him down. Tajaa, Divine and Malik turned and observed Lite and Rassa mess around with each other.

Born, a smallish, brown-skinned Blackman with a short fade haircut that was barely a six feet, hundred and fifty pound guard, worked out in the isolated gymnasium. He shot the ball from various and specific spots on the court. He ran lines, worked on his dribbling with both hands and numerous styles along with perfecting his moves that he went over and over until each movement was smooth, easy and instinctive. Each moment on the floor, Born attacked with a single-minded focus that had the objective to be the best. After a group of twenty straight three-point shots was taken, in which he hit twelve, Born moved over to the side and drank a bottle of water.

Here was the last one of the group. The gifted superstar athlete who last season ripped up the college court and made a name that was regarded highly by those in the professional league. Born, or Wallace Burchin, averaged almost twenty five points as a junior and now bigger things were expected by those on the outside rather then those close to him who only looked for Born to be Born. Yet what made him so special was his dedication and humility when it came to his brothers that he grew up and hit the playgrounds with. Malik pushed him, taunted him, and made him work just as hard as any guard had every Saturday when they played at the local city courts.

And Tajaa and Rassa made sure of his toughness when he drove inside on them, as they would deliver countless shoves, jabs and pull downs to the ground. Rassa, DJ and Malik were always the main core that headed out to the courts with him and ran it all day. Divine and Pops were the two that pushed him to go to college even when it looked like he might remain in the city and work an everyday job to take care of his mother and his little brother. Pops made sure that certain people knew about Born, especially after he wrecked shop at the summer Pro-Am league. Then there was Lite and Tajaa who made sure that nobody, and that included the bloodsucking drug dealers who thirsted to befriend Born, came near or even thought about touching a part of his body. Or Benji and Seven who assisted Born in finding the right people that could be of legal and professional guidance and help in the manner of college, rules, agents and contracts. Born was well aware of the reason why each one gave a hand to get him to the point that had him working out at midnight in an empty court.

It was done to assist in improving himself to be an asset that could be of benefit to himself, Malik and his brothers. Born was well aware of his role and was prepared for any consequences to follow.

Born ended his brief break and returned to his workout on the court, repeating a crossover move until it was perfect. Shooting free throws while doing push-ups. Working on a step back three-point shot. He repeated each move, each drill, and each action over and over. His determination was reflected in his late night commitment while others where partying the night away. The sweat poured from his toned and muscular body with the vision of Malik, Divine, Seven, Pops, Rassa, DJ, Benji, Lite, and Tajaa each looking on with full support within his mind. So that was what he gave back, and then some.

Back at the house party that was in full swing at Freddie's pad that he opened his door and extended a bed to Malik who in turn paid the utilities as his rent. The large group of young people had grown since Malik, Divine and Benji had arrived and so had the festivities, the emotions and the egos.

In the back room, the dice game had enlarged with sightseers who reacted with excitement at each roll. Big money sat in the middle of the circle of bodies with even more in side bets that lay in between of specific individuals whose Air Jordan's or AI's held down to make sure the green paper didn't go no where.

DJ held the dice in his right palm that he shook in his hand. In his other hand was a thick and crumpled wad of bills that illustrated he was on top of his game tonight. The dice flew out of his grasp with a slick comment to all the players along with a slight spin of the wrist.

More and more people gravitated to the back room and stood and watched the dice roll out of DJ's hand followed by point being hit and money being picked up. Energy had encased the room and flowed thru each body present at the current winning streak.

Lars was growing more and more enraged at each winning roll that DJ released out. Hate was building up inside of him. Was he cheating? Did he switch dice? Lars could only think that DJ was hustling him, which he was. DJ had learned the way of the dice and the way of the game from his father who was known in the streets as 'Naturals' when it came to the dice game.

Malik, Divine, and Tajaa glanced on the game from time to time but their focus was more on the lovely ladies in skirts, smooth-fitting jeans and shorts that accentuated their figures. Benji remained sitting off in the other room, engrossed in the health book that Rassa gave him.

Lars slapped some money down to the side of him and made a few disrespectful remarks on some of the clothing attire wore by DJ and Lite that drew some laughs from the bystanders.

DJ ignored the words and let the dice go. They flipped, turned and landed on a six and a two that made eight. DJ knew he had hit his point and reached over into the middle to collect that large hill of cash. "We builders here, yall betta know."

Lars rose up that caused Malik to easily notice that his once partner had gained some weight that had been turned into muscle. He quickly stuck his foot on top of the money. DJ came to a stop and looked up at a serious glare cast on Lars' face. "Slow your roll partner. Point was six. The six/eight was side," said a graveled voice Lars as he motioned to the side of him were a group of bills laid. "This is what you pick up."

"Stop trippin' chief. You know what point was."

"Nigga, the only one trippin' in here is you. You rolled two three's."

"A three and five. What are you on?"

"I'm not even going to argue with you. Point is six."

"Come on L, get off that shit. "What? Are you on acid tonight?"

"Fuck you nigga!"

J-Rob, a young Blackman who was about two years younger than Malik, Divine and the rest of them and was looked to as Malik's little brother who was always in Malik's presence, rose up and stood with arms crossed and extended a steely glare that looked right thru Lars.

Rassa and Freddie remained kneeling with their heads lowered to the floor. Freddie, cause he didn't want to catch sight of Lars bloodshot eyes. Rassa, cause he just wanted to concentrate on Lars' voice and his intentions.

Lite remained lowered to the floor on one knee. He picked his head up and took out the toothpick he had been chomping on and threw it to the side. His eyes stayed right on the jeweled up young man who had once hustled deep with Malik.

Lars continued to stand right in the middle of the circle, on top of the money with the wrinkled brow revealing his anger. "You might sucker those poo-butts who fall for that shit but I'm not them partner," said Lars with spit flying out in stressing the p sound.

The crowd that had formed around began to sense a threatening displeasure that was intensified by their very existence. The group began to moan and argue about what the point really was and who should pick up the money.

With the argument becoming more and more heated, Malik stepped forward out of the crowd of people. "Lars! Lars!" Shouted Malik who finally got Lars' attention away from his boys and onto him. "Everyone here saw point was eight."

"Hold up, hooolldd up! Who in the fuck invited you into my street?" Exclaimed Lars with a small grin that quickly was wiped off as he peered at Malik. "This has nothing to do with you player so I'd advise you to stay the fuck out."

J-Rob who was in some long baggy jean shorts with a 'Stop Snitchin' white t-shirt focused his eyes even more on to Lars.

DJ, all that time, had kept his eyes on Lars' boys and their demeanor. He took a breath, scratched the side of his face and rose up off his knees. He could see the pistols that were tucked inside their jean jackets into their waistbands. And he was well aware of what these boys where capable of. They didn't where those pieces for looks.

An unmoved Malik took a couple steps closer to Lars with a relaxing smile. "C'mon B. What's right is right, and my brother's point was eight."

"I don't give a flying fuck if he's your Lord and Savior. I'm telling you to stay the fuck out of my street or," said Lars who at that moment turned his back and shared eye contact with his boys. "This ain't no fuckin' game Leek."

Lite and Rassa jumped up at that moment with serious expressions that gave a look toward Malik that expressed the seriousness in the situation then turned and surveyed Lars and his boys. They only needed for the signal from Leek for this to be on and they were ready and willing. As cool and friendly as Lite and Rassa could be, they were just as vicious and merciless when it came to unwanted drama with devilish intent. There was no bitch in these fellas.

Divine stepped away from a young lady with a short 'Halle Berry' hair-do and hips for days and moved up beside Malik, crossed his arms and fixed his eyes on Lars. Benji heard the commotion that had taken center stage in the place and slowly rose from the chair and made his way into the room where he took his place a few steps behind Malik and Divine.

Malik took his time with a calm grace that addressed every move he made as well as what surrounded. Malik viewed the money pot in the middle and took it into consideration the amount that scattered about on the floor. He knew Lars. And knowing him and what pushed him, this could get ugly quick. He knew only two or three of his brothers were holdin'. DJ never carried but this was a house party. Lite and Tajaa were about their hands but Lite was known to carry from time to time. Maybe Tajaa had a piece on him and for sure Rassa did. Benji never entered his mind. But Malik knew that Lars and his three boys were packing for sure. And he also knew that Lars' boys were young in the head and high on emotions, which meant that they would just start squeezing. And that meant that a lot of young people would be in harms way. Malik didn't want this to go any further. This was the wrong time at the wrong place. Knowing all this, Malik gave that look toward DJ who read it perfectly.

Lars continued to stand and glare at the group of men that stepped in his direction and after a moment began to mock Malik with a stare. "What? Y'all gotta problem here?"

Lars stretched out his arms as if too say, 'come with it, please, so I can blow your fuckin' heads off'.

The large group that had gathered around, where now well aware of what this had led too and where it was going. Some had started to leave in a rush, not wanting to catch a bullet in the ass on accident or be one of the innocent casualties that are always heard in the news.

DJ moved passed Malik and toward a teeth-sucking Lars. "Yo-yo! Aright, point was six. Where's the dice?"

Lars dropped his arms to his side and stayed glaring at Malik who turned around with Divine and headed into the other room. Lars failed to realize what he had just done. They had gone from girl chasing, late night talks and sharing a box of cereal to the confronting and threatening the taking of a life. J-Rob gave one last look at Lars who spoke with his boys in a hushed tone then rose up and left the circle where he joined Divine and Malik who walked away unmoved and aware.

The circle, which had decreased in size and energy, formed once again. DJ lowered to the ground, shook the dice in his palm and let them roll out. The dice rolled, flip and stopped on a four and two to make six. He leaned over and picked up the rest of the dough that Lars could only watch with a displeased scowl.

Lars stood up over the circle with his boys to his side and angrily threw some more money down to fade DJ. He looked up from the money and watched Malik with a disgusted facial expression. "Bitch ass mutha fucker," commented Lars in a low-tone that was only heard by his boys. "Need to get his bummy ass out on the block and make me some money."

Lars' boys cracked a smile that showed the gold teeth that filled their front grills.

DJ, with his head down and focus on the dice, sensed the animosity that was still carried by Lars. This was much deeper then a dice game argument.

Rassa laid back in one of the chairs and puffed on a blunt as he wrote in his book of rhymes, structuring a few bars. Lite and Tajaa stood facing each other and worked on a few defensive moves with their bodies and hands. DJ spoke with Cherise on everything from Hillary Clinton to Jaime Fox to BET as she sat across from him, next to Malik, attempting to debate with him. Divine and the young woman who had snarled at him earlier in the night at the phone, sat close in each other's arms and shared words of care and interest that went back and forth with a comforting smile. Freddie sat quietly on his couch and observed the video game that took place on the television with a drink in hand. Benji, laid up in the loveseat with the book resting on his chest, had snoozed off. A few other young ladies socialized, lounged and relaxed back with each other in the front living room area. The party had come to an end and the place showed it with the mess that invaded each room.

J-Rob and Malik enjoyed the battle with each other in a game of Madden football on the Playstation. The others continued to drink, smoke, eat, and share conversations that filled the room.

Benji, looking comfortable and peaceful, remained at rest with his eyes closed and his head leaned to the side. DJ and Lite, who was in the middle of a hand movement to deflect a punch that Tajaa showed how too, spotted this particular sight. DJ moved over to him and made sure Benji was out.

Tajaa looked over at DJ who tickled Benji's palm that got no response. "Is he resting again?" Asked Tajaa who attempted to hold back a smile.

DJ turned from Benji with a grin. "You know what time it is?"

DJ gave a smile toward Rassa who knew what that meant and returned the expression with a nod. Rassa vanished into the other room for a quick second and returned with a cup of ice water and some shaving cream.

Benji snored away. Rassa placed the cup of ice water in Benji's hand that he cupped around it and hooked the fingers into the handle so to hold it in place. DJ took the shaving cream and squeezed off a white mound of it into Benji's other hand. DJ put the can down and searched the room for some type of tickle instrument he could use. He found the stem from the weed plant that had been used and moved up next to Benji. Every one in the room stopped what they we're doing and turned their attention on to the sight. DJ gave his neck a twist and cracked his knuckles. He moved the twig slightly over Benji and then ran it slowly and lightly up and around his nose.

At first, nothing. A second try came and this time Benji flinched. The whole room drew back, trying to hold in their laughter at the expected outcome. DJ gave it a third try and brushed the twig lightly but quickly along the bridge of the nose. Benji shook his head then brought both hands up to his face that dumped the ice water on his face and smeared him self with shaving cream that covered his eyes. The room erupted into laughter. Benji snapped up to a sitting position, wet and creamed, and looked at the group that was cracking up and in tears either on the floor, in the other room, or in the corner. No one could stop, not even Malik who was on the floor, holding his stomach. Benji sat there and looked at him self. After a moment of realization at how he must look and what he just did, he joined in on the laughter. Just another night with his brothers.

CHAPTER THREE

A new day brings a challenge to look into the mirror.

INSIDE THE LAVISH, heavily, high-priced furnished living room of Lars' grand two-level home situated out in the suburbs, just outside the city, sat Lars with an attractive blonde-headed bombshell of a woman named Cleo and a flashy dressed, pinky ring wearing older white man named Georgio who had his hair slicked to the back. Cleo, with a voluptuous body that was accentuated by the tight and short skirt along with a revealing top, stood behind Lars on the other side of the oversized couch and applied her fingers to his neck that gave him a sensuous massage which he enjoyed being the fruits of his labor. Georgio sat opposite the couple in a black leather lounge chair and smoked his expensive Dutch cigar and drank a glass of gin on the rocks amongst the laid back setting. The two men shared a few laughs as they spoke on a past happening that took place in the city that involved their business together, which in the end benefited both. Lars slid his hand up her arm to her shoulder to pull her in close and looked up at her, realizing that the conversation had reached that moment that required some private tending too. "Baby, could you excuse us for a moment. I gotta speak with my man here on some things."

With no questions and not a trace of debate, Cleo applied one more sensuous rub that moved from his neck area and too his bald head with a seductive expression and gave Lars a kiss to the top of his gleaming scalp. As she began to step away from Lars, it was clear that this girl had a rear end that was not like any ordinary white girls. This young female had some junk in the trunk and she knew how to flash it and move it well. She seductively turned from Lars and with a sexy appeal, moved out of the room that kept both men's eyes focused on her behind and the disposition of her frame.

Georgio shook his head in amazement, captured by the thought of what he would do to her if only, and let out a breath followed by a drink from his glass. "That is one hell of a piece of ass you got there L," he commented in between sips.

Lars, with a bottle of Cristal in hand, poured him a drink. He sat the bottle back on the glass table, leaned back in the plush couch, and took a gulp to satisfy his thirst. It tasted too good to him. After the drink cleared his throat-way, he picked his eyes up and fixed his glare, in a poker-face manner, on Georgio. "Hey, hey now. Show some respect. That's my number one bitch right there."

"I am showing you some respect. It's not true what I said?" Cracked back Georgio.

Lars bowed his head in acknowledgment and gave a slight grin that Georgio recognized agreed with his assessment. He conceded that Georgio was right about the ass but he demanded respect, even from Georgio, who held his leash. Georgio was the go-between, the middleman, who connected the product & the resources with the bodies to distribute. Lars leaned over on to the circular table that had eight to ten razor thin lines of coke on it, and he sniffed two of them up with each nostril. He sat back up and adjusted his nose along with a snort. "So," said Lars with a couple sniffs. "What do you want from me?"

Georgio took a moment to answer his question that threw him a little off balance by it. He raised his hand to make sure that Lars realized whom he was speaking with. "If I do remember correctly, we have a partnership in this. We do for each other because it's good for business. Remember?"

"Aright, aright. Man, didn't mean to ruffle ya up there. So what's up?"

Georgia was comforted by the recognition, even though it was only a token, and leaned his head down on to the table and snorted a few lines in succession. He sat up, wiped his nose and moved up a little closer to Lars. "It's come to my attention that we have some new palms in the candy store and we need a taste-test session. We would like you to see how they like the candy," said Georgio with a treacherous grin that was demanding an order in a polite way.

"Are they professionally established?"

"Nope. And that's why I come to you with this. I know you have access to other, let us say, subsidiaries that can be of some use. You know, expendable assets."

Lars picked his eyes up and focused them on to Georgio who sat and looked back at him with all seriousness. He was well aware that Georgio was not asking him. Lars took a moment, leaned back and cracked a grin to illustrate what power he thought he had with the situation, then nodded. "What about them A's?"

Georgio and Lars shared a knowing smile and tipped their glasses together. He accepted the order.

Divine entered into the low-lit hospital room and observed his ailing mother, Deanne, who was laying in the inexpensive bed with tubes, machines and monitors hooked up to her. Divine slowly and quietly moved up to her side and gently took hold of what was left of her hand. Deanne awakened from her semi-rest with the touch of her hand, and slowly opened then turned her eyes on to her oldest son. He broke out a slight smile to bring some comfort and leaned down and embraced his old and weak-looking mother who had been plagued with what a great number of the population on the planet had been stricken with. Divine rose up and kept his adoring gaze on her. "How you feeling momma?"

She licked her lips and gathered up some strength. "Tired. How about you, how you?" Requested Deanna who was groggy from the drugs being pumped inside her to temporarily stop the cancer from spreading within her body.

"I'm good. I got that job."

"That's great," said Deanne attempting to sound excited thru her weakness. "Now, don't let them work you too hard cause you know they will." Deanne took a moment and with a focusing of her murky pupils, looked closely at Divine and the expression on his face that revealed the immense amount of hurt at the sight of what was happening to his mother. "So, how do I look?" Asked Deanne. Her strength was still visible even with the little hair she had on her head, the dark circles that had deepened into her dark face and the frail frame that was basically whittled down to bone.

"Like my mother," said Divine with a tear building up in his eye.

Rassa opened his eyes to the crack of light that broke thru and shined thru his bedroom door from the light bulb in the hallway of his parent's home. Night had descended and the young man had just awakened from a full days rest since he was out all last night. Rassa might get home from a night out at 5 in the morning, sleep to around one or two, check on things and handle immediate errands then find a few hours to nap, wake up around eight and get ready for the night. The night was his. That was his life and it definitely didn't sit to well with his parents, or more specifically – his father. Rassa slowly and deliberately rose up after taking some time to get his thoughts together as he laid back on the lumpy mattress and sat on his bed for a quiet moment. He rubbed his eyes, scratched his head, and checked his balls then looked out the window that revealed the night that sat outside. Rassa took his finger and pushed play on his CD player.

With music that revealed a beat that he had put together, he stretched out his limbs, let out a yawn and picked up a notebook that contained his many rhyme verses. Rassa found the page and began to work on an unfinished rhyme. He constantly repeated a verse over and over as he moved out of his room and disappeared into the bathroom just down the hall.

Not that far away from Rassa, at the same time, Malik and Cherise laid in the bed, side to side, together and shared kisses that were gently pressed all over her face, neck and chest area by Malik's smooth lips and the massage of his tongue. Malik was in his boxers while Cherise laid in her cherry red bra and panties. He used his hand to feel on Cherise's curvy body, from her shoulder to her back to her c-cup breasts down her side and on to her butt that he cupped and grabbed with a powerful intensity. He moved gracefully on top of her with his manhood erect and ready for action. Cherise, with her lips connected to his, opened her eyes in a moment of doubt that led her with a forceful thrust to push Malik to the side of her body that allowed her to roll away out of his grasp. She hopped out of the bed and gained her composure from the sexual tension that was gaining momentum. She searched the floor for her pants and shirt that she located at the foot of the bed. Malik was well aware of the reason for her stoppage and he turned over on his back and slid his arms behind the pillow that gave comfort behind his head.

Cherise, with her pants on, placed her shirt on her body and began to button it up. "You know, I'm beginning to feel this is all I am to you. Isn't it?"

Malik remained lounging back in the bed, nonchalantly, and gazed on Cherise who stood at the foot. He let out a breath and turned his eyes up toward the ceiling in a moment of 'here we go again'. Malik asked himself how come she couldn't just be happy with the present? How come everything to her is a dam soap opera? He turned his eyes back on her and examined her closely.

Pops exited the high school gymnasium doors and made his way toward his 1989 Nissan Maxima. He unlocked his car door and threw his bag, followed by his brown suitcase, inside. Just as he was about to get in, he caught the site of two groups of boys that faced off toward each other next to an open field.

The tough-looking, grim faced boys exchanged heated words of threats at each other along with accusations involving a minor incident that had now escalated to a serious manner. Reps were at stake, egos were in full exposure and words and emotions were uncontrolled.

Pops had seen this before and sensed from the expressions that it was only going to get worse unless a cool wind entered in. He closed his car door and made his way toward the boys in sweat suits, tennis shoes and bandanas.

One of the boys peeked his eyes to the side just as the dance was about to move from taunts to actions, were they saw a large man who they knew off approaching in their direction. A yell was made to inform that caused all the young bodies to scatter in every direction.

Pops went after two specific bodies that he snagged with great agility as they felt his long arms reach for them, and them only. By the neck, that Pops held on to with immense pressure, was two of his basketball players, Samson and Jett. The two boys crinkled their faces up in pain and discomfort with a cry to let go.

"Now, what are you boys up to tonight?"

"Just hanging out," squeaked the taller Samson.

"Yea, you know, talking with our boys," added the stronger looking Jett in a high pitch.

"Hanging out huh. Just talking. You boys must think I'm an ass."

"That's all we were doing, really coach," said Samson who was unable to loosen the grip.

"Then what was all that tough-looks and flexing about?" Asked Pops.

"What?"

"What were you all talking about then?" Asked Pops knowingly.

"Uhh, you know, things, girls, school. Coach, your grip is too tight," cried out Jett.

Back at the hospital room were Divine stood over his mother and caressed her hand and forehead. "What are all these tubes and wires and things doing for ya?"

Deanne opened her eyes for a second and gazed on Divine's concern. She closed them then re-opened her eyes again that remained aimed toward Divine. "Looks. Just for looks baby." Deanne reached up and touched Divine's cheek with a weak hand that was almost all bone with her skin wrinkled and discolored. "It's good that you see what this cancer is and what it does. Now you know."

A moment of silence fell as Divine, in a still stance, brought his eyes to scan over his faded away mother who only had a few strains of hair left. He placed his eyes back on to her face with her eyes closed that she opened to meet up with his. The two traded a loving eye connection that reflected the deep bond between mother and son. This might show him what cancer does but that doesn't help in bringing his mother back to the strong and beautiful woman she once was.

The night continued to expose itself out over the city area but that wouldn't stop Seven and Tanisha from hitting the jogging trails and getting in a little exercise. Side by side they ran at a steady pace amongst the peaceful surroundings of one of the many lakes that the city was full of. After the couple rounded the corner, Tanisha slowed down gradually and eventually came to a slow and measured walk in an effort to catch her breath but also to have a moment. Seven, who continued to jog, realized that Tanisha had fallen off the pace. He continued to jog in one place as he turned his body toward Tanisha and passed an 'are-you-quitting' look. "Come on love. We still got another mile. Let's finish this out."

Tanisha walked up to were Seven was jogging in place at and put her hands over her head to open her breathing up. "Let's just walk the last mile together." There was something on her mind that was bothering her and becoming more and more of a presence in her life. Questions along with concerns were filling her up, becoming a heavy weight, and they needed some answers and some direction. And if they were going to walk together and be together, then the only one who could giver her what she needed was he.

Tanisha took hold of Seven's hand that she looked at for a moment then turned up with her lovely brown eyes and gave him a 'please baby' look with a clear face that was full of love and care and could not be dismissed by the young man. Seven understood and broke out a smile that agreed as he came to a stop and took hold of her hand. The two began to stroll thru the dark area with no fear, side by side, hand in hand along the trail.

Benji sat at a large table inside a well-furnished conference room in a high-rise office building downtown with Dean Mason, a forty-something year old Blackman who was decked out in an expensive and flashy Armani suit and silk tie. Dean was one of the aids to the powerful state Senator Henry Raskaskuso. With a moment of silence held in the room, Benji calmly observed Dean thumb thru a file loaded with papers that described Benji's life and accomplishments. "I have to admit, your record Mr. Makkir," said Dean who pronounced the name wrong. "Your record is very impressive. From high school straight to college, in which you graduated in the top half of your class, and then three years of law school and again tops in your class. Along with various fellowships, internships and study abroads in between. Very impressive indeed."

Dean closed the file and began to tap his fingers on it. He looked across the table at Benji who sat patiently but bored. Did this guy really think he was saying something? Benji knew of his accomplishments. He didn't need to be told any of this. This was nothing more then pure hot air to gas up an individual on his achievements. In other words, Benji was being shoveled straight bullshit he didn't need. He took a deep breath and broke out a facial expression that communicated to the young aid to just get to the point of this meeting and what he had to offer.

Rassa moved out of the bathroom where he finished doing a number two then washing himself up and made his way down the stairs. He continued to recite the verse over and over as he entered the kitchen area, looking for that right lyric to make sense. He was searching for those words that described the 'Elvis' tactic being done to Hip-Hop. Over and over the verse was spit, working on that last bar to fit right and feel right. He gave his mother Merrissa, who sat at the hand me down, mid-sized table, a kiss and then proceeded to fix him self some toast. Merrissa, with a comfortable smile on her strong face, turned her eyes on her son as she enjoyed a cup of green tea to fight this little cold she had. Rassa poured a glass of juice when his father, dusty and dirty, who just got home from a long days work, entered in and watched his son wait for his toast. The big, strong, and rough-looking, older Blackman with many wrinkles that laid into his face, unbuttoned the dirty and sweaty shirt. "Well, well, look who decided to get up finally and join us?"

"What's up dad?"

"What's up dad? How about a job boy."

Merrissa lowered her cup of tea that she sipped from to her saucer and turned her head to her husband. "Hal."

A disappointed tension had built up between the father and the son and now it was only growing into a wall that disallowed them from constructive communication. The only words they would share would be few, if any, and they would always be brief in nature. Hal especially was fed up with his son playing around with his life, so he thought. He wanted him to get serious and do something that brought in a steady check. In other words, Hal, in his mind, was looking for his son to become a man. Merrissa thought that it was going to take some time and she had decided to not pressure him and instead just be there for him. She understood the creative side of Rassa and appreciated it, which was something that Hal was unable and unwilling to do.

Born, with a young Blackman named E who was a 6'9 ball headed ballplayer with a diamond in his ear, and a number of their teammates engaged in a highly competitive pick-up basketball game that showcased each of their abilities, their teamwork and the high level of skill possessed by both E and Born.

Deep jump shots, nice moves to the hole, laser passes that led to buckets, high-flying dunks that brought reaction from courtside, and shots that some felt could not be accomplished, but where.

Seated to the side were a group of young and attractive ladies, a young Caucasian man with flip-flops on and a towel draped around his neck who was the team manager, and an assistant coach with a Ron Jeremy moustache who stood and observed the action. In the corner of the gym stood, with arms crossed, a sharp dressed young light-skinned Blackman who was in his early thirties named Alex. 'What was he doing here?' wondered the assistant coach who turned his eyes in his direction then turned back to the action, only to find his eyes back onto this unknown body in the gym.

Alex shifted his eyes from Born on the court doing his thing over to the assistant coach who quickly turned his head away from the dashing young Blackman with a gold watch, a silk tie and a pair of sunglasses that sat on top of his head.

The action intensified. Born was putting on a display that had the observers reacting to his every move and his teams every score. With the ball in his hand, Born jerked his body to the right, crossed over to his left that had the defensive player tripping over his own feet, and laid it up and over the larger and bigger looking center for game point. With no emotion and no reaction, Born casually walked toward the bench area where his things lay at as he received hands and acknowledgments of a good game played.

Alex glanced over toward the assistant coach with an amazed facial expression at the performance he just witnessed and gave a nod and a smile of approval. He then turned his focus up into the rafters of the arena were a dark figure stood and looked down on the action from.

A still sitting Dean Mason brought his hands together as he placed his elbows on the file and set his chin on his clenched hands that had come together. "So tell me, what is it that you can bring to our office?"

Benji took a moment. He dropped his focus from Dean to down on to the file that lay on the table. He then picked his beaming light-brown eyes up and stared right at Dean. He licked his lips and took a breath while he moved up in his seat, closer to Dean. "Now, doesn't that right there, answer that question?"

"It can and it can't," responded the prideful senator's aide.

Benji took his bottle of juice in hand and gulped down a swallow. Dean observed the young man's demeanor, confused and somewhat surprised at how he handled the question. Doesn't this guy know who he's speaking and meeting with?

"You know, I have been on so many of these interviews and meetings, and I have to say that almost all you guys deal in the same manner. You just don't get it, or maybe you do. The fact of the matter is my words can tell you what you would like to hear. Maybe that will bring a smile to your face and I'll get the position. But my past works, that says it loud and clear. See, what I'll bring is someone who will strive for perfection and do the job right from beginning to end."

Benji alternated his look between the file and Dean's eyes with nothing more to be said.

Cherise moved away from the bed and over to the other side of the room. Malik kept his eyes on her closely as he continued to lie back in the bed. "What did you come over here for?" He asked.

Cherise turned around and met up with Malik's eyes. "I mean if that's the way you feel, or the way I make you feel, then why bother coming?" Said Malik comfortably and honestly.

"Because maybe I'm the only one who really cares about us. And that's why it hurts when it seems that you and I are only about this," said Cherise as she motioned toward the bed. "We never go out or, or we never do things like normal people."

"Normal people?" Malik stated with amusement. Was she for real? 'General Hospital' in full effect.

"And when we do go out, it's always with them."

"Them huh?" The amusement ended as Malik's face went cold and emotionless. "So, let me get this straight," said Malik who rose up from the bed to a sitting position with a sort of laid back but serious expression on his face and in his demeanor. "What your saying is that you dislike the present arrangement that you and I have at this time. Is that right?"

Cherise moved toward Malik and nodded her head. She hoped he understood were she was coming from and what she desired from him. What she truly wanted came from different worlds that made it impossible to have both.

DJ stood in the small kitchen area with an apron fastened around his waist and a pair of house slippers on in his boxers. The five foot nine light skinned hustler banged pots around and prepared some homemade soup with music on that he danced to.

His mother, Brenta, a beautiful lady in her mid-forties awakened in her bed from the noise of the pots and dishes. She raised her chunky frame up and slowly moved into the kitchen were she saw her only son cooking. DJ, who was unknown of her appearance, did a dance move that involved a spin that brought him face to face with his straight-faced mother staring at him with crossed arms. "Boy, what are you doing in here?"

"Hey momma," DJ said as he advanced toward her with a smile and planted a kiss on her forehead. "How was your rest? Get enough?"

"It seems like it but that can change quick. Now, what in Lord's name is it that you're doing in my kitchen?"

DJ gently and lovingly took his mother's arm and led her to a chair at the small kitchen table that he pulled out. She took a seat being somewhat dumbfounded at what was going on or what was about to happen.

"Here, take a seat, relax and let me serve you a little something."

Tajaa was laid out on a workbench, doing a set of bench presses with roughly 245 pounds on the bar. Raekwon's newest CD pounded out from the boom box that gave a hand in the workout. Tajaa finished the set and put the bar on its holder and sat up, perspiring heavily. A knock was heard at the door. "Who is it?!" Thundered an exhausted but rejuvenated Tajaa with a firm voice. He got up from the bench and reached for the door.

"It's me . . . Zach!" Said an unsure but loud voice outside the door. Could this really be his older brother? Tajaa thought he was locked up for two more years and hadn't received any word on any change.

Tajaa stepped to the door and opened it up where there in front of him stood the tattooed up older brother, Zachary, who was dressed in khakis, an old sweatshirt, a baldhead, and had a strut in his stand and walk.

"Look who finally showed his face," growled Tajaa with a steely impression that glared on the thirty-five year old man who had trouble keeping eye contact.

Lite stood on the downtown street corner, near a popular nightclub, with a drink in hand among a group of older men in their late twenties to their mid-thirties.

Words followed by laughs filled the air. One of the older men, dressed in knock off clothing that dated back some years and could be found on the sale racks of discount stores, dominated the conversation with a barrage of boasts and put-downs. Minister, an intoxicated, know-it-all, thirty-seven year old ex-high school basketball superstar who now was relegated to memories and spiteful feelings stood with his fake jewelry, turned off cell phone and a bottle of cheap beer.

"I'll tell you young niggas something that you might not know about myself," said the slurring man. "I could go up into that club right now and pull five bitches easy. No problem"

Lite glued his eyes on to the swaying man and looked right thru him. "There you go," challenged Lite as he turned his head in utter disgust. He slowly took a drink from his glass of Schnapps' and observed the area and smelled the night air. He thought about Malik and Divine who told him about the jokers in the hood who avoided and ran from responsibility. And here stood such a person across from him that had been flipped.

Dean adjusted his tie, cleared his throat, and slid back in his chair, feeling a little disrespected by Benji who casually looked over at him. "Mr. Makkir," Dean said as he tapped his index finger nervously on the file. "I can understand how you feel with these type of proceedings and I'm sure they can become monotonous. But Senator Raskaskuso is a very important man in the political system, which I'm sure you're well aware of. And those that join our family here must be of the highest moral, ethical and social standing who work to only increase the power of this office, this government, and this country. This type of position that you're up for is basically a launching pad into congress, the house or whatever other appointments that are available. So that is why we like to hear from you and get to know who you are and what you have to offer and bring to this office," explained the Senator's aide.

Benji worked on getting a piece of lint, hair or dust ball out of his eye followed by a yawn. "Mr. Mason, what I bring is exactly what you've seen and what you see. There are no words that I can express that will allow you to fully understand what I am capable of. My past works fill in that blank there. For you, my abilities and what I may have to offer this office are right there in that file," said with a confident voice that tapped on the file to stress his point.

"I see," said an exhausted Dean, who was all but frustrated but yet still calm. He leaned back in his chair and ran his hands thru his hair. "I must say, you are a very different personality than your father."

Benji was unmoved by the apparent jab by Dean.

"Yes, well. I thank you for coming in. We'll be in touch." Dean got up from his chair at the same time as Benji did and they each extended a cold handshake.

"It was good that I met you." Benji said as they held eye contact with their hands still locked together for a moment. Benji then turned and left out the room with Dean at a loss for what just took place and could only think of what a joke that young man was. But the real joke was on him who lost a gem that walked out the door with an amused grin.

Pops stood in the middle of the field in the night air as he tightened his hold around the neck and shoulders of the two boys who lacked discipline. He had just stopped a fight that might have escalated to knives, chains or guns from taking place. "You know, I remember the group talks we use to have back in the day when I was your age. And they usually ended up with one of us getting knifed, shot or beaten bloody and spending a few days in the hospital. Some times even worse. You hear what I'm saying?"

"Yea, yea but no one had a gun," said the helpless Samson.

"Did I say any of you did?" Asked Pops in a forceful nature.

"No but . . ." Jett leaked out.

"And I got some news about you two missing history class these pass few days."

Samson and Jett remained silent as they turned their eyes from on each other toward the ground.

"I take that to mean that my two players have decided to skip classes these days. Aright, then both of you will understand the punishment to come. I'll see the both of you after class, in my office."

Samson and Jett turned their eyes toward each other in a knowing fashion cause they understood what was going to go down after school.

The bedroom was still and silent for a moment as each traded examining looks back at each other. Malik lifted himself off the bed with a sly and amused smile pasted on his face at the present situation that had taken form. He knew what he had to do and gradually moved toward a gazing Cherise who was anticipating Malik's care about to be expressed with a change to come for the better. Malik strolled by her, with his eyes kept focused on her. He passed her and stopped at her backside. He grabbed her softly by the shoulders and began to massage them, which relaxed her as she closed her eyes and felt the touch of his fingertips. Malik spun Cherise around calmly so that she ended up facing toward him where they locked eyes on each other once again. Malik looked on the young woman and only felt a feeling of disappointment. Disappointed cause she had failed to enjoy where they were in their relationship at the present moment. Disappointed cause she failed to see or understand him and them. Disappointment cause she failed to have patience with the course that they were taking. She was like so many women in these days that were always attempting to change men into what they perceived as being right. But right for who? What was so wrong with were they were at in the relationship? How come she couldn't find happiness with the present situation? And here stood Malik, a young man of twenty-five, who lived his life as he saw fit for the moment. He was about self-improvement but it would come from him and it would be in his own time. He was about the kind of love that showed being at peace with self. He was about truth that stood in the mirror and looked back at all times. He knew the best thing to do was throw everything fake out and care about the real. "So tell me, what would you like from me?" Asked the strong and confident voice of Malik.

This was what Cherise had been waiting for and she jumped on it with vigor. "I'd like to go out to dinner. I'd like to go out to a concert. I'd like to go out to plays and fairs and shows. I want us to visit museums and galleries and take trips together. You know, things like that," said an excited and passionate Cherise searching to make her point.

Malik calmly and slowly moved from Cherise's eyes and retrieved his shirt and jogging pants that were folded on a chair that he begun to put on. "Well yo, it looks like the time has arrived for us to make a change here," exclaimed Malik who took a seat in the chair to put his socks on.

Cherise was overcome with a sense of happiness that she was getting thru to him. Pleasingly, she kneeled down to him and sensuously wrapped her arms around Malik who finished getting dressed despite the embrace. He stood up with Cherise who rose up with him to a standing position face to face in close contact. He put his hands to her cheek and gently held her head in his hands and stared into her eyes deeply and caringly. He realized at that moment that he had to do the right thing.

DJ wiped the table that Brenta sat at then placed down a spoon. "I've made a little something, something for you moms. Get you on your feet and give you some of that natural energy after a long nights work." He took a few steps over toward the stainless steel pot on the burner and took a taste to make sure it was just right. He gave a nod of approval to himself and reached for a bowl to his side that he filled with the vegetable soup.

"When did you learn to cook?" Asked Brenta with a pleased but surprised voice.

DJ placed the steaming bowl of food down on the table, in front of his mother and took a couple steps back and set his eyes on her about to give his soup a taste. "What do you expect when you've lived with three females all your life. Now, go ahead and give it a taste."

Brenta lifted a spoonful to her mouth and blew on it to cool it down. After a brief moment, she took it into her mouth and savored the taste that, to her, was astonishingly good. "Impressive," Brenta said as she took another spoonful in hand. "This is real good baby."

DJ, with a bowl in hand, pulled out a chair and took a seat beside his mother. He moved up close to the table, took the spoon in hand, scooped up some carrots, potatoes and broccoli into his spoon and gave a blow to cool it off. He gingerly placed the spoon in his mouth in which the hot food began to burn the inside of his mouth that he continued to cool down in between bites. "How's things at the nursing home?"

"Crazy and chaotic," his mother said quickly with no hesitation. "Do you know that I got to pull a double shift this upcoming weekend because we're short again? On top of that, they got the wrong people administering the wrong measure of meds that's causing some serious problems. We have aids that are being run ragged, having to cover two floors, which affects their work. And who do you think catches the hell?" Said Brenta with a touch of aggravation. "I'll tell ya baby, all these women who say they don't need a man and want to work in this job market, don't know what they're getting themselves into. I'm tired, so tired. You just don't know baby," said Brenta in an out of breath tone with a lowered head that took a rest for a moment. She raised it up and continued to eat.

DJ with his eyes stuck on her and her tired body could only think of what was happening to his mother. Slowly she was killing herself. The very life that taught him how to dance, that had a smile on when bills piled up, that had an upbeat word of encouragement along with the strict hand of discipline was slowly draining from her. The system was killing his momma. The mother that loved him thru all was being taken from him, piece by piece. Sadness and anger filled him up as he looked with care on his mother who had done so much for him. How could he help her?

Divine spotted a chair in the corner of the hospital room. He pulled it toward himself and took a seat close to Deanna's side. He kept his dark brown eyes placed on her who could barely keep her eyes open for a long length of time. Just long enough to make sure her oldest son's face was still in the room.

"I love you so much momma," Divine said as he leaned over her and rested his head on her shoulder that she began to rub gently, with a motherly touch.

"I know you do baby. Hey, listen to me."

Divine lifted his head up and straightened his look at her.

"Have you seen Franklin lately?"

Franklin. Divine's little brother of eighteen years old who had dived head first into the sea of crack and alcohol. He was known on the streets as a fiend who will take any thing and everything from any one at any time to support the only thing he cared about – getting high. Divine took his time as he thought about the young man that he had reached out to a number of times in a variety of ways. And the same thing came back to slap him in the face each time. Either money was stolen or borrowed, things were taken or lies were told. It never seemed to change with him and it never seemed to matter or care. Divine was aware that the only one that could really help him was himself and nobody else. Not mother, not Malik, not the clinics that got people off one drug only to hook them onto other drugs just to get a rep, or not him self. Divine thought about his little brother and what had become of him but he knew it was his choice. The decision was upon him on what he wanted to do and where he wanted to go.

Divine lowered his head toward his mother and shook it from side to side. With a feeling of lost ness and sadness in her eyes, she turned her head toward the window and stared out to where the night sat outside. She thought, what had happened to her youngest?

Born sat on one of the plastic chairs that were one of many placed to the side of the court. He exchanged hugs, handshakes and praises from the other players in the game who enjoyed the competition and an opportunity to taste what Born had to offer. He got a hold of his duffel bag and pulled out a dry shirt with a bottle of water and a towel and began to dry himself off. The group of young, white and black ladies approached Born with eagerness to make their presence known to him. Born immediately caught the sight of the attractive ladies heading in his direction.

"Whheeww! Nice game Born," said the white girl with dark hair and green eyes who arrived in front with a sexy smile that had no problem moving in his arms for a hug.

"Yea, I love how you play. You make everything," followed the other white girl with red hair and a nice figure that included a pair of big titties and a banging rear end.

As Born broke from the clutches of the brunette, he cracked a small smile as he finished drying off his body that the ladies took an interest in. They moved closer in, all except for one, who stood on the outside, behind the small gathering of adoring girls.

"You were aright. You're outside shot looked a little off today. You better hope teams don't throw a zone on you," said the light-skinned Black woman who had her long, thick hair in a braided ponytail.

Born fixed his eye contact on the lovely looking, yet with an inner toughness that still had a gentleness to it, young lady. He extended his hand toward her that she took and pulled her in close for a hug as they exchanged knowing smiles with each other. Born was attracted to the deep honesty and the realism this young lady expressed. Cessy was known for being blunt and upfront and Born respected that in her which also increased her beauty and her attracting.

The two other ladies took an amazed look at each other and cracked a smile feeling the connection that they were witness too. They knew.

Born backed himself up from the deep embrace and searched for his shirt. "So you think my jumper needs a little fine tuning huh?"

"It's just a hunch."

The two smiled at each other. Born licked his lips to eliminate the white crust that had developed from the sweat and nodded his head to agree with her assessment.

The red head stepped in front and placed her hand in a way that only a female can do on Born's shoulder. "Anyways, are you going to that thing tonight?"

Born, who had his eyes fixed on the sweet piece that spoke some truth with conviction to him, turned his eyes on to the sexy thing that undressed him with her sexual look.

Tajaa and Zachary stood at the door and stared across at each other in silence. Tajaa's eyes burned deep at Zachary who was unsure of what to say or what to do. So much time had passed and what the fuck was he doing out so early?

"How you been little brother," said a somewhat shameful Zachary, not really knowing what to expect from his baby brother or how to act.

"I've been good. Thought you never get out," said Tajaa who sharpened his glare on his stone face that revealed no emotion.

A silent period was held that had Zachary contemplating turning around and leaving from the entryway.

"Bra, come here." Tajaa broke out with a smile and grabbed his thin brother who looked like he hadn't ate in days, and gave him one thunderous bear hug with those huge arms wrapped around. The two animated individuals moved into the small apartment.

"When did you get out?"

"A month ago."

"And you're just coming to see me now? I ought to whip that ass just for neglecting me like that. What's up?!"

"Please little brother, come on now, don't hurt me," begged Zachary with a relieved smile attached. He took much notice in how his baby brother had filled out in the physical. "Dam, you got big but I, I had some loose ends that I had to untangle and tie up, ya know."

"True, true," he took a seat and observed Zachary who stood and looked around the place that was barely furnished. If any one could help him out, Zachary thought, it would be him, his little brother who he practically raised by himself.

Seven and Tanisha walked hand in hand, with their shoulders lightly touching, thru the night that had draped itself around the lake that provided a jogging trail that connected all the way around. Tanisha came to a stop, which in turn brought Seven to halt his calm steps by the tug on his arm. Something was on her mind that was most visible on her delicate facial features and Seven took notice.

"What?" Asked Seven as their hands released slowly from each other.

"Do you ever think of the future and us? I mean, what is to be?"

Seven took a slow step toward her and touched, with his swinging arm, her hand. "I'd rather live in the present with you building for the future. That's what really matters."

Tanisha was looking for a better answer that would bring comfort to her, which she needed at this point. "You know what I mean. Don't you have any regrets or concerns or worries that – "

Seven understood what was on her mind and what she was really asking. "Regrets?" Seven spoke up, cutting her off. "I have none, love. And as for concerns and worrying, that takes up too much time and energy."

Seven looked deep into the young ladies' eyes. Where was this coming from? They had been thru so much together and had experienced the highs and the lows and survived it hand in hand. And now, on this muggy night in the city, she asked of regrets. Her eyes had a seriousness in them that was filled with too much concern that Seven clearly saw. Seven thought for a moment that they were stepping into a part of their lives that would bring them to face the ultimate test. Their love for each other was unquestioned, but the direction, Seven saw, was the key to the growth of their love for each other.

Pops, who kept his tight hold on Samson and Jett's necks with his two large hands, gave a disturbed look down at the boys who begged to be released while standing in the middle of the more dirt then grass field.

"Come on coach. This is hurting," both pleaded at the same time, one over the other.

"Tell me, who's the teacher of that class you two are skipping?"

"Mr. Wheeler," cried out Jett with no hesitation.

"Wheeler huh," Pops said with an inner concern for the welfare of the children and what was happening behind school doors. He was aware of Mr. Wheeler's liberal ways that allowed students freedom without consequences.

He finally released the hold that allowed the boys to massage their necks and regain circulation. They each turned and faced Pops who had a serious glare stuck on his face. He was disturbed at the name relayed to him and began to plot in his mind the action to be taken.

"Coach, that man doesn't care what we do. He just throws us the books and then likes to listen to himself talk. It's mad boring," Samson spouted out with a high pitch.

"And he treats us like, like we're nothing. Like we don't exist and I don't like that," Jett chimed in.

"And you don't like that. It's boring," Pops said with a touch of ridicule mixed with anger and disappointment. The large man became silent as he stared down at the two boys who felt the pressure coming from his tender but firm brown eyes.

DJ ate a couple spoons of the soup he had just put together, and in the middle of digestion his eyes caught the picture of a tired woman leaning onto the table that brought him to take his mother's hand into his. "What can I do for you momma? All you gotta do is tell me"

Brenta ceased from lifting her spoon to her mouth let it down into her bowl then turned and looked straight at DJ with a determined glare that was held for a quiet moment. Brenta took a breath and released it. "Baby, the only thing I want you to do for me is survive and live," said the sweet voice. She placed her other hand on top of his. "That's it. I don't want to see you end up like your father – shot in the streets over a dollar. Don't let a fantasy or a nightmare destroy you."

"I know momma," spoke a knowing DJ.

"I want you to remember that all this; the job, the problems, the bills, the pain, the tough times, this I can fight and overcome. But if you give up, that's what would kill me."

DJ, for the first time, really felt what he meant to her. It finally made sense the connection a child has with its mother. He leaned toward Brenta and gave a kiss to the top of her head.

"You deserve so much more momma."

"This will do for the time being. Now, back to this soup. It's delicious baby."

DJ cracked an accomplishing smile and picked up his spoon. Brenta returned her focus back to the soup. DJ slightly turned his head and observed his mother who he wanted to do so much for but understood that the last thing he wanted to do was be the death of her.

A disturbed and agitated Hal stood over the kitchen sink, popped a couple aspirins into his mouth followed by a few gulps from a glass of water to push them down. He picked his head up from the sink filled with a few dirty dishes and looked straight ahead at the wall in front of him. "This boy lays around, sleeps most of the day, and comes and goes as he pleases," the grizzly voice harped that turned around and looked at the lanky young man who stood at the toaster. "Running the streets in the night. You must think I'm a fool. Is that what you think I am?" Hal glared at Rassa for a moment then took his seat at the table with a worried Merrissa who rose up to fix the larger, older man a glass of tea, thinking it may calm him down.

Rassa's vision followed the older man and looked on him sit at the table and drink the tea that was set in front by Merrissa. "Stop bugging old man," with a playful laughter in his voice and a small grin, trying to ease the situation and break the tension building up.

"Boy, you better . . . don't even go there. This ain't no joke."

Rassa quickly realized that his father was in no kidding around mood and placed his eyes back on his bread that was in the toaster that popped up at that moment. Hal had always been on him to do something other then this 'hip-hop thang' but every time an opportunity came at Rassa, he kept his focus on his rhymes.

Hal reeled his head around and set his eye contact directly on Rassa at the kitchen counter. "My question is, when are you going to grow up and do something with yourself? Take some responsibility and stop with all this foolishness." Hal spun his head from Rassa's sight and met up with Merrissa's brown, soft and caring eyes that were filled with a deep concern. Rassa remained quiet as he played with a verse underneath his breath and spread some jam and butter on his toast that had popped up and took a drink of his orange juice.

Malik and Cherise stood face to face in the bedroom that was lit up by a small lamp that was placed near the bed, on a side table. The two were so close they could basically feel each other's breath on their faces as their eyes were firmly placed on each other. A smile sat on her face with pleasure in anticipation of Malik's next words.

"Let's start with those wants you desire," stated Malik plainly.

"Yea."

"Well, I'm unable to provide you with them, and so – " Malik moved away from a surprised and stunned Cherise, whose mouth was opened, eyes were blinking and finger-tips were twitching at what she just heard. He reached for the door that he pulled open to reveal the outside hallway to her. "You've got to go."

Cherise stood still in silence and disbelief. Did he really just say that to her? Men don't act like this when it comes to a fine girl like her. Maybe he was playing around. This could not be happening. She turned her head and gazed at Malik as she took one step toward the door, and it was at that moment she realized that this was for real and so was he. "Wh, what? I, I can't believe you," stuttered and stumbled Cherise, searching for breath of control.

"I know and that's the reason why this has to be done."

"What is this? You know, you know what you're . . ."

Malik threw up his open hand immediately that stopped her cold from speaking anymore. He then gently, with grace and command, led her out of the room with a smooth, guiding push and into the hallway. She shuffled out in complete amazement. Malik closed the door, took a breath and headed back over toward the unmade bed. It was necessary. He had to do it for her and himself. Cause if she wasn't happy then there was no way he could be happy. This was the best move for them at that moment in time.

Cherise stood still at the closed door for a brief period and stared at the cream colored wood with the rusted doorknob. She then slowly spun away from the door and began to stomp away toward the front door entrance. She passed Freddie and a lounging J-Rob who relaxed back on the couch in the front room. Their eyes turned away from the television and on to the young lady whose face was flushed and grim looking. Cherise pushed the door open with a violent thrust and she was gone.

Malik stepped out of the bedroom and joined the two other young men out in the living room area, watching the sport highlights on the television.

"Decided she wanted to take the other road?" Asked a cognitive J-Rob who was aware of the whole scene without needing to go into details and with out glancing toward Malik.

"Yep, and it's too bad cause mommy had a lot of potential, and some of the softest skin."

"Yea, and a banging ass," Freddie added.

J-Rob and Malik turned their heads to each other and exchanged eye contact. They then burst out in laughter at Freddie. He still didn't get it when it came to women and relationships. Malik wasn't all about the banging ass, big titties and gorgeous faces. He was after a woman who respected her self and what he was about. And if they were unable to see that, and love that, then the door would always be shown.

J-Rob knew this. He had learned this from Malik and felt that a new stand, a new way in relating with each other, had to come for there to be a solid connection between man and woman.

Freddie remained in his chair, unaware of what the laughter was really about. He thought he was just being funny with the added comment. How wrong he was.

The two young in the head boys stood in front of Pops with their caps on backward, their oversized t-shirts wrinkled and their dark jeans sunk low, almost falling off their behinds.

Jett looked up with a disgruntled expression on his hairless face. "I mean, it's like in history, all we were was slaves. That's all he ever teaches about black people."

"And he doesn't care. He let's us come and go as we want, so," Samson chimed in with. "We actually didn't skip, we just left and didn't return."

"Don't cop out and don't punk out. Be accountable. It's still on you though, even if he looks away and doesn't care. It's up to you to do what's right, otherwise suffer the consequences – like the both of you will with me tomorrow," Pops said as he took a moment and thought about the state of young people and how they were being allowed to get away with small things that eventually became big things. "You young brothers have to start using your minds instead of losing them to emotions. Because this world, no matter what they say, is very unforgiving. And I don't want to see you behind bars or in a grave. You hear me?"

Pops and the two boys stood still in silence for a moment as they traded caring and understanding looks with each other. The boys had felt what Pops was saying and took notice in the vibration of words that came from the heart to only make a better way.

"Now, the both of you, get out of here and go home. And do some studying."

Samson and Jett, who felt cared for, walked off across the field side by side. Pops kept his eyes stuck on the two boys who moved farther and farther away from him. Pops didn't feel good. He didn't feel good about the boys and what they had to say. He didn't feel good that a group of black boys were preparing to kill each other. And he definitely didn't feel good that teachers were negating their duty as teachers and allowing students to skip classes. This had to change. And for it to change, Pops had to make a stand that many refused to do when it came to the city and public schooling. Pops looked back toward the school and after a moment of thought, headed back in that direction from which he came.

The group of men of various ages, continued to gather on the downtown street corner. Lite broke into a loud yawn and moved his eyes around the area to give it a quick canvas.

Minister sipped from his plastic cup and made a few catcalls to a couple passing women. "Ain't nothing but a pimp thing going on here baby. Y'all need to come and holla at a nigga."

Lite turned his eyes and plainly stared at Minister with a straight face that exposed no emotion, no care, just plain disgust. Lite was the type whose thoughts quickly got put into words and expressed verbally. Minister ignored the young man's intense eyes. His only concern was to show how big of a man he was. "I got twenty that at the end of the night, you don't have nothing but some facial pains. Not even a mud-duck's name," challenged Lite.

"Ahh young nigga, you must not know. Bitches ain't shit to me. I'll pull a bitch with just the smell of my ass. That's how raw I am out here. And bitches know this. You better ask somebody."

"Yea, yea, yea," said Lite who turned away, unconvinced and unimpressed.

Laughter erupted from the other men in small jewelry, old shoes and meager clothing, who were amused at Minister's antics and Lite's reaction. Lite took a drag on the pinner-joint that was making the rounds. He passed it on and took a drink from the bottle of wine cooler in his hand and looked away nonchalantly. A young lady driving by recognized Lite and hollered out toward him. Lite returned the greeting to the young lady with a smile and a hand-finger gesture. Lite was the burning example that was shown by so-called leaders of what was wrong with the youth. Standing out on the corner, pants low with a bottle of wine and a joint in his hands. But what they failed to see despite all that was he had sense to know of loyalty and courage, something the so-called leaders lacked immensely.

Born, with the group of three young ladies still encircled around, placed his wet, sweaty shirt that he played in along with his towel and an empty bottle of water into his unzipped duffel bag. "What's going on tonight?"

"There's a party tonight over at Cynthia's. It suppose to be crazy wild there," said the dark-haired girl.

"You should go Born. Both you and E," the redhead added as she turned toward E who was off on the other side of the court, speaking with the assistant coach.

Born finished off the rest of the other bottle of water as he passed a smile that communicated 'maybe', keeping his intentions to himself. "Are all of you going to be there?"

"Of course, you know us," the red head said with a seductive smile that yearned for him to take her to bed. She dreamed of being his girl.

"I don't know if I am," interrupted the light-skinned young woman confidently.

Born focused his eyes off the two ladies front and center, and placed them directly on an unassuming Cessy. She stood tall and observed the area as well as Born's disposition in between with quick looks. She was interested but she knew this wasn't the moment to openly reveal what she felt.

Deanne laid in the bed, facing away from Divine who kept his eyes on his ailing mother. Deanne crunched up her face and closed her eyes as a burst of pain in her stomach rose up and attacked with a great kick.

It passed after a moment that allowed her to gather up some strength to speak. "I don't know how much longer I have. Each day takes another little piece out of me," Deanne weakly let out. "There's one thing I like to ask you to do, for me."

"Anything."

"Find Franklin," Deanne said with her eyes straightened out and aimed at Divine who looked away and lowered his head.

"Momma."

"I'm asking you to reach out to him. Find him. Help him."

Divine lifted his head and looked directly at his mother who was asking a difficult request of him. "Don't you think I've already done that? That boy is on his own road. It's up to him if he wants help."

Deanna stayed silent and fixed her cloudy whites that surrounded her small pupils on Divine. This was her last wish. Both of them saw this.

The school hallway stood still, quiet and in darkness, after hours in the high school that was located on the south side of the city. Mr. Jack Wheeler, a small, bald

Caucasian man with glasses, exited his classroom on the first floor and began to walk down the isolated hallway with briefcase in hand and a whistling tune coming from out his mouth. The history class teacher passed a break in the lockers that was covered in darkness.

A voice raised up that echoed out loud and clear toward Mr. Wheeler from behind. "Jack. You have a minute?"

A shaken Mr. Wheeler froze for a moment in fright. He spun around and adjusted his glasses so to get a clear look at the large man standing before him. "Walker?"

Pops stepped out of the darkness that encased him and into a speck of light that revealed his face. "Yea."

"You startled me," said a relieved Mr. Wheeler. He took a deep breath and composed himself.

Pops remained silent with a stone face and stared at Mr. Wheeler that provoked a sense of discomfort in the cheap suit-wearing teacher who liked to claim his liberal activist roots.

Seven and Tanisha came to a stop on the paved walkway and faced each other with a deserving care in their eyes. Seven lifted his strong hand and brought it to her face were he lightly caressed Tanisha's brown cheek. He moved closer. "What is it?"

Tanisha took her time and searched for the right words to describe her feelings. A feeling of intense moments of fear had shaken her and her sense of belief. She wanted badly at times to remain under the blankets and never come out. There were days were she felt she could do anything but every so often this feeling of despair would raise it's ugly head to bring doom. "There are times when I stop, look and listen, and all I see is pain, misery and chaos around me, and it scares me. I don't like that feeling Seven. I ask myself, what about the children? Our children? Are they going to have to live thru the same mess? What's going to happen to us in this? And there are times when it has me doubting everything in life. Even you sometimes."

Seven pulled Tanisha into his arms that wrapped around her and merged the front of his head with her smooth forehead. Seven felt her pain, her fear, and her confusion. It made him think of his purpose and the importance in it. After a moment of physically comforting, the couple pulled their heads apart and looked on each other. They both felt the love that existed between them that was manifested without words. Their actions said it all.

"The doubt is there to test you, and me. Use it, learn from it, and see it for what is really is. All that matters love, right now, is us, you and I, building a home. This world is what it is, but don't let it stop you from growing together with me, ya know. The child is the best part, regardless of that which surrounds you and I. We have a duty. So let's do it."

Tanisha looked up at Seven, strong and firm, and broke a smile out on her face. She saw what he meant by the duty of each and she also saw that he understood her concerns that he made his.

She understood that the only ones who could create a place were babies could grow, children could learn and teenagers could be teenagers that could correct mistakes, was them. And she valued what she had in her life

"I love you," said Tanisha who was the same height as Seven.

"There's that smile. And I know what would feel good right now." Seven began to caress her body at each point and slowly began to move toward and on to Tanisha in a seductive way. Their bodies came close together and their arms wrapped around and embraced each other.

"And what would that be?" Asked Tanisha knowingly.

Their faces and lips came extremely close together with out touching. Seven lowered his hands from Tanisha's face and on to her waist. He slowly and gingerly placed his lips on hers with a kiss engaged in. As their lips and tongues massaged each other, Seven moved his hands to her mid-section and after a brief rub, started to tickle her. She began to laugh uncontrollably and then turned and ran from Seven's long fingers. He chased her thru the dark trail and finally caught her and made a two-hand tackle in the grass, to the side of the jogging trail. The couple rolled around in a loving embrace then came to stop and shared a passionate kiss in the night, under the stars.

Tajaa took a seat on the floor and began to stretch out his legs and do a set of crunches. "You represent in there?"

Zachary was in a state of not knowing how to act after all the years away. He stood and held onto his bag in the middle of the room and just looked around. "You know I did, even though I had to use them things a few times."

Tajaa took notice in Zachary failing to comfort himself. It must be jail, he thought. Prison was able to make people so dependant on being told what to do, when to speak, how to live, that they carried that same type of dependency out in the world. "Take a seat brother, make your self comfortable. You want something to drink, eat or what?"

"A soda if you got it."

"I don't have no acid in a can but there is some grape juice in the fridge. Get your ass in there and help your self to whatever. What the fuck I look like," said Tajaa with a slight smile.

Zachary, with a touch of hesitation, dropped his bag and moved into the kitchen. He looked around at what his little brother had made for himself with satisfaction. He opened the fridge and got out the pitcher of grape juice. "Still the same old scrub that followed me back in the days. Out here living now. Look it you."

Tajaa finished his crunches and turned his eyes toward his brother and broke out a grin. He remembered the days of tagging along behind Zachary, playing football with him, getting taken care of by him when their parents left their lives. His older brother was always there for him and he made sure to instill an inner toughness to survive in a cold world. They had their many fistfights but grudges were never held.

This was what he passed to Tajaa who wanted to give back in whatever way he could. And now he returned from incarceration for a stick-up job he pulled that only netted him $110. Tajaa knew that his brother and his crew of bandits thought very little of the system and even less of the working-class structure that collected taxes and provided enough just to get by. Zachary was on the path of fuck getting by, he wanted it all and stealing was just a racket that he saw as necessary in a place that was built on taking from. Tajaa, with an understanding smile, kept his eyes focused on his brother and all he wanted was for him to be straight and upfront. Tajaa knew he was a thief, so be it. But just be honest with him and on the level. It was the only love that meant something in this day. "Yea, yea I sure did. I was right behind you. Runny nose and all. Especially when dad was sent away. You remember?" Agreed Tajaa in remembrance of past times.

Zachary moved back into the room. "Some."

"You were my influence, my guide, in those days. You showed me a lot."

Zachary took a seat and exhaled a breath that revealed a moment that he had found to relax. "And now what?"

"And now we're young men out here in this who are responsible for the choices and decisions we make," plainly stated Tajaa. "There's no more following. We have to make a bed now and then lie in it."

Silence fell over the room with their eyes locked on each other. Zachary knew what he meant by that and what it called for from him. There where times that you had to show how strong you really were and what you were loyal too. Cause one way or another, it would eventually come out and be revealed.

On the festive basketball court that saw a variety of people engaged in conversation, E broke away from the assistant coach he was speaking with and made his way over to where Born and the ladies were gathered. He extended his arms out to each woman who fell into them with a little girl fancy that included smiles, jokes and playful gestures. They loved E and his party all the time personality that was beyond friendly. He was down right big brotherly and loved to flirt, which they didn't mind at all. Matter of fact, they encouraged it. After a few small words were thrown back and forth, the ladies said their good-byes and left out the gym. Born kept his eyes on the light-skinned beauty who returned the glance all the way until she vanished out the doors. E observed his friend and teammate and the attraction the young Black woman had on him with a small smile.

In the background, Alex, the mystery man in the gym, and the assistant coach shared some words and gestures that illustrated his interest in Born.

E joined Born and took a seat in one of the chairs next to him. He saw that Born was taking his time, relaxing, and letting his body cool down and calm down. Born was never one to make unnecessary moves. He took his time until the moment came to make that dash to the goal, at the defender or whatever brought about that feeling of urgency to go. And here he was after that performance acting like Yoda did after he had that fight with Count Dooku, slow, old and measuring each step to make sure not to over-exert him self. "That was some nice play out there. That's what I'm talking about," said Born with a laid back casualness.

"Just remember, I'd also like to go top ten." E added with a flashed smile that Born picked up on and flashed one himself. Their teammates, who adored, admired and respected the two stars, along with the student observers, passed by the young men on their way toward the exit. Born and E extended handshakes and hugs to each with Born informing some of the young guys who idolized the basketball star about Cynthia's party that brought a wave of excitement. Everybody was apprised of that girl's pool parties at her parent's home because they would get loose, wild and fun.

Born remembered the last time he went. It was the first time he had ever had three women at the same time. It was incredible for him. As for the girls, well, only one was satisfied. He chuckled and looked over at E who rocked his neck side to side, attempting to crack it. "What are you getting into tonight?" Asked Born.

"Come on, you know better then to ask me that with Cynthia's about to pop off."

"What? You might want to stay at the rest and watch some Sanford and son re-runs."

E cocked his head to the side and curled his lip. "Funny guy."

"So you decided to come out after this year?" Asked Born.

"I got feelers out there. See what they're talking about, but if I can get that top ten money, I'm gone."

"Yo, yo, all I'll say is be aware of the long money over that short money. There are a lot of players who left early and weren't ready. And even though they got picked in the first round with guaranteed money, in the end, after a couple years, they're over seas somewhere playing for that small money in a foreign land. I don't want to see you be one of those cats who leaves just cause some numb-nut said that you'll go top ten and you get your three year-seven and half mill, team option contract, which is really around a mill for each year after taxes. On top of that, being unprepared in the head, fall off to the bench of some second rate team that doesn't make the playoffs and collect your four hundred grand, maybe seven hundred, and float around the league. You know? I'm talking about being the one the team builds around and make that long paper after three years. I'm talking about seven year-ninety-six mill."

"I hear ya sun," said an open E to what was being shared to him by Born.

"Now do the math and really study yourself son and love what you do, cuz if you don't love it, fuck it."

E was somewhat overcome at what was just laid out to him. Born had ran down what only a select few had mentioned to him in passing. And here was his teammate relaying the whole story that made sense to him. Too many in this game were taking the quick, short money without fully developing and being aware of ones own self-potential. Instead of realizing where one was at in the moment, they were caught up, looking too far ahead.

Just at that moment, Alex and the assistant coach parted hands and went in separate directions. The sharp dressed young man who sported a thin moustache made his way toward Born and E. He stood in front of the young hoop stars on the campus and was well aware of the man whom he extended his hand out toward. "How you doing Wallace?"

Born looked up in the middle of changing his socks. He knew that this dude was from the other side using his government name. "What's happening with you?"

E lifted his eyes and looked on the laid-back young man who stood with a supreme confidence. E shifted his eyes back toward Born. "Another fan of yours?"

"Hi Edward."

"What's going on my man?" Said a surprised E who returned the handshake with Alex.

"Traveling, watching, evaluating. You looked really good out there. I see you're in top shape. That's impressive, really impressive, especially these days. You coming out after this year?"

E, stunned by the reply of questions and the assessment, looked Alex up and down with a 'who is this guy' expression. Then he turned to Born who was studying the young man's demeanor. "Who is this guy?" Questioned E who extended his thumb in Alex's direction.

"What's up man? Who are you?"

"Just a friend of someone important in the game. Can we speak in private Wallace?"

Born and E shifted their eyes toward each other. Born made a gesture with his face that had E grabbing his things. E and Born shared a hug with hands gripped and the tall, slender young man moved out of the gym but not before he gave one last look of concern in the direction of Born. E exited the doors that slammed shut with a loud thud and left the gymnasium quiet and deserted, except for Born and a standing Alex.

Hal sat at the table in the middle of the kitchen with Merrissa who worked and stroked the older man, attempting to keep him calm. Merrissa was a lady who looked her age and did it with grace. Tall and full in weight but not fat and not chunky with tender hands that were taken care of.

She watched Hal closely, searching for any sign of understanding that he might have of the younger man. She was well aware of his anger toward his only son and were this could lead. Hal took a drink from his cup of tea. "And do you know what this boy wants to be? A rapper!" Hal started to beat box with his mouth and very badly with spit flying all out.

Rassa turned and looked with a crazy expression at his father with a half amused half disgusted expression.

"Yea, a rapper. You believe this shit? Here I am busting my ass all day and I come home to this. A grown man waking up. But that's all good cause he's going to be rapper."

Rassa took his plate of toast and grabbed a seat next to his irate father. "And what is it that you like me to be dad, huh? Do you want me to be a twelve-hour a day, menial labor employee that only makes enough to pay the bills but can't stand looking at himself in the mirror cause he never took that shot to do what he loves? Or would you like me to be one of those robots out here who has a salary but no mind and no life?"

Hal turned his head and glared at his lanky son for a moment, itching to stand up from his chair. Rassa had hit a soft spot that Merrissa took notice in that pushed her to hold a little tighter on to Hal's hand in an effort to restrain his anger rising.

"Boy, I've done told you once. Don't you raise your voice in my house."

"Dad, I'm an artist. How come you can't see that? I'm an artist. What's so wrong with that?"

"An artist huh? Well, let me tell you something. What you need to do is start getting serious, especially around here. Cause it must be nice to be an artist and not have any bills. But that can all change. And you better be aware of it boy."

Rassa saw that his father refused to hear his voice. A quiet ultimatum was being made in a non-direct way. Instead of an older man who saw the beauty in the words expressed by a young one, he saw a resentful, angry old man in front of him whose only way to communicate came out of frustration. Maybe this came from slavery, maybe from his full time job that kept him pinned in one position, maybe from his own father who exhibited the same cold nature. Rassa coolly ate his food and swallowed down his juice as he kept his eyes away from the fire emanating from his father with the room dipped in silence.

Back in the dim hospital room that had that sour, anti-biotic smell, Deanne picked her head up a little and looked over on Divine with sadness in her eyes. She needed the thought of her youngest son, Franklin, getting that needed hand of help out of the hell he was trapped in. "For me, do this, please. He's so lost out there."

"But he's . . ."

"What, on drugs? I know. But please, give me your word that you'll try one more time with Franklin. He needs you"

Divine paused for a moment and lowered his eyes to the cold floor. His then picked his head up, looked at his mother and began to gently rub her forehead. "You have my word."

"Good, good," said the weak voice of Deanne who placed her head back down into her pillow. Divine remained looking on her. She deserved a peace of mind and should this bring some to her, then he would do what it takes. And this would not only be in words, but he would surely follow thru in actions as well.

Zachary, nervously and fidgety, with a touch of anxiety, attempted to relax back in a raggedy old chair to the side of the room that definitely needed to be retired to the dumpster. Tajaa stretched out his limbs to make sure each ligament was given the proper attention. "Have you been up to see dad?" Asked Zachary.

Tajaa rose up and moved to the bench were he took a seat. "Not for a couple years since he told me that he didn't want to see my face."

"You know that was the hurt and pain talking. Prison, the bars, they can do that. They can make you refuse any contact with the outside world so that you harden and forget. It's demeaning in there bra, it's nothing nice."

"You don't have to tell me that."

"I'm just saying, it's a family breaker. You should really go see him."

"Maybe."

"Fuck maybe."

Tajaa turned his eyes on to his serious looking brother and saw the importance in what he was saying and what he was asking. Tajaa slowly nodded his head. Zachary was right. He did need to see his father and his father needed to see him. So many years had passed since that night when anger squeezed of six shots that laid down two men who had jumped a friend of his and in return he got life. Tajaa felt both sorry for him and angry with him for leaving his sons all alone in a frigid world.

The street corner downtown began to pickup with traffic as the hour increased into the night. Lite stood a few steps away from the overbearing Minister who was becoming increasingly drunk with each drink from his cup that strengthened his courage. And with each gulp brought an egotistical boast. Lite swung his head around and glared straight at Minister. "Yo, how come it's bitch this and bitch that from you?"

Minister took a moment and exchanged humorous looks with the other men of the group that surrounded him. He moved his eyes directly back on to Lite with a deep and crooked smirk. "You must be a young nigga talking like that."

"For real, you have a low outlook on our women. What's up with that? Cause that's a lot of bitches you keep hollering about."

Minister straightened up his facial expression, took another drink and then wiped the drip from the corner of his mouth. "Because that's what they are little nigga."

"Come on duke, you know there are some lovely, precious young ladies out here who are searching for the right one to devote themselves to. And they are far from bitches."

"Look it here young nigga," said Minister who moved up close to Lite as he refused the rest of what was left of the pinner-joint. "They're bitches because they're out here for one thing – the paper. They want to drive luxury cars, wear Gucci, Prada and all that bullshit, flash diamonds and pearls, and act like their shit don't stink. That's what makes them bitches."

Lite took a drag from the other weed joint being passed around and blew the herb smoke in Minister's face and then shook his head in disagreement and disappointment at the older man who chugged from his cup. The older man was becoming more irritated with Lite and the way he was coming at him. He thought this young kid needs to check himself and know who he was speaking with. The alcohol continued to push him toward a confrontation.

The gymnasium sat still as the overhead lights began to dim down slowly. Alex pulled up a chair and took a seat across from a relaxed Born who made sure everything was tucked in his duffle bag. "So what brings you here my man?"

"We have a mutual friend, whose name shall be unmentioned, who is very interested in representing you and your future career," said Alex in a professional yet laid back tone.

Born realized what this was all about. College was suppose to be unbridled fun. Days and nights of unlimited laughter, non-stop partying and freedom from a parent's hand. It wasn't. It's a business and here it was at his doorstep with a cool smile. He turned his eyes on this guy who sat with the utmost confidence. "Yea?"

"Yes. And he will definitely make it worth your wild if you would consider signing with him a little early in the process. On the down low of course. I'm talking about all the cash, jewelry, vehicles, homes and big asses you can dream of, he can provide. And I know you like that."

Alex reached across and gave a playful tap with a smile to Born's knee. He picked his eyes up and turned from Alex's sight and out to the court area. Agents and Agent's agents were disallowed from having any contact with college players. But that never stopped them from finding ways around that.

Rassa finished off one of the two pieces of toast that he chewed in his mouth. He looked in Merrissa's direction, across the table. "Did you listen to that track I made?"

"Yea. I like it, but I just don't quite understand some of things you say."

"Did you like the hook?

The last face the days in the worst place that got the mice trapped in a maze, a maze. The last face the days',

Rassa with animated arms swinging about.

Merrissa watched her son rhythmically speak out the verse with a prideful smile on her face. She loved his expression, even encouraged it. But there was Hal. At the site sitting at the table, he grew more and more agitated with Rassa and Merrissa's positive reaction that she gave back. He sprang up from the chair with no words and stormed out of the room, cursing and talking to himself.

Rassa stopped reciting the hook as he watched his father leave the kitchen area. He lowered his head with a disappointed air. Merrissa took her time and watched Rassa's reaction. She reached across the table and touched Rassa's hand that slowly moved inside his. "He's only concerned about you, as I am. He doesn't want to see you end up like so many young men these days who get caught up, give up and then are dead." Merrissa rose up from her seat and moved behind Rassa were she wrapped her arms around him and rested her head on the top of his. "Always remember that he loves you more then he can say. And I love you so much that I pray for you every night."

"I know yall do but if he would only understand my point of view. What this means. What this really is. This is who I am." Rassa leaned back into Merrissa's arms and felt the motherly care coming from her.

A variety of noises sprang up as the high school laid it self out in the night on the south side of the city. Inside, Pops and Mr. Wheeler stood in the dark hallway, face to face.

"You never know who or what is going to pop up around here," said Mr. Wheeler who was still a little jumpy and nervous as he attempted to calm himself down.

"Well, as long as people are doing their job then there should be no worries. Right?"

"I agree. We all have to do our job around here to keep some type of order."

"See, that's what I want to talk to you about," said Pops in a matter of fact way as he moved closer toward Mr. Wheeler. "What job is it exactly that you're doing here?"

Mr. Wheeler felt caught off guard at that moment and took a step back from Pops. How dare he come at him in this manner thought the man who had put in many years in the public school system. "I don't like the way you just said that Walker. Is there – "

Pops, with force, moved up into the offended man's face that attempted to express some act of control and cut him off from going any further. "I don't give a dam what you do or don't like. You're supposed to be a teacher. But that's something that I see you've failed to do around here."

Pops had seen this non-caring, prop act many times at the expense of the young minds that were suppose to be nourished and elevated. But this was one moment he would not, and could not allow it to pass. Strong, good teachers were what was needed in the city, not these half assed cowards. He stared at Mr. Wheeler with a cold glare that the history teacher felt go right thru him.

Tajaa lay back on the worn out work bench with the sweat from his body leaking on to the floor underneath, and looked up at the bar that lay across, above him. "Where you staying at?"

A tired and worn out Zachary hesitated for a moment then moved his eyes over on to Tajaa, trying to find the right way to approach his younger brother with a valid request. "That, that's what I like to talk to you about Taj," clearing his throat. "Would it be straight to rest my head here, just for awhile, until I get some things up and going?"

Tajaa turned his head as he rested back on the bench with his hands firmly clenched around the bar that held a large amount of weight. He beamed a firm, direct look with intensity that expressed the seriousness in the request and what it called for. "Just so you know, a lot has changed. A lot."

"Four years, I hope so," shot back an overlooking Zachary. He knew a lot had changed between him and his brother. He just didn't know how much things had changed when it came to doing their share, staying focused, and keeping things tight so that stupid stayed outside.

Tajaa remained fixed on his brother. This was no game. Tajaa did not want any funny business brought into his home. More importantly, Tajaa was trusting Zachary with a responsibility and it was on him to respect that. Silence filled the room. Tajaa released the bar, got up from the bench and walked over and extended his hand to Zachary with eye contact sustained all the way. "Aright. As long as you understand what you're asking and what I'm saying, you're welcome to stay."

Zachary and Tajaa gripped each other's hands and shook them firmly. The street general returned to the bench and began to do a set of bench presses.

"Good looking baby boy," said Zachary with an air of calm finally found. After the years of being imprisoned, this felt like paradise that his body embraced. The smell of incense. The clean floor. Music playing without screams. No stare downs. No walk byes. Just him with his brother in a room that filled him with ease and comfort.

Zachary took a deep breath in and released it smoothly as his body sunk into the chair with his eyes closed and he fell into a deep sleep.

"It's good to see you bro," said the voice in between breaths that pushed the bar up and down at a steady pace, pushing until his arms could do no more.

At the same time in the college gymnasium, Alex moved up and deepened his concentration on the smaller statured Born who had a variety of tattoos on his biceps, forearms, back of his neck, and chest area. Alex leaned in even more closer to Born and into his ear, making it more personal and more about business. "Don't worry. Everything will be kept on the low and taken care of behind closed doors. He'll make sure those ears and mouths that could be of damage will be kept closed."

Born continued to look out at the basketball court. "He likes my game?"

"For sure."

"He likes my style?"

"Definitely."

"He likes me?"

"Very much. And to show how much – " Alex reached inside his suit jacket and pulled out a white envelope filled with cash. "Here's a little taste. Just something to wet your lips and stimulate your fingers. He sympathizes with you guys in college receiving shit for the work you do. And that is what it is – work."

Alex handed the envelope toward Born. The young man in long black shorts turned his eyes and looked at the envelope that was in Alex's grip. Then he placed his eyesight on Alex who sat with a smile and the envelope held out to him in a tempting fashion.

Lite was in closer contact to the group of older men standing out on the corner that was surrounded by a nightclub, a few bars, a magazine stand and an abandon lot to an abandon building. The flames of animosity had risen with the consumption of alcohol and the words of disrespect. Lite was focused strictly on Minister and his lips that continued to move with no care. He firmly interrupted the older man who was busy yappin' about how he treats and takes care of his bitches. "So just cause they like nice things, that's what makes them bitches? Sounds more like weak men who feed their women that shit and act like little bitches themselves."

Minister turned to the other men in the group and let out a chuckle or too in a mocking fashion as he pointed at the younger man who stood with no emotion and no expression. "You all hear this young nigga?" Minister turned his eyes on to Lite. "There bitches because all that shit means more to them then their pussy."

"Then it's time for men to stop being weak."

"Who you calling weak mutha fucka?!"

"Well nigga!" Lite quickly stepped forward into the drunken man's face. A couple of the other men stepped in between and quickly restrained him as best as they could from getting at Minister. He had grown tired of his non-stop blabbering and decided that it was time to put an end to this non-sense. Lite was always quick to address ignorance in a physical manner, never letting anything slide and confronting anybody at anytime.

In a moderately furnished two-bedroom apartment in the heart of the city, DJ sat and wrestled in the living room, on the floor, with his two children who were filled with laughter and excitement. DJ attempted to pin his small but cock-diesel strong son and counted one, two, three.

Aiesha, a young twenty-four year old Black woman with braided long hair and a slim figure that she took care of, finished up in the kitchen area, putting the dishes away and making sure the area was spotless. She moved over to a basket of clothes that sat on the floor. She picked it up, placed it on the table and began to fold the children's pants, shirts and towels. She shifted her eyes from the clothes, as she folded, on to DJ with an angry and disturbed expression pressed on her young-looking, caramel-brown face. Something had been building inside her, but then again, she was always looking for something to pop off about, no matter how small. Drama was Aiesha's middle name

At that moment, DJ's cell phone rang that was on the living room table. He stopped the wrestling match, answered the phone and talked in a hushed voice that

Aiesha was unable to hear. This only made things worse and increased her agitated manner.

Who DJ was speaking to was inconsequential. What mattered was it gave Aiesha an opportunity to address her anger at him as the feeling over ran its cup with her. She had heard all the stories about him, but that's what they were – just stories and she failed to understand that. DJ hung up the phone and returned to playing with his little boy and girl who were three and two years old. He didn't get to spend that much time with them but when he did he made sure it would last until the next time. Yes, DJ was out there hustling in a creative manner and it was all for his babies, making sure they were properly fed, clothed and housed. He devoted the majority of his time and earnings, swinging out in the streets to make sure his babies and her had the real jewels in life.

Aiesha, failing to understand their situation together, kept everything pinned underneath being unsatisfied, which had led to numerous blow-ups the young couple had been having the past year. Aiesha exchanged a few more dirty looks at the three of them in the living room, the two children on top of a smiling DJ, trying to hold him down. "So, who was that on the line? Talking all low too."

After a quick glance to check out here stance, "Don't start Esha," said the young man as his son showed off his strength with a flying body tackle that surprised DJ.

Aiesha finished folding the clothes and moved into the living room area where she pretended to straighten things up that needed no straightening. "Don't start what?"

DJ took his time and settled the children down so that they just sat with him on the floor and started to read a book that DJ pulled off the table. "You know what. Let's just enjoy the night together. I'm here, you're here, are children are here, safe and with us. Let's just enjoy this moment."

The well-fit young woman in a white tank top and dark colored jogging pants that fit snug up against her lower body refused to change her stiff expression that was filled with a jealous rage. She moved in front of DJ and glared on him who listened to his children talk about the pictures as each page turned. "And when was the last time we did this? Can you even remember? A week ago or was it two, three or four – "

"What does that got to do with right now?" Said a calm and low-voiced DJ

"Who were you with? At least be a man and admit it." Here she went again, questioning his manly nature.

DJ lowered his head in disappointment. How come she found it so hard to believe in him? Yea, he might have had a lot of women come at him and yes, he was one of the most sought after men in the city. But he loved Aiesha all the way and knew she was for him. Her strength, her tender nature, her ability to do what was necessary at tough moments all appealed to him and was what drew them together. But here she was, standing in front of him and questioning him on matters that she knew nothing of. He looked at a jealous woman who had went from beautiful to ugly, love to hate, and from his mate to his enemy.

The hospital room seemed darker and colder at that moment as Deanne moved around, from side to side, in the hospital bed and attempted to find a comfortable position. Which was hard to locate on these five-dollar mattresses the county provided. She pulled the cheap and thinly made blankets up that Divine gave a helping hand with. "I'm going to take a little nap now. I'm so tired baby," said the weak woman with a touch of finality in her voice. "And tell Franklin, tell him, tell him, I love . . . him . . . . help . . . him . . . ," said the voice that trailed off slowly with each word as her eyes closed, her body slumped deep into the bed and in a flash she fell into sleep.

Divine stood still and looked over, with salty tears building up in his eyes, on his mother whose head had slowly turned to the side. "Rest momma." Divine bent over and kissed his mother on the forehead and then took a moment and looked closely on his mother who was having trouble breathing. He rose up from her, turned and moved to the door, but before he walked out of it, he stopped, turned and looked at his mother one more time. He knew this would probably be the last time he saw her and he hated seeing her like this, cancer-ridden. He only wanted to remember when she was strong, active and alive. When she showed him how to dance to Kool & the Gang's 'Celebration'. When she came to the park in her nightgown and slippers and rung his neck for staying out past his curfew. When she sang him and his brother to sleep. That's what he wanted to remember, not what he was looking at now. He slowly turned away and left out the room that stood dark, lifeless and quiet.

Only the two older men stood alone in the high school hallway. Pops took a step toward Mr. Wheeler who adjusted the glasses on his face. A nervous teacher of twenty plus years made sure the words that came out were strong and with authority to confront the questioning nature that Pops had released at him. "What do you think I've been doing for more years then you?"

"Good question. But see, we don't need people here who allow children to move aimlessly and recklessly so they themselves can be thought of as a cool teacher or so these same people can talk down of the children here, and make themselves look-," said Pops who reached out and adjusted Mr. Wheeler's jacket collar. "-well, like their big stuff, you know what I'm saying."

An offended Mr. Wheeler jerked away from Pops' hands and focused his look on him. "Look, if you got something to say or if you are accusing me of some kind of infraction, put it in writing and we can take it up with the school board," said the high pitched voice attempting to come off with some sort of power. He picked his finger up and pointed it at Pops. "But you better make sure you're sure buddy."

Pops glared at the man for a moment then quickly took hold of the pointing finger and began to twist and squeeze it that inflicted much pain to Mr. Wheeler who dropped his suitcase and yelled out that echoed thru the bare hallway.

Born and the young Blackman who had been recruited by the mystery admirer for a specific purpose, sat across with an envelope extended to him. Alex urged him to take it. Shook it in front of his face. He deserved it. Born gave one last look at the envelope that sat in the hand of a messenger. Someone who wasn't an agent or linked to an agency. He was only a man from off the street who was having a man-to-man conversation, nothing more. Born was aware that if he took that envelope, he was then theirs. He would belong to this dark person who he knew nothing about. He would become their property and under their control and all for the price of an envelope. Born picked up his eyes and placed them on Alex. "Let me ask you something. Are you mentally challenged?"

A surprised and stunned Alex sat in a frozen state of 'What' for a moment, threw off balance by the posed question. "What?"

Born stood up as the word slipped out of Alex's mouth, slipped on his college sweatshirt and placed his duffel bag around his shoulder and across his chest. "Tell your man, I'll meet with him when the time is right – face to face, when the season is over. Then we'll see if likes me, and how much."

Born walked away from a sitting Alex, with a feeling that he had done the right thing. Fuck feeling, he knew he did the right thing. He recalled the talk he had with E just a moment ago – the long money.

Alex followed Born with his eyes in stunned amazement at what he just heard and saw. He placed the thick envelope back inside his suit jacket then shifted his focus up into the rafters at the dark figure who disappeared into the back.

Born left out the gym, leaving Alex alone for a moment. A small part of Alex was proud of Born. He liked what her heard of the young man and after this small insight into his character, that respect grew for him. He had done the right thing but he had failed the mission given to him and he felt repercussions to come from not being able to get Born signed on the dotted line. Alex strode out the gym doors that slammed shut. The lights cut off and the court sat in silence and pitch darkness.

Tajaa and Rassa arrived on the block and met up on the street. A few steps away, they saw Lite, Minister and the other older men gathered up on the corner. Tajaa and Rassa spotted the rough and rugged looking young man who was causing the nature of the older man to become emotional and tense. The two, side by side, walked over in that direction.

A settled and calm Lite set his bottle down and looked across at Minister. "What I'm saying is women are more then a bitch, a hoe, a groupie, a jezebel, a gold digger or whatever. If one out of ten of them choose to act like a hoe, bitch, you know, then that's how they should be treated. But to stand up here and say all women are bitches, and no-good dikes, is fuckin' idiotic and nothing more then a reflection of your own inadequacies Negro."

"What the fuck did you just say?" Questioned the mean mug of Minister. "What? Are you a fuckin professor or something? Look it here young nigga, if you don't want to admit that your momma is a bitch, that's on you," said Minster with a suck of his teeth that revealed his one gold tooth.

The group of older men who had been gathered around, drinking and smoking, dropped their mouths and reacted to the comment in a comical sense, but not Lite. He saw what he had to do so to get thru and leave an impression that needed to be left on this flower head.

Tajaa and Rassa stepped up on the corner and observed their brother and knew at that moment, from his demeanor, what Lite was about to do, since they have seen this many times.

Lite, who didn't see his brothers behind him, calmly took a drag on the joint, passed it to one of the smirking men then socked the life out of Minister who was lifted off his feet and threw onto his back that hit the ground first. The crowd of men let out a gasp of excitement at what they just saw, and they were happy someone did what they were unwilling to do themselves.

Pops continued to twist and tighten his hold on the smaller teacher's index finger and hand that vibrated the sounds of pain thru the isolated school hallway. The man writhed, begging to be released, but Pops made sure he went no were and felt some discomfort at the same time. "I don't make accusations like some people. And there will be no need for the school board. This is just some staff advisement, from one to another," said Pops who leaned into Mr. Wheeler's ear. "Clean your shit up or you could find yourself in a tight," Pops squeezed tighter, putting more pressure on the hand and wrist area that brought a shot of intense pain to Mr. Wheeler. "Tight situation. These children need strong teachers, good teachers, teachers that teach, not play. And we don't need any pity-filled weaklings that let them run wild. You hear?"

"Okay okay," said the voice in between the shrieks of pain that his scrunched up face expressed. "I hear you. Please let me go. I got your point!"

Pops released his finger from the awkward hold. His point had been made. Mr. Wheeler moved a couple steps away from Pops, holding his hand. Pops brushed himself off, straightened his dress shirt and tie and made sure his suit didn't have a wrinkle seen with a smile. "It was good we had this chat. It feels so liberating to get things off the chest. Don't you agree?" Exclaimed Pops who took a deep breath in and exhaled it out.

Mr. Wheeler picked his head up as he held onto his hand, and looked at Pops and gave a nod of recognition, hoping this will end their meeting – for his sake.

Pops returned the head nod back and then rubbed on his stomach. "I'm hungry. It's about that time to eat. You have a wonderful night."

Pops moved toward a flinching Mr. Wheeler and gave a couple pats on his shoulder as he passed by him and moved on down the hallway, disappearing in the darkness.

Mr. Wheeler slowly and with nothing but hurt filling his body, picked his suitcase up with his other hand, and at half speed, shuffled down the hallway in the opposite direction.

Silence had fallen in the small and cozy apartment that DJ had set his lady and their children up in. DJ, with his son in his arms, gently placed him to the side and rose up in front of a standing and glaring Aiesha who folded her arms and twisted up her lips. "Girl, let me tall ya somethin'. Your dam jealousy is going to be the end of us. You know that right?"

"Is that a threat?" Shot back a disturbed Aiesha.

"All I'm saying is the way your behaving right now is ruining this, this time we have together. And it's all because of some silly notion that you have that I'm with different women every night. There's always gotta be somebody else with you."

"Silly?"

"Yea, silly," reiterated DJ who looked down at his son who kept his big, brown baby eyes on his parents and the way they conducted themselves with each other.

"Well, are you?"

DJ picked his head up, took a slow and deep, calm breath, and slowly turned his eyes on to Aiesha. "What I'm doing is battling thru this war zone out here and putting food on the table, clothes on my babies backs and a shelter over our heads."

Aiesha rolled her eyes and spun away from DJ, moving out toward the kitchen area. "And you can barely do that."

How could she say that under the circumstances in which they existed in? Especially when a majority of black men were leaving their women, children, and responsibilities. And here he was, doing the best he could under the circumstances that surrounded and doing his part as the provider. DJ took a look at his babies who could feel the tension that was reflected in them both turning their eyes toward DJ and Aiesha. DJ stepped forward and moved his eyes from his little girl and boy and on to Aiesha who was in the kitchen for a moment. Then he dropped his head, leaned down to his children and gave a kiss to both of them on the top of their heads. He moved to the closet, grabbed his black leather Minnesota Twin jacket and started to open the door, cracking it just a bit. He came to a stop and remained facing toward it for a moment in thought. "You know, you're going to have to decide whose team you're on, because we can't go on like this. We're losing."

DJ calmly and slowly walked out the door that closed behind him. Aiesha, with her back toward the door, threw her dark-colored dishtowel against the wall in frustration. She left the kitchen area and stepped into the living room were she took a seat on the floor and began to hold her daughter in her arms as she stared off. DJ's son remained sitting on the couch, alone, where he looked around the apartment for his father that he was unable to find. His facial expression went from comfort to distressed.

The streets didn't stop. Not just cause somebody got laid out on the concrete. No way, things kept going as if nothing happened. Minister got up slowly and wobbly as he attempted to shake off the shot he received from a right hand cross. After getting his thoughts together and realizing what just happened to him and who was the cause, he rushed toward a standing and unmoved Lite. Before the older man could take two steps, Tajaa stepped in front and cooled the drunk and heated older man out and made sure he didn't take this any further. Lite, with no reaction one way or the other, turned away and began to walk in the opposite direction with Rassa who threw his arm around the cock-diesel young man with a slight smile. Minister continued to make threats over Tajaa's body that disallowed any movement toward Lite.

Rassa, with his arm around Lite's neck, shook his head at what he just witnessed. "You are a live wire G!"

"Fuck that dark cave. I can't stand these mop heads out here who act like they know."

"No doubt son. Kids jaw might be shattered. That was ill B," said an animated and laughing Rassa.

"Soft butter heads."

Lite and Rassa continued to walk down the block. Tajaa advanced on them from behind and the three walked off cool and calm, like nothing happened, together. Tajaa made it known to keep his eyes open to that kid Minister and his next steps that he might take on him. Lite didn't care, he wanted him to make that move, it would be his pleasure.

Back at the spot were a backside fell back flat, Minister took a crazed drag on a cigarette as he kept the corner of his eyes on Lite. He moved his hand to his jaw area were he soothed the bruise that had developed on his face. Instead of letting it go and acknowledging what brought the right hand, his mind was only plotting on how to get back and find some revenge.

Benji sat back at a small table, big enough for two, in a local deli café located by the lake in the city. Benji and his father, Roger, ate their salads that were drenched, one in a French dressing and another in balsamic vinegar. Roger placed his fork down in his bowl and picked up his cup of tea that he slowly drank from. As he set the cup down, Roger shifted his eyes from the people around him and on to his son who was enjoying his lettuce, cucumbers, carrots and croutons. "The word is out that you blew Senator Raskaskuso's aide off. Whatever happened to the internship with Councilman Kelley that I lined up for you?"

Benji chewed and swallowed as he looked across at his father. "Word travels fast out here."

"You know I was going to receive a phone call."

"I just wanted to check it out since they called. What a waste of time. You know what that guy asked me after running down my political history?"

"What, how are you able to help?"

"Yea, now is this how the system runs? I felt like a little boy."

"It's politics son, you should know that."

"It's bullshit dad. Straight up. I don't need to be on no ones roster of helpers, gophers and ass kissers." Benji lowered his head into his salad and dug around in his glass bowl until he found the last cucumber that he ate with satisfaction.

Roger eased back in his chair with the grace of an elder statesman. "Look whose getting a little cocky these days. This is the political life boy, better get use to it," said Roger with a calm yet stern voice that signaled the seriousness of being professional. "You're going to come face to face with individuals who are so below you when it comes to intelligence but they'll hold a lofty rank or a high position. And that's because they know the political game and how it's played. The ins, the outs, the angles, the weak spots and the difference between the real players from the fake players. They might be stupid but they're not so stupid and you better never forget that."

Benji picked thru his salad, unable to find any more cucumbers. "Father, I just want to work with one who has a true sense of purpose in this racket. Somebody who is about more then money, PAC's and positions."

Roger broke out a small prideful smile at his son. "I know you do, but the higher up you look, the less you'll find of what you're really looking for. But Kelley – now there's a good one. Believe me."

Benji finished up his salad when a young attractive Native American woman entered in and passed by Roger, who noticed immediately, while Benji was more concerned with cleaning his salad bowl. Roger took his gaze off the lovely toned woman and turned his attention on to his son and his lack of attention toward such a beautiful site with a body that curved in every area and a face that radiated thru out the room. Roger took his hand, reached across the table, and knocked Benji upside his head. "Wake up youngen!"

"Hey! What's up? What was that for?"

Roger, with his eyes and a head motion in the desired area, pointed toward the young woman, whose long, black and silky hair reached down to the middle of her back. She took a seat alone at a table toward the back of the place.

Benji turned around and looked at her briefly then turned back and eyed his father. "Come on dad, I'm too busy for that right now. I got other things to focus on." In fact, Benji was partially intimidated by women. Not because of the sex or the attraction but by what it could mean to his political career with a woman involved in his life and the changes that would come with their presence.

"Son, son, son," said Roger slowly with light-hearted frustration as he shook his head in disappointment. "Don't make that arena be your only home. Only a part. Otherwise, you're going to miss life, cause it will pass right by. And that right there is something you do not let pass on by. You hear me? Now, go on over there and say hi."

Benji took a moment and stared at his father. There was no backing out at this moment of challenge. His father's words made sense. Maybe he was right. His young eyes took another look at the young woman who sat respectfully and elegantly. She definitely was fine and worth what he perceived as a distraction to his career. "Aright, aright. If it will make you happy."

"Shit, it should make you happy boy," threw back his straight-faced father.

Benji rose from his chair and started to walk over in the direction of the water-drinking woman whose lipstick left her lip's imprint on the glass. She lifted her eyes and locked on to Benji's who she noticed coming her way. They held eye contact between the two for a brief moment as movement drew closer. Benji continued to move thru the crowded place. As he passed by the counter area, a customer unintentially stuck his leg back that tripped Benji. He fell into a passing waitress face forward who was carrying a tray of drinks that ended up getting spilled all over Benji who was laid out on the floor.

Roger burst out into laughter, uncontrolled, all over the table.

Benji picked his head up and looked at his laughing father, then at his soda pop drenched clothes then at the young lady who was also laughing. Benji saw what was funny and joined in on the laughter that the place had also broke into.

CHAPTER FOUR

A knife in the back can only cause death when there is separation.

MALIK AND J-ROB sat in separate lounge chairs that looked like they were just bought, situated in the living room at Freddie's home and watched the martial arts flick 'Five Deadly Venoms' on his large screen TV in his nicely furnished place. You could definitely see how his hard work paid off and where it went.

Divine entered in from the night and into the place where the two faces immediately shared an inviting look and feel that was followed by shared hugs and handshakes then Divine took a seat next to J-Rob, who moved from the chair on to the long couch near the open window.

Malik turned his eyes from the television screen and looked closely on Divine. He could see the hurt that was visible on his face from the visit he was just returning from. Malik knew what it was about and what it meant. "How is she?"

"Weak and drained, but still fighting, and still loving."

"Just like a mother," said the younger J-Rob who, with a pick in hand, shaped up his medium length Afro that was thick and well rounded on his glistening dark frame.

"You know," agreed Divine. "She asked me to find and help Franklin."

J-Rob turned with a slight alarm of caution on his face that he aimed toward Divine. "Is he still basing?"

"Come on now sun. That kid is married to the pipe and needle"

"One thing about fiends, it has to be them that first helps themselves," said Malik with a relaxed voice as he lounged back in the chair to the side of the television.

"No doubt," confirmed J-Rob. "Take one step only after they've taken two."

"Yo, I gave her my word that I would make an attempt."

Malik and J-Rob both moved their eyes on to each other and shared a knowing eye contact for a moment then turned to Divine and looked at him. Their eyes communicated to him the delicate nature of the territory he was about to venture in and how this task called for another to be open to the helping hand.

"Be aware sun," Malik advised.

Divine acknowledged with a head nod and left it at that. He was well aware of the 'what' and the 'how'.

The three young men turned their attention to the television and the movie that played on DVD.

Divine quickly recognized the picture that sat on the forty-plus inch screen. "Is this Five Deadly Venoms?"

Malik nodded, lifting his brows to signal a necessary purpose that threw their intention on the specific scene. Freddie, a twenty-five year old light skinned Blackman who was known around the way by each and stood to the outside of the group, walked into the room and grabbed a seat in the other chair that was placed next to Malik.

A scene from the movie played that showed and spoke of how the main character was unable to defeat the Master's ex students by himself. He was informed that only by befriending and linking himself with one of the five students was he able to have a fighting chance in battle to put a stop to their greedy, and destructive acts that were taking place.

As Malik, J-Rob, and Divine dropped commentary here and there on the movie, a sound began to be heard coming from outside. The windows began to shake from the base that resonated The Ying-Yang Twins. Outside the window, Divine and J-Rob observed a vehicle pull up and park near Freddie's house. Lars stepped out of a black, newer-model Lexus GS300 with a full body kit, Sprewell wheels and tinted windows. Lars blew thru the door, ending a call on his cell, like the house was his own. "Yo! What's happening niggas?"

Malik set his eyes over on an approaching Lars. "Lounging, watching this piece. What's good with ya playa?"

"You know me. That paper," said Lars with a swinging chain and a bottle of beer in his hand. "Yo, my fault on that thing that broke out at the dice game the other night. I got a little over excited, my bad," Lars stated very casually as he moved around the room in a name brand navy blue jean outfit with a pair of mid-cut Fubu boots and exchanged hands with each in the room.

"Ahh, ain't no thing," shot back Malik with no emotion.

Divine and J-Rob met up with each other's eyes that gave off a feeling of concern that they both were hit with. You're dam right it was your fault, they thought, but what was he telling Malik this for? He was never one to apologize or acknowledge his wrongs.

"You Fredo! Let me holler at you for a minute," said a standing Lars with arms crossed. "In the back."

Freddie got up from the soft leather chair situated in front of the television with a black love seat on the other side. The scrawny young man joined Lars as they disappeared into the back of the kitchen, out of sight.

J-Rob, Divine and Malik continued to focus their attention on the movie that saw the 'Toad' sit firm in the little water spot.

After a moment, Lars and Freddie emerged from the back of the house and joined the laid back men out in the living room area where laughs and words were being traded about the movie scene that just played out.

Lars took a seat in the chair spot that Freddie had occupied near Malik and leaned back, lighting up a cigar. "Chop suey movie time, huh? Yall like this stuff?"

Divine, with no smile no more, remained still and focused on the television. "No doubt. You watch any of these?"

"Nope. I like that menace type shit, ya know, Boys in the Hood, Dead Presidents, Superfly, that American ghetto shit. This really don't do nothing for me except put me to sleep – ya know."

"Yeah, I like them pieces too, especially Dead Prez, but the fighting scenes in this are ill B, and the stories are full of self refinement," said Malik with calmness in his voice that was in a relaxed tone, comfortable and confident.

"See, I'm not feeling that Leek. Them scenes are way to fake. Climbing walls, fighting on tree branches, one man kicking twenty niggas asses. Get the fuck outta here with that bull shit."

A concentrating silence spread out over the room for a moment. A scene in the movie played that saw the 'Snake' speak about his plan in taking down the 'Toad'.

Lars sat in the chair with his head in his hand and bored to death. He quickly glanced over at Malik then straightened up in the chair and moved up toward a focused Malik. "Yo Leek. You down to make a lil scratch?"

"Doing what?"

"Delivery."

Divine and J-Rob moved their eyes from the television and on to each other in a knowing eye contact when that word came out of Lars' mouth. That answered their question.

"Delivery? What's up with you and your troops?" Malik immediately smelled funny business but remained himself.

"Right now we got some heavy heat and extra eyes on us. We need a change up, ya know what I'm saying."

Malik took a quick moment and thought about the proposal being made, as he remained laid back in the chair, legs crossed. He shifted his eyes over to Divine and caught his baby brown's locked onto his. Was this kid for real? Or was he on some bullshit? He turned from Divine and met up with a staring Lars. "I don't know."

"It's simple dog. All you got to do is drive to the spot, make the drop, collect and be out. Boom, boom, boom."

"Still."

Lars felt at that moment he had Malik and all he had to do was put out a little cheese. "Check it, here's a little something up front," said the influential voice of Lars. He reached into his jean pocket and pulled out a large amount of folded hundred dollar bills. He peeled off five of them and laid each on the table.

Malik took his sweet time, patient and calm in total observation mode, as he alternated his eyes from the money on to Lars. "Whose the contact?"

Lars cracked a sly grin, took a drag on his cigar and a swig from his bottle of Heineken. "Some kids from out of town that have some loot to spend."

Malik took a breath, wiped his eyes and gave off the sense that he didn't want to go thru with it with a little hesitation. "Aright B. Make the arrangements and let me know the deal."

Freddie, nervous, confused and unsure of what to do, took his eyes off Lars and scanned the room, meeting up with each face as he sat on the loveseat that was situated to the back of the room. Freddie was the type of young man who had nothing to stand on of substance. He was unsure of himself and those around him. He attempted to create bonds of friendship thru giving money, allowing those to use his house, and live with him. Freddie was unaware that he was a pawn in the game. He wanted to be liked by everybody but that was hard to come by when built on fragile ground. He possessed no strength, only an illusion that gave him a feeling of false power with his good paying job, his car and a home. But in reality, he was at the mercy of those who would use him for their own purpose, good or bad. He ran from the ultimate choice of were his true allegiance lied. But you can never run forever.

"My nigga. I knew you had my back," said Lars with a wide smile. "Just like old times. Don't worry, I'm going to hook you up."

Lars extended his hand that Malik took and the two joined in a quick hug that had little feeling that came with it. It was only done for looks and effect.

"Cool," answered Malik with no feeling one way or another.

Lars broke contact with Malik and moved toward the door. "I'll get with yall the next day. Stay up niggas," the voice rang out as he moved out the door and toward his vehicle.

After the booming base coming from the Lexus disappeared, the room sat in a silent stillness with the movie taking center stage that all eyes stared at.

Malik began to stretch his arms and legs along with letting out a loud and thunderous yawn. "Freddie! What's up b-boy?"

A startled Freddie jerked his head in Malik's direction. "With what?"

J-Rob and Divine looked at each other. They realized why he was acting a little funny. Lars had done some re-con. Freddie had allowed himself to be entered into and used to further some plans that might not be of the best of intentions.

"You. What's going on with you B? You've been kind of quiet," said Malik with a small smile to bring some comfort.

J-Rob, moving straight up in the couch that sat to the side of the love seat that Freddie sat nervously in, peered with a penetrating look at Freddie that brought a wind of discomfort. J-Rob leaned back in the couched and looked on Freddie from the corner of his eye.

"Nothing. Nuttin's going on. I'm just chilling," said a stuttering and uncomfortable Freddie. He didn't want to get in the middle of what Lars was doing and felt he had done nothing wrong, but somewhere underneath, something wasn't right. He was in rewind mode, checking the words he spoke to Lars.

Divine remained lounging back in the couch with his feet kicked up on the table. "He's lounging. Boy, you always lounging."

"You sure," said the serious tone with a stern expression on Malik's face. "Nothings going on?

"Naah, naah, why? What's up?"

Ignoring the questions. "Aright." Malik spoke as he turned away and met up with Divine's eyes. Freddie nervously looked around the room and then settled in on the movie.

"He's the snake," mocked Divine toward one of the characters on the television screen in a hard tone that vibrated the room.

J-Rob and Malik let out a laugh as Divine hardened his eyes on to Freddie then took them off his face and turned to look out the window. The eyes all turned back on to Freddie for a quick moment then back toward the movie that the three resumed commentating on the action while Freddie just gazed off at a spot on the wall.

Malik, with every move measured, crept thru the city night on foot, around parked cars, thru bushes, up over a broken fence and up to a dark bedroom window of a large two-story house. He gave a couple soft taps to it, making sure they were loud enough to be heard but not hard enough to shatter the glass. After no answer, he gave it another shot with a little louder tap.

The curtains sprang open to a sleepy young woman in her mid twenties who was in a long t-shirt, which revealed her sexy figure even more. Roberta had grown up since the last time her and Malik had been together. Now they had been apart for some time, going in different directions. She stood before Malik, adjusting her eyes to see who it was at three in the morning was pounding on her window. She noticed the face and pushed her head to the side in disbelief and surprise. Slowly she opened the window.

Malik stepped forward and leaned over into the first floor windowpane. He had been told of some news that he himself had to come and check out.

"Malik," Roberta whispered in a high tone. "This is a bit too late for a visit. What the hell is wrong with you?"

"You think so love?"

"Are you aright?" Asked Roberta in a moment of concern.

"True, true. How you doing?"

Roberta paused for a moment and looked around the area. She was stunned by the brashness of this young man who out of no where showed up at her window like she had read in one of her romance novels. It was both romantic but crazy at the same time. "Do you know what time it is?"

"I haven't seen you in awhile and you know, thought I stop by and see how you living these days."

"And whose fault is that?"

"Come on now. We both agreed to go our own way. We we're trapped in a corn field together. And you didn't feel I could give you what you wanted."

"And how come?"

"Cause you want the bling-bling of this world and I'm about something else that you couldn't see. I am what I am and there is no denying that."

"Yea, well, I'm going back to bed Popeye," said in a disgruntled and upset accent. Even when she was upset, Roberta looked extremely sexy and Malik took notice.

"Hold up, hold up. Can I come?" Asked Malik with a straight face that illuminated his seriousness.

"No."

"You know you want me to come inside," said Malik who looked over her magnificently shaped body. "Yo love, you look good."

"Come on Malik, you know I'm seeing Lars."

"Ohh word. That's your new love interest?"

"Far from love but you know."

"What? You don't make love no more like we use to?"

"Malik," said Roberta with a glare in her eyes to lay off.

"Aright, aright. So, hey, check this out. Let's say Lars was going to do something that would hurt me and you found out. Would you let me know before?"

"What?! What are you asking that for?"

"I'm just throwing stuff out there. You know, checking the waters. Answer the question."

Roberta took a moment as she leaned over the window and looked deep into the young man's eyes that she would forever feel deeply for. "Yea, you know I would definitely let you know if anybody was planning to hurt you – no matter who."

Malik cocked his head to the side in a questioning way. "Are you just saying that?"

"I thought you knew me. And if you did, you would know that I'll always care about you."

Malik flashed a closed mouth smile and nodded his head in acknowledgment. It felt so good to hear a lovely woman express their care for him. "That feels too good to know love. So, can I come in and rest with you."

Roberta let out a smile as she turned her head to the side. "No Malik," her eyes betrayed her answer.

"Aright, then I'll let you get back to bed. Now you're sure you don't want me to come in and rock you to sleep?"

"Bye Malik," answered Roberta sweetly.

"Peace baby girl."

Roberta closed the window and pulled shut the curtains as Malik stepped away. She lifted the curtains a little bit and looked out at Malik who was moving out in the darkness. Her eyes again told a different story for her deep feelings for him. But he was right. She wanted the nice things; European cars, designer jewelry, houses with pools, vacations to tropical climates. She was hooked, addicted, there was no going cold turkey for her, at least she thought. Roberta pulled the curtain shut and climbed back into bed. Her feelings for him betrayed her wants and she knew this.

A couple days after, Roberta and her group of girlfriends that came in all shades and styles with bodies that hit those curves in the right places and faces that defined pretty, lounged by the hour glass shaped pool that was located in the back of Lars' spacious back yard. The air had the mixture aroma of barbeque and marijuana on a muggy evening with the sky clear, the sun setting, the stars taking shape, and the night moving in.

The ladies laid out on the pool deck, swam in the pool, drank at the wet bar and socialized around the area of Lars' lavish home with his boys and hanger-on friends who tended to be his best customers as well as his source for cheap labor.

Roberta stayed clear of the various extra-curricular activities that were taking place and instead chose to lay back in a chair with a two-piece swimsuit on her well taken care of skin and observed the gathering. The young men and women in their mid to late 20's sat, laid, and stood as they each made that attempt in some fashion to hook up together. A couple ladies, enjoying the warm rushing waters in the jacuzzi, gave a few men a show that involved the ladies touching on each other, undressing each other slowly and seductively while kissing with passion on each others bodies. The young men couldn't get enough and were fabously getting off on it and each sexual gesture that only brought the lust for more.

Roberta turned her head from that scene and focused on another group of five men sitting at the poolside table and playing blackjack for big money that sat scattered on top of the glass tabletop. Sounds of winning and losing came at each turn of the cards as the blunts and drinks were consumed in a non-stop motion. Roberta noticed that everywhere her eyes turned, there was coke, weed, guns, money and sex that sat out in front of with no shame and no respect. Was this what she wanted? Is this better then what Malik could offer which was a night kicking it at Freddie's watching a movie or reading each other a book? Where was she really in her life? Roberta rubbed her eyes and rose up out of the chair and moved into the house to find some coco butter. She noticed that her skin was in bad need of a little moisturizer.

Roberta entered into the small bathroom that was situated in between the hardly used kitchen and the main room that was littered with clothes, cd's, video game with a number of games and a large screen television, along the long hallway that led to each room from one side of the house.

She opened the door, clicked on the light and searched thru the many cabinets for some lotion that she was unable to find. As she leaned down to look under the marble sink, she heard Lars and two of his boys enter into the house from the front door. They passed thru the main room, thru the hallway and into the kitchen area were they came to a stop near a counter that was full of bottles of Jack Daniels, Alize, Seagrams Gin and a few green bottles with no name.

"Is everything set up for Malik-leek Friday night?" Asked one of the young men with a chuckle in his breath at what they had planned.

Roberta heard the name she cared for, and moved quietly to the door that was slightly opened and leaned in just enough to get a good listen.

"Yea, it's all ready. Green light babay. We find out if these cowboys are about business or on some retarded shit, and we lose nothing in the trial," said Lars confidently as he checked the time on his platinum Rolex.

The other young man threw the empty duffel bag up on one of the other kitchen counters and poured himself a drink from the no-name green bottle. "What about the product?"

Lars glanced over at the two empty duffel bags that were going to carry the merchandise in and checked inside to make sure it could hold the product. "If they are on that funny stuff, then we'll deal with them. Let's take it one step at a time niggas. First, we'll let our guinea pig do his job."

Lars cracked a sinister grin and was handed a glass with some Alize and pineapple juice in it from one his boys as they all tipped their glasses together and toasted to Malik.

Roberta backed up from the bathroom door with a serious and horrified expression on her face. She took a moment to realize and understand what she just overheard. She recalled what she spoke to Malik the other night outside her window and the question he asked.

Lars and his boys walked out, more like strutted out, of the kitchen and on to the pool deck as they finished up their business talk and turned their attention to some people that needed to be met with.

Roberta silently peeked her head out from the cracked open door. Seeing the coast clear, she moved out of the bathroom and toward the living room where she exited the front door quickly.

At that second, one of Lars' boys stepped back into the house to fill his glass when he observed the light on and the door open to the bathroom. He thought for a moment. Was this like this before? As he moved forward to inspect a little closer and was about to move toward the front door area, a young, sexy light-skinned woman in a one piece bathing suit joined the young jeweled up man and threw her arm around his wide shoulders from behind and seductively kissed his ear and onto his neck that halted his steps. Lars's boy could contain his sexual urge no longer that had overtaken his investigative nature. Forget about that bathroom and the light, his mind was thinking only about ass, tits and what position he wanted to put the young vixen in. He grabbed her by the hand and moved off with the quickness toward the upstairs bedroom.

Outside Lars' place, in the driveway, Roberta sat in her new ride, a sporty Acura Integra, and stared at the steering wheel. She knew what she had to do, but could she do it? Cause it would mean the end of this way of living, a way she liked at times. She knew exactly what this all meant and where it was going to lead too. But Malik's face, that all that kept popping into her mind and the love he showed her.

Five hours later, Malik pulled into a dark, empty parking lot in the back of an old abandoned building, turned off the ignition and sat for some minutes alone. His mind was racing thru all the possibilities that he might have to deal with after this meeting. He thought about Lars and the things they've been thru. Brim came to mind and how Lars snaked him. He thought about were this job he was going to do for Lars might lead to. He recalled the sound in Roberta's voice when she called him and asked to meet in private. She was speaking in a low tone and in an impersonal way, very unlike her. And what was up with the late hour? Something was definitely up. As bad as this all seemed from the start, Malik saw the possibility in what could come from this and what could be obtained if gone about right and exact, and it was this forward thinking that allowed Malik to push along and take this meeting at just after two in the morning. But he kept telling himself that things had changed since the days of cuddling, laughing, kissing and loving. She was with Lars and he had to keep that front and center.

Five minutes later, Roberta drove up and pulled along side Malik. As she turned her car off, Malik stepped out of his and got into her freshly waxed vehicle that sparkled, even in the dim of the night. The two sat under cover of darkness and all Malik did was listen to Roberta explain what she heard at Lars' place. She laid the whole story down for him, piece by piece. The who, the what, and the why.

Malik gave a calm nod with an appreciative smile and a parting kiss to her cheek. With no words, he stepped out of her ride that started up and drove away. Malik watched her disappear into the night. He scratched his chin and looked out at the city landscape.

An hour later, Malik, J-Rob, and Divine drove around the city area with no specific destination. Just driving. They each took a turn behind the wheel of the caravan, and discussed the situation that faced them and how they should go about it. They had a few choices they could choose from. One was to back out completely with no explanation and continue to stand on the sideline. Second would be to confront Lars at this very moment on his purpose of use, which they all realized would lead to a violent end right then and there and gain absolutely nothing in the long run. And then there was the third option. The one option that appealed to all three and made the most sense when it came to the current situation with themselves, the streets and the children. It was agreed.

On a rainy night a day later, tears filled the eyes of Divine, Malik, Seven, Pops, DJ, Rassa, Lite, Tajaa, Benji, Born, J-Rob and Freddie along with a few other people that were close to Deanne, who paid their respects at a city cemetery. Divine's momma had left the physical plane and returned to the essence. The informal service had no preacher, no body reciting words from a book, and no religious hymns recited. It was quiet, respectful and remembering. All began to leave the grounds after about an hour except for Divine who remained standing and looking on his mother's grave. His memories of her where fresh that passed thru his mind one by one. He then lifted his head up and spotted a dark body who when noticed by the eyes of Divine turned and quickly ran away. "Franklin!" Divine hollered out to no avail. He was gone.

A couple nights passed with relative peace. Malik and J-Rob relaxed back at Freddie's place with a game of chess and 'Duck Season' by the Wu-Tang Clan playing on the CD player. Freddie stood in the kitchen and talked in a hush tone on the phone. It seemed he was becoming more and more secretive.

With Malik using his queen to unseat J-Rob's rook, Cleo, Lars' chick, showed up at the door. She refused to come in and just handed Malik an envelope along with a set of keys. With out any words and just a brief smile that revealed her seductive powers to Malik, he headed back inside and took a seat on the couch, putting the chess match on pause, and thought for a moment. The choice had been made, the side had been taken, and the plans had been set into motion. The keys were for the vehicle that the product would be sitting in. In the envelope was an address written down on were to pick up the aforementioned ride at, another address on were to meet the Cowboys at and instructions on were to meet up with him at afterwards. He grabbed his apple that was sitting on the table and began to eat it.

Freddie walked into the living room and took a seat across from Malik who turned his deep eyes on him and glared at Freddie as he chewed on his apple. This was a chance, his chance, for the straight-haired young man to come clean and let Malik know what he knew. But fear and pride choked Freddie up. He had nothing to say.

A group of young Black men of all shades of Black and physical forms huddled together in a deserted, dirt lot in an empty and isolated part of the city, on the north side. They stood by three dark colored SUV's with their headlights on and windows smoked out. They drank, talked shit with each other, laughed at jokes that were thrown around, smoked Philly fat blunts and waited for the expected visitors to arrive.

The Cowboys, as they were known, were a young group of twenty to twenty-three year olds who loved getting that money no matter what the avenue. They had arrived from out of town and were able to get linked up with Georgio due to the business and reputation they had garnered back home.

Sherriff, a heavy-set light-skinned Black man, sat calmly inside the sparkling midnight blue Lincoln Navigator, with the dubs spinning, and puffed on his cigar. He leaned back and surveyed the scene outside the vehicle.

A pair of headlights moved forward that was reflected on Sherriff's window. His eyes, covered by a pair of dark glasses, observed the old beaten up Ford Escort approach. The group of young men turned their attention from each other and on to the car that came to a stop and sat still for a moment with it's headlights remaining on.

Malik and J-Rob stepped out of the car and looked over the group, the area, and then on to each other. With a duffel bag over each ones shoulder, the two men started to make their way toward the Cowboys.

Before they could get five feet from Sherriff's SUV, a large, dark young man with bad skin stopped Malik and J-Rob and began to search them in every area of the body that could conceal a pistol.

He found nothing and allowed the two to step forward.

Petey, a slim, frail-looking Blackman with round looking glasses who looked more like a computer geek, tapped on the SUV's window. Sherriff exited in a cool nature and walked over with a confident and cocky swagger. He came to a stop and stood in front of the observing young men who each held on to a duffel bag filled with fifty pounds of that new enhanced THC substance that Georgio had talked to Sherriff about were it could be obtained. Sherriff needed new product, better merchandise, plus his supplier was cutting his business back due to some legal problems that had arisen. So here was an opportunity to find out what this was all about. Punks or Players.

Sherriff stood face to face with Malik and J-Rob who watched the group of men take their positions behind their pretty boy leader who might have been a little heavy but they could tell he worked out and it was far from being sloppy fat. The undisputed leader of the group grabbed the toothpick out of his mouth and tossed it to the side. "What's up playas?"

Malik took his time and looked closely at Sherriff, seeing how his hands moved and his garments sat on his body. He moved his eyes around the area and on to the set of mean, thirsty eyes that were all focused on them. He brought his focus back to Sherriff. "Nice outfit B."

"I know this," said sharply. Then the high school drop out in a 'Ray Lewis' jersey with a pair of black baggy jeans to go along with a pair of black Iverson's shifted his focus from Malik and J-Rob and on to the rusty car that sat in the back of them with it's headlights on. Sherriff returned his look back on to Malik and cracked a grin. "You gonna buy a new ride with the dough from this deal?"

STRENGTH & HONOR: BOOK ONE

Laughter was heard coming from the group of Cowboys. Malik and J-Rob took a look at each other and also laughed along. Malik returned his attention to Sherriff. "You don't like my classic?"

Sherriff brought his laughter and smiling to an end and sharpened his glare straight at Malik. "So, what you bring for me?"

"Just a little something you requested from your man. You got that paper?"

Sherriff mumbled to one of his men that Malik was unable to make out what was being discussed. J-Rob moved his eyes out beyond the group of men to a specific spot covered in the darkness. Sherriff returned to Malik as he rubbed his hands together, anticipating the business transaction to be profitable. "Let's see what you brought us first."

Malik thought that it had to pop off some way, so he decided to concede and get it started first by stepping forward and swinging the duffel bag around toward the Cowboys' eyes.

He nodded, moved his hands on to the heavy load, unzipped the duffel bag that revealed the plastic bound pounds wrapped tight with Lars' symbol of a dollar sign over top of a star labeled on each package.

A pleased Sherriff backed up as he rubbed his chin in satisfaction. His eyes ablaze with want and desire. Greed reared its ugly head and took control of the large young man who was fully aware of his next step that had been planned ahead.

Malik zipped up the red duffel bag, took a few steps away from the looming group that glared at the two of them and straightened up toward Sherriff. "Now, how does that look?"

"That's what we're talking about right there."

"Let me see the paper," demanded Malik in a laid back but firm manner.

"Come on dog. What do you take me for? You think I'd come to a deal with no money? That's like coming to a gun fight with out a gun." Sherriff turned his head in a mischievous way and smiled to one of his guys that stood to his side.

Malik carefully read the faces, dispositions and expressions and concentrated on Sherriff and his every movement as J-Rob stayed focus on the area and the group action.

Sherriff raised his hand. "Petey!"

His partner in crime, Petey, made his way from the back of the group with a tan suitcase in hand. He stepped in front of Sherriff, popped the latches, and opened it up.

Malik and J-Rob glanced at $85,000 wrapped up and laid neatly inside the case. Malik picked his head up and looked at Sherriff. "Let's do this."

Petey closed the suitcase and moved away, toward the back of the group. Malik knew at that moment what kind of deal this was and swiftly got into character.

Sherriff took a moment and began to pace back and forth with his hands clasp behind his back. "First, we need to do some renegotiating. This price your man is hitting me for is, well, it's a little high."

"Do you know what you're getting for it?" Malik stated more then asked as to reveal in a salesmanship way that this was some good shit.

"I think it would be better to just take it."

Guns started to cock in all directions from the eight bodies present with Sherriff and Petey. J-Rob and Malik took a step backwards and looked over the area with a surprised and taken back expression. These young men weren't here to do business. They came to make a name for themselves that would eventually lead them to takeover this market. Malik could see it in Sherriff's eyes from the start. He wanted to start a war, take some heads and build a rep in the street 'the nigga that took Lars out of the game.' And to do this meant he had Georgio's blessing. To Malik, this was nothing new. Now, not only was he caught up in Lars' backstabbing game, he was also about to be used as a message sender for the Cowboys. Malik dropped his head in utter disappointment mixed with submission and gave it a shake. "Aright, aright. Check it, no problem this way. Here," Malik said as he threw the duffel bag down in front of him and raised his hands high to show there was no fight in him.

At that moment, J-Rob burst out in a fearful-anger and dropped to his knees. "Yea, you can have it all! We don't want no problems!" He cried out as he opened the duffel bag and started to toss out the packed pounds of weed in an uncontrolled fit. "Take it all!"

Sherriff smiled wide as him and his crew of bandits became disarmed at that moment. He looked on his prey with a comical amusement. "If it only could be that simple." He reached into his waistband and pulled out a black 9mm pistol. Sherriff moved toward Malik, raised his steady arm that held the steel sideways and aimed it between Malik's low lids. "Lars will get the hint."

A blast was heard that cracked the night air. But it wasn't from Sherriff's pistol. Another shot was let loose and this one struck one of Sherriff's soldiers who dropped to the ground with a hole to his stomach that turned a dry shirt to a wet one. Everybody spun and looked in all directions to find where the shots were coming from. Boom, boom, boom! Where was this coming from?

As this commotion was taking place, J-Rob, who had tossed the elbows out of the bag, got a hold of two pistols and extra clips in the bottom of the bag that he grabbed up, tossing one to Malik.

The barrage of shots continued, and now they were joined with Malik and J-Rob's barrels who fired on the Cowboys from the front. The Cowboys, with pistols drawn, fired back in chaos. But they were so off balance and so confused, they became easy targets. The larger group that out numbered Malik was now being eliminated one by one to even the odds.

Malik and J-Rob dropped low to the ground, on their bellies, and one by one they began to lay the Cowboys out.

The shots that came from an area in the back of the lot continued to confuse what was left of the Cowboys who had taken cover in a panic. J-Rob and Malik spit bullets that hit legs, chests, shoulders, and asses.

Sherriff saw Petey lying on the ground, dead after taking two shots to his chest, with the case of money near his side. Sherriff made a dash toward the case. He was looking to grab the dough and hit the SUV to make a quick get away. However, Malik spotted the large figure zigzagging his way toward the money. Malik rose up, popped in a new clip and began to fire constantly at Sherriff. The bullets found their mark, hitting him in the leg and then the shoulder that threw him to the ground, near the tire of one of the SUV's.

Then all of sudden the gun fire ceased. Silence took center stage. A number of bodies laid scattered about the area that was filled with the smell of hot gun smoke. J-Rob stood up from the ground and let out a whistle.

From the dark area in the back of the lot rose Divine with shotgun in hand. He walked over and joined Malik and J-Rob who stood tall in a sea of bodies, guns, jewelry and the suitcase. Malik moved over, picked it up and gave a grin to Divine who made his way in their direction as he observed the area. Part one of mission impossible accomplished and it was seen on each one of their perspiring faces.

J-Rob and Divine arrived face to face and came hand to hand, sharing a breath taken in and released out. J-Rob moved over to where Malik was with the suitcase in hand.

As the two shared some words on the job just done and the case of money secured, Sherriff blinked open his eyes. He spotted a gun near by and slowly reached for it without being detected. He got it in his hand and then took a breath to gather his strength. The young man, whose clothing had been drenched in blood, jumped up and began firing in the area of Malik and J-Rob. The young soldier saw that Sherriff had an open shot at Malik and there was only one course of action to take. He pushed Malik to the side and stepped in his place as he raised his gun. But before he could pull the trigger, one bullet struck J-Rob in the chest and the next bullet entered his neck and exited out. Blood spit out on to Malik and J-Rob fell over. Divine sprang in and emptied his clip into Sherriff who was thrown against the Navigator, then to the ground, face first.

Malik picked himself up off the dirt and moved over J-Rob's bloody body that was gasping for air. He gathered the young man up into his arms and comforted him the best he could with encouraging words, gestures and sounds, wiping the blood from his face. "My brother, come on, my brother, hold on. Hold on!"

J-Rob tried to speak as his hands held on and squeezed tightly to Malik. Divine made sure everything else was secure then slowly, and with hesitation, walked over to were Malik held J-Rob. He observed the deep neck wound that had severed an artery and was gushing blood from. It was only a matter of time.

"Sssshhhhh. Save your strength baby boy. We're going to get you to a hospital," said Malik who rose up and struggled to get J-Rob firmly in his arms. He dragged him a few yards toward the Escort.

Divine stepped back and watched knowingly. He was aware of the condition J-Rob was in, what J-Rob meant to him and Malik but he also knew what had to be done. A hospital room wouldn't help, it would only mean this was all for nothing as the bars would be closed on them all. Sacrifice was necessary and J-Rob knew this.

Malik continued to attempt to drag J-Rob and get him to the clinic. "Put me down," ordered the wounded young black man.

"What? Fuck no!" Declined Malik, moving a couple more steps.

"Yo! Leek, put me the fuck down," demanded the voice with out any base or treble. "You know this is how it rides brother. And I'm not going to jail and either are yall."

Malik stopped and fell to the ground with J-Rob who took his hands and grabbed his face to look him in the eyes with the last ounce of strength he had in him. "This, this better have been," a pause to gather his last breath, "-this better have been fuckin'worth it G." He gasp for another gulp of air as blood spit up out from his mouth.

"I can't leave . . ."

"You're not leaving, ya know," spit out J-Rob in a moment pause that brought of understanding of what he meant. "I love you G." J-Rob took a deep breath in and then expired with is eyes slowly closing.

The young wirery man, who had followed behind Malik since the days when they played touch football in the streets and hit cars with snowballs and then ran, died in his arms.

Malik pulled him up and hugged him tight. "No! No! Not you, come on B, get you, I'm a get you there – "

Before Malik could make any last attempt, Divine stepped over behind Malik and placed his hand on Malik's shoulder that stopped him from the struggle and made him realize the situation. "He did his job son, now we have to do ours, otherwise he was right. This will be for nothing."

Malik agreed and gave a slight nod. His calm returned with his awareness as he focused on the present situation and what had to be done. He slowly and gently set J-Rob's limp body down on the dirt ground. He kneeled beside the well-preserved young man and stared at him for a moment.

"We got to get out of here sun, come on." Divine moved away to other areas of the lot and began to pack up anything and everything that had worth; guns, jewelry, the pounds of weed and any carrying money that was in the Cowboy's pockets.

Malik reached down and removed J-Rob's chain that was around his neck then placed his hand on his forehead.

Divine placed the duffel bags along with a couple of other bags full of items into the car. He started it up then got out and took a step toward Malik who was still with J-Rob. "Let's get the fuck out of here bra!"

Malik rose up, spotted the suitcase near by, took it in hand, and made his way toward the car. J-Rob's body lay with the others in the dust. The ride backed away and peeled off down the road, leaving the place in darkness and silence.

Divine navigated calmly down the many avenues and back streets they took in the rusty, beat up old two door car to get to their next destination.

As Divine handled the wheel, Malik changed his blood splattered clothes that he placed in a large black trash bag and wiped the blood from his hands, face and

STRENGTH & HONOR: BOOK ONE | 117

arms with a wet towel he got from the back of the car on the floor. They were fully prepared for both sides of the fence. Malik sat in the passenger seat, dressed and cleaned up with his head looking out his side window. "Dam, J." Malik lowered his head and gave it a slight shake of sadness as a tear fell on to his lap.

Divine looked over at Malik and saw him somewhat distracted and trapped in the past moment. He had to get him back into the present otherwise they needed to stop right then and there. "Focus son. Snap out of it! We still got some work to do."

Malik picked his head up and looked across at Divine and passed along a look of realization. He brought the gun into his lap, pulled out a clip, checked it, pushed it in and pulled back the hammer. "Time to serve justice."

Divine kept his focus on the road and the mirrors that allowed him to check if any problems were heading in their direction.

Divine and Malik arrived at the back of a fish and chips spot that them and the rest of their peoples had used as one of their many hang-out joints. They parked the car, wiped it down, and threw the dirty clothes and rags in a trash bag that they took with them then left the keys in the ignition with the windows open. The two young men dressed in all black jogging pants and black hoodies took the duffel bags, suitcase and garbage bags in hand and walked over to the caravan that was parked around the corner on a residential street. They threw everything in except for the suitcase, closed the sliding side door and made their way to Lars' Lexus that was parked a car down in front of the caravan. Malik and Divine, silent and concentrating, got in the luxury ride and pulled off.

Divine and Malik entered into a part of the suburbs were politicians, corporate VP's, real estate tycoons, divorced mothers living off alimony, and drug dealers made their home. The houses were orderly, and lined up with manicured grass fields and basketball hoops that littered the driveways. Divine slowly turned on to a specific street and then cut off his headlights as he found a spot to park on the side.

The two of them sat inside the vehicle for a moment and looked ahead at a specific house in their eyesight that was about a half a block away. It was where Lars' lived.

They exited the luxury ride that Cleo handed the keys too, moved to the back trunk that Divine popped and they each began to prepare themselves in silence.

Malik slipped on a pair of football gloves and then picked up a 9mm that was taken off one of the Cowboys. He pulled out a silencer attachment and spun it onto the barrel then tucked it into the back of his waist.

Divine, with the same type of gloves on, grabbed the forty-five that Sherriff had used, attached the silencer piece, and placed it in the pouch area of the hoody.

Malik snatched the suitcase, closed the trunk and then joined Divine, side-by-side, moving out towards Lars' place among the quiet and peaceful surroundings.

Down in the game room of Lars' lavish and beautifully furnished home, equipped with all the toys one can desire, Lars and one of his boys played a game of pool for five hundred dollars that sat on the ledge of the pool table. Each of them enjoyed their drinks while making fun of each other in a one ups-manship contest.

In the bedroom, Lars' other boy, a little tipsy and horny, sprawled back in the bed and spoke sweet words to a young woman on the phone. He was working on getting a little late night nookie.

The front door silently opened. In entered Divine and Malik who made their way down the stairs slowly and cautiously, and into the room fitted with a large screen television, a Playstation, a dartboard and a poker table to go along with the pool table that was being used and an expensive sound system.

Malik moved forward into the room with the suitcase in hand were the pool game was being conducted. Divine fell back, with hands stuck in his hoody pouch, and took a seat on a bar stool near the bar.

Lars picked his eyes up as he was sizing up a shot and noticed Malik standing and looking at him. "Malik. What the fuck?" Said a stunned, surprised and confused Lars who gave a look toward his boy who kept his eyes on Malik. "What are you doing here homey?"

Malik remained quiet, calm, and in control as he moved toward the pool table, set the suitcase down at his side, picked up the eight ball and began to sling it across the table, back and forth against the felt edge. His focus was on the black ball and the spin he gave each push that moved it in a certain direction back towards him. After a moment of awkward silence, Malik picked his eyes up toward Lars. "Surprised to see me?"

"You dam right I am. Fuck! I said we get together the next day. Remember! At Freddie's," thundered an upset Lars, attempting to get control of the situation.

"Well, I just couldn't wait till then. Especially after the job I just did."

Malik had to remain in control cause all he wanted to do was leap at Lars and choke the life out of him. It was necessary to stay in control of his emotions and intentions.

Malik reached down for the suitcase. Lars' boy quickly whipped out his gun from his side holster. Malik looked over at him and broke out a small grin from the corner of his mouth as he picked up the suitcase and placed it on the pool table. Malik opened it.

Lars observed what cash was in there as he broke out a grin and moved toward Malik and the open case. "So they were legit, huh?"

Malik leaned over on the pool table with his arms holding him up and kept his head looking down. "Sounds like you weren't too sure."

"You never know in this game, you know what I mean."

"Yea, yea, I know what you mean," Malik said as he moved away from the case and took a moment and observed Lars going thru and counting the money. "Do you remember that kid J-Rob?" Malik asked in a matter of fact way that was calm and friendly, without any menace.

Lars was focused on the money and failed to realize the awkwardness of the question. "Yea, didn't he go to high school with us? I think I know that cat. What about him?"

Malik turned his back, and took a few steps away from the pool table. He locked eyes with Divine who continued to sit calmly, focusing on the movements coming from one of Lars' boys while attuned to the sound of a voice coming from the bedroom. "Him and I went way back, even before you and I."

"Didn't know that dawg. I knew he hung around here and there. Saw him in the halls with you and on the court but . . ."

"His mother took care of me when mine went away at first," interrupted Malik. "We, along with Divine, basically grew up together. From peewee football to late nights with girls playing touch and tell to house parties and MGDees. I loved him, ya know." After a brief smile between the two, Malik broke his eye contact with Divine and lowered his head. A tear rolled down his cheek that went unseen by the once friend who had now become an enemy. J-Rob's face was so clear in his mind. A young heart who loved his friends that he saw as his family. Whose heart was pure and filled with courage to do what was right and whose ears listened and understood purpose.

Lars and his boy looked at each other with a 'who cares' expression and gave a shrug with their shoulders along with a smirk. Lars glanced, for some inner reason, at the pistol that lay on the ledge of the table.

Malik turned back to face Lars and stared at him, straight into his eyes with a cold look. "You have no fucking clue what I'm talking about, do you?"

Lars stood, with money in hand, and closely observed both Malik and Divine who remained in the back with his hands stuffed inside the pouch in the front of the hoody. Lars didn't like the way this was going and knew he had to go on the offensive. "Should I?"

Malik turned his head back to Divine. "He's not listening to what I'm saying."

With 'Big Pimpin' booming from the speakers, Lars ignored Malik's comments and slammed the money down into the suitcase in disgust. "Look, this all touching, ya know, strolling down memory lane with you but you're a little short here."

"Am I?"

Malik, who had been holding the eight ball the whole time, spun around toward Lars and threw a perfect strike that hit Lars in the head and knocked him back on to the floor.

Lars' boy aimed his gun at Malik but before he could fire, Divine had already whipped out his piece with the silencer and let out one shot to the heart that stopped him cold and laid the young man out on the floor.

In the bedroom, Lars' other boy, unaware, continued to talk on the phone, being involved in some hot and heavy sex talk with his hand in his pants and on his dick, messing with it, and begging the girl to come over.

Lars, in pain, crawled in an effort to get to the gun that lay on the ledge of the pool table.

Malik stood and watched his ex-running mate for a couple seconds then pulled out his pistol and shot him in the knee that caused Lars to let out a loud yell.

Lars' boy quickly dropped the phone and rushed with a full head of steam and eyes closed into the game room area.

He was met swiftly by a standing Divine who pulled the trigger one time that hit the chest and stopped his movement abruptly.

Malik casually walked over to were Lars was rolling in pain, picked him up with no remorse and threw him up against the wall. "Looks like you're in a little trouble here dawg." Malik cracked a curious and amused facial expression. "Isn't this how you started? Remember?"

"Fuck you," spit Lars in between the throbs of pain.

"Irony, huh?" Malik paused with the smile leaving his face to reveal no mercy. "Now, where is it?"

"Where's what?"

Malik took the butt of the gun and knocked him in the mouth that cracked a couple of his teeth along with busting his lip wide open. Divine secured the money and closed the suitcase then grabbed a large pillowcase and began to bag up anything of value.

Malik pulled Lars close to his face and looked him deep in the eyes. "Where do you keep your shit?"

"Bitch, I'm not telling you a god dam thing."

"Aright, aright. If that's the way it's gotta be, so be it." Malik backed away from Lars and smiled at him for a moment. He then spun around to Divine, gave a non-chalant shoulder shrug, then rotated back around to Lars, and as quick as an eye can be blinked, raised the gun and plugged one into the shoulder.

Lars dropped to the floor and cried out in pain with his blood splattered up against the wall. He wasn't dead but he was being picked apart, piece-by-piece, which was worse then dying.

Malik moved back over him with ferouciousness, picked him up viciously again and slammed him up against the wall even harder. "How about the other knee this time."

Just as Malik backed up and aimed the silencer barrel at the knee of Lars, he quickly threw his hands up and opened his eyes wide. "Okay, okay! It's in the back bedroom, behind the picture, above the bed."

"The combo."

Lars hesitated for a moment in pain and then recalled what it was. "Six . . . Fifteen . . . thirty-three."

Divine moved to the back bedroom upon hearing the vault numbers relayed and located the safe. He opened it up with no problem and gleamed a smile at what he observed inside.

Malik continued to stand over Lars and look at him with utter disgust at what he had become and the choices that he made that led to this point in time. He slowly, and with an easy calm, placed the gun to Lars' forehead. "Black devils like you are going to burn. Fuckin' blood sucker."

"Yea, you think so? Well, if I am, then so are you. What do you think you are? How are you any different or any better then me nigga?"

Malik moved closer in and extended his lips into Lars' ear slowly. "The difference is, you accepted it and I rejected it. The judges have arisen mutha fucka."

"Then go ahead, kill me bitch ass nigga!"

"What for? You're already dead. You just don't know it"

Divine returned from the bedroom and shook his head to Malik, letting him know it wasn't the spot they were looking for. It was only a diversion hole filled with 25G's and some jewels that was aimed to satisfy a possible robbery attempt, giving them the idea that they came up.

Malik spun around and faced Lars for a moment with a cold stare. Who did this drug dealer think he was? Malik walked right up to him, picked him up and pushed him on the pool table. "Are we suppose to leave now that you gave up your little safe?"

"You got what you wanted. You'd be smart to just leave it at that."

"Really." Malik said with an air of amusement and a smile toward Divine who shook his head in disappointment that dropped to the floor. Malik turned back to Lars, took him by the head and slammed it down on the pool table. A hollow sound ushered out loud from the custom hand-carved wood table. Both Divine and Malik raised their eyes to each other and shared a knowing look with a slight grin. They had just found Lars' G-spot. Malik ripped open the felt that revealed a hidden compartment built on top of the table. He opened it to find a few kilos of coke, ten pounds of weed, a large amount of cash, guns, jewels and ICE. Divine peeked in, then picked his head up and met up with Malik. Their smiles grew and each turned to Lars at the same time.

"All wise," said a calm Malik.

Divine and Malik quickly began to load the bags up with the rest of the things they came up on. Divine showed the packages of coke to Malik who took a moment and thought as 'N.Y. State of Mind' came on the high tech DVD/CD player that continued to play through out the confrontation. Malik slowly cracked a sly grin and nodded in the desired direction to Divine who read his mind and knew what his plan was. "Bring all that shit," ordered Malik. Divine gathered up the kilos of coke, letting out a laugh at what they were about to do. It was something Divine had dreamed about doing since this white poison was flooded into their streets and homes. Lars, who was lying on the floor, was snatched up by Malik and dragged into the bathroom in a roughhouse manner, followed by Divine and the coke. "I want you to see this house negro."

Malik stood by the toilet. Divine tossed one of the kilos of coke to Malik who split the bag open with a switchblade and then began to pour the coke into the toilet, and with a hand motion on the toilet handle, it all flushed down.

Lars lay off to the side, and watched in pain and anger as his money was going down the sewer. "You mutha fucka! Man, fuck you! Punk ass bitch! You better kill me niggas!"

"Nigga?"

Malik grabbed Lars' head and dunked it in the coke-filled toilet water bowl while pouring more coke on top of a gasping for air Lars. "Get high Lars. Get high!"

As Lars was getting whitewashed in the bathroom, the last of Lars' three main boys who he recruited after taking down Brim to run with him, drove up in a convertible Ford Mustang and parked in the driveway. He got out, took a slow sniff of the night air and then headed to the front door where he disappeared inside.

The six foot one, young black man with a baldhead, long platinum chain, Rolex watch and an iced out pinky ring stood in the entry way and heard some voices that he was unable to make out coming from the downstairs area. He slowly made his way in that direction, and the closer he got to the bathroom, the more he was able to make out the situation Lars was in. He drew his pistol out and slowly and cautiously stepped toward the bathroom from were the voices came.

Malik continued to dump coke on Lars, yell his displeasure at him and dunk his head into the toilet water, all the while Lars gasped for air and yelled out in anger.

Lars' boy drew closer to the oversized bathroom with a jacuzzi in it. He spotted Divine who was focused in on the activity that took place at the toilet from the entryway. He fired a shot that hit Divine in the shoulder and threw him to the ground with his pistol knocked out if his hand that lay in the hallway. Lars' boy began to move toward the bathroom door and fire wildly, hoping that one or more of the bullets fired hit the desired target.

Malik quickly left Lars at the toilet and as he moved toward the entryway, pulled out the silencer pistol. He slid up against the wall on the far side and thought for a moment as he looked at Divine who had dragged himself up against the opposite wall in the bathroom and out of harms way from the shots that spilled out.

Malik shifted his eyes around the room area until they locked on to the doorknob and the tall door that swung in. Shots continued to ring out, then came to stop to change clips. Malik sensed the opportunity and swiftly jumped on the door knob, and leaned from up high into the hallway where he got off a clean shot that struck the young man in his head and sent him falling backwards. Malik hopped off the door and checked to see the status on Lars' boy. He was dead, done, no more. Malik moved back into the bathroom and attended to Divine who gestured that the bullet went thru clean.

Lars, with coke all over his head, sopping wet, bleeding non-stop and in immense pain, pulled a small twenty-five from underneath a pile of magazines that sat near the side of the toilet. Lars got his strength up and aimed the gun at Malik. Just as Lars was about to pull the trigger, Divine, who saw Lars with the gun in hand, pushed Malik out of the way. He grabbed the gun that was to the side, on the floor that Malik had used and set down.

Lars pulled the trigger. CLICK! The clip was empty and there was nothing in the chamber.

Divine cracked a smirk to the click that he heard come from Lars' small gun then pulled his finger that pumped a bullet right into Lars' face. Lars fell back up against the tub that pushed him forward were his face fell into the toilet.

Malik looked at Lars then on to Divine and the two exchanged a relieved expression in an appreciative nature as they sat on the floor together for a moment.

Malik helped Divine up and they moved out of the bathroom, and into the game room were they gathered up the bags, packed the rest of the merchandise up and double checked that they got it all.

Divine moved back into the bathroom and threw Sherriff's gun on to the bathroom floor, near Lars.

Malik was already out the sliding back door with no second thoughts and no remembering moments. It was what it was and it only took a blink of an eye. Divine stopped at the entryway that led out to the backyard and took one last look at the carnage left. He saw what money and power abused and gained by an ill body had led too and so, earn by the steel, die by the steel. He looked down at his shoulder wound that had a folded t-shirt, tucked inside his hoody and raggedy t-shirt that lay over the bullet hole in his flesh. With a slight grimace of pain as he made a slight adjustment to the piece of cloth that at the very least slowed down the flow of his own blood. Divine took a lick of his lips, turned around and then disappeared out the sliding patio door and into the night. The fabulous home stood still and quiet as the five hundred dollar bills remained sitting on the edge of the pool table under the glass.

CHAPTER FIVE

Authority has standing with moral substance.

IN THE DESERTED lot that was situated in an isolated part of the city where fireworks popped off at, an unmarked police car pulled in, kicking up dust with flashing lights, and came to a stop amongst the array of bodies that laid in pools of blood mixed with dirt, the shot up SUV's and the immense amount of ammunition shells that were scattered everywhere.

Captain Robert Sagen, a middle aged Blackman in a suit & tie with a gray fedora on top of his receding hair and chomping on a cheap cigar, exited from the unmarked Grand Marquis and stood and looked over the large number of police, medics and media that arrived in full force, looking for a story to put their face on the ten o'clock news with.

Captain Sagen walked over toward a familiar and helpful face he spotted surveying the scene, but was quickly pounced upon by a young lady with nice legs, too much make-up and a microphone and her cameraman who rolled off one question after another in an attempt to find out what went down. Captain Sagen failed to break stride as he declined comment at each attempt and moved away from her with a little help from a couple police officers who escorted the feisty woman from his physical space. He met up with police Lieutenant Jack Blackmon, a younger black man with a thin moustache and short hair, who stood over the body of J-Rob.

Captain Sagen joined Lieutenant Blackmon in gazing down at J-Rob then the wily Captain picked his head up and scanned over the area that was surrounded by darkness. "What we got here Jack?"

"A real mess Captain. No drugs or money have been found. I would say a robbery but I have no evidence of that yet. But this is an excellent place for it to go down."

"Well, that's why you're a lieutenant," remarked Captain Sagen with a slight smile. "Put your thinking cap on. You know any of these?"

"None of the spots look familiar. I would say they were out of towners who came in. But for what?"

"What do you think – to get paid. From what I can see, some one or some bodies made a clean come up tonight. Nice job." Captain Sagen said as he kneeled down and observed J-Rob's body. He looked for identification, jewelry, and tattoos, anything that could tell him who he was, but he found nothing that caused him to pause and think for a moment. Here was a golden opportunity for the Captain to make a name for himself. Just what he had been waiting for. Lt. Blackmon looked a little closer at J-Rob's face and noticed something familiar but was unable to put his finger on it. No long chains, no large bills, no watches but all these shells. What was this? Who was this? Where was this all leading too? Captain Sagen questioned to himself.

"You think this was more than just a robbery Captain?" Asked the deferring lieutenant.

"There was definitely another party. I saw a pair of footsteps back there and some tire tracks leaving out. As for a robbery. I'm not too sure that was the real motive here. Too much time was taken. Too much care."

"What makes you say that?"

"Because too many personal items on such a large number of men are missing, which means this wasn't just about a robbery. It's like revenge. I hurt you, you just don't want to hurt me. You want to take everything from me then hurt me. That's what I believe happened here. A feud. Between who, I don't know."

"What do you want me to do?"

"Run I.D. checks on all these spots, then cross-reference them and, ohh yea, check on the street with any and all U.I's. You come up with anything, call me."

"You got it Captain." The young lieutenant quickly made his way to have a word with a couple of the officers and relay the instructions.

Captain Sagen stood with his hands in his pockets and a cigar chewed down to a tiny stub. He pulled it out of his mouth and threw it to the ground. "A new player. A new player," said the Captain quietly to himself.

Captain Sagen walked back to his vehicle and lit up another cigar that he puffed on to get it fired up as he stood at his car door. While he looked out at the scene, his ears overheard a call come over the radio that caused him to immediately jump in the car and speed off.

Tajaa relaxed back on his two-piece couch in his apartment that was a little messy since Zachary had arrived and brought his messy ways with him. He was out in the streets at that moment that gave Tajaa some private time.

As Tajaa sat comfortably and sewed up the crotch of a pair of jogging pants, a knock sounded at the door that he answered. Malik entered in with a wounded Divine that Tajaa gave a quick hand to with out any questions. Tajaa helped him into the bedroom and with no hesitation, addressed Divine's bullet wound. Malik after handing off Divine to Tajaa, hopped on the phone and made a few phone calls in an urgent and quick nature. He had to unload all the materials that he had just obtained and who better then his brothers to call on for a little assistance. One by one, each was contacted and told to meet with him at Tajaa's now, and with no explanation, they each agreed.

A hour or so later, Malik, one by one, met with Seven, Pops and DJ in Tajaa's tiny living room area that also served as a dining room. He handed each of them a package. Seven received a manila envelope with some cash and a couple garbage bags full of guns and jewelry. Pops received the suitcase full of cash. DJ received a backpack full of jewelry, cash, and the ICE. It was all about business. Socializing was left for another time. With a hug, a handshake and a knowing nod, each moved out of Tajaa's well aware of what was asked of and how they would go about it. Malik took a little time to himself to catch his breath and rest as he laid back in the chair then glanced over at the two duffel bags that laid full of weed. Malik had one more face to meet with but he also had a face that he had to make a visit to. He had to confront in the physical and find out were another body stood and what he knew in regards to the evening's outcome.

Malik rose from the chair, picked the duffel bags up and moved to the bedroom were he stood at the doorway for a moment and watched Tajaa clean and dress Divine's wound. The large man showcased his steady hands that revealed his caring nature that took his time in making sure the job was done completely and accurately.

Malik moved inside the cramped bedroom and pushed the duffel bags inside an already full closet and shut the door. Tajaa stood up with a pleased and satisfied expression at his handy work. Malik walked over and stood right beside Tajaa. Both of them observed Divine who worked at getting himself comfortable.

Tajaa turned his head toward Malik. "It's got to be all that good food the God eats."

"Feels like a quarter burned thru and now it's trying to close up with it still inside," said Divine as he fought the shots of pain.

"How's he looking Trapper John? I see the medical class in first aide came in handy," said a tired and exhausted Malik.

Tajaa began to throw the gauze, scissors, tape, rags and soap into a large bowl. "You're right about that. Never pass up on an open invitation to learn something. But he's doing good. He'll survive. The bullet did a clean get away. He's just being a Nancy Kerrigan. Why, why," fake cried Tajaa as he moved out the room.

Divine extended his middle finger at both Tajaa and Malik who shared a smile. Malik walked over to the foot of the bed as Tajaa exited the room. He took his time and observed Divine with care in his eye.

"Make the necessary arrangements?" Probed Divine.

"It's all taken care of."

The two held eye contact silently with their thoughts focused on J-Rob and what he did on the battlefield tonight.

"You know he went with more honor then a lot of these fake thugs out here," Divine gingerly expressed so to not upset the dressing on his wound.

Malik took a seat on the bed. A flood of memories over came him. All the moments he experienced with J-Rob. The good and the bad. "You remember that time when you, J and self got pulled over with those two dime sacks on you and I . . ."

Divine lifted his head toward Malik. He remembered with the moment clearly envisioned. "And he grabbed them and took off running on foot with poe-poe chasing after him."

"That was beautiful. He always said and lived that an individual should take the weight so that the group can continue forward."

"Did he get caught?"

"You know they weren't catching him."

The two dirty and musty young men shared a laugh. Malik got up from the bed and started to make his way toward the door. Divine kept his eyes on Malik. He was well aware of what Malik was about to do and where he was going.

Malik stopped at the doorway and stood still for a moment, facing away from Divine. "Get some rest son."

"One more thing to take care of?" Asked Divine.

"Gotta make a visit."

"Be wise," said Divine as Malik turned and locked eyes with him then spun back around and left out with calm and grace. Divine finally found a comfortable position but he was unable to close his eyes and rest. He just laid there and stared out the window. He took everything in that went down and made sure that everything was done in a right accord. They were not there to take life but to deal with death.

Malik arrived at Freddie's front door and with no knock. He plainly, with no regard, entered inside where he found Freddie sitting on the couch with his arm around Cherise as they watched 'Love Jones' in close comfort.

Malik immediately thought to himself that she found some one who will definitely give her what ever she asked. "Hey Cherise. How you living?" Asked Malik casually.

"Hi Malik," said sweet and innocent with a grin.

Freddie jerked his head around at a serious-staring Malik who stood with his arms crossed to the side of the couple. Freddie was shocked that he was looking at the young man who had lived with him for the last six months. Words were choked up.

He was sure that after his talk with Lars that either he would make some serious money and stay the evening in a hotel or he would be in trouble, and for some reason he disregarded the word and that thought of trouble. Either way, Freddie was not expecting to see Malik's face for a while.

He straightened up, pulled his arm from around Cherise and changed his whole body disposition and facial expression, from seductive to concerned. "What, what's up Leek?" Said a shook Freddie who was searching to gain his composure to seem calm.

Malik took his time and moved slowly and purposely thru the living room, dining room, kitchen areas and then back toward Freddie who remained sitting, unsure of what Malik was doing or feeling.

Malik laid his eyes on the TV screen that was at a part of the movie when Lars Tate's character is in fiend mode for Nia Long's character while lying to him self. He moved his eyes on Cherise and glared at her revengeful pupils that met his for a couple seconds that she felt the heat from. Malik wasn't mad at her. He was disappointed that this was the course of action that she choose, but so be it.

With a stank attitude, she swung her head away from his and rolled her eyes to give the impression that she could care less.

Malik switched his eye contact from Cherise and on to Freddie who continued to sit nervously, unable to keep his eyes and attention on any one thing for too long. His mind was moving to fast in too many directions.

"My fault kids, didn't mean to disrupt your mating session here. I just stopped by to collect some things." Malik cracked a small grin as he headed into the bedroom and began to bag the little clothes that he had kept at this place.

Malik had scattered his things in various places. Tajaa's apartment had some of his higher priced clothes; button down shirts, polo pullovers, designer jeans, and a number of tennis shoes such as the new Iverson's, the white throw back Jordan's edition #4, and some timbo's. He also had things at Rassa's parents house, Seven's place and Pops' apartment. He only had some t-shirts, a couple pair of long basketball shorts, socks and a pair of Nike trainers at Freddie's.

An unsure Freddie slowly, and with caution, rose up from the couch and stepped into the bedroom were he observed Malik packing his things up from the doorway.

"What's going on Malik? Watcha doing? You leaving out?" Each question tripping over the next.

Malik went thru a pile of dirty clothes that lay in a corner of the room. He found the white wife beater tank top that he played ball in the other day. He took a smell and then curled his face up cause of the stink that reeked from it. "What did you say? Ohh, what am I doing? Well, I think we both know the answer to that question." Malik picked his head up and looked directly into Freddie's eyes. "Don't we?"

"Well, what, what happened tonight? Everything work out?"

"No. But that's not your fault. You didn't know what was going on. Right?" Sarcastically put by Malik. "You were blind, deaf and dumb." Malik turned away and continued to gather his clothes and throw them in a black garbage bag.

Freddie threw his eyes away from Malik in shame. He did know something. He only chose to remain quiet and play dumb. When Lars spoke with him on that day,

Freddie was asked about Malik's work and money situation. He was looking for an opening and Freddie was the avenue. Lars mentioned that he had a job for Malik and that he needed to know Malik's status. Little did Lars know that he was asking the wrong person. And little did Freddie know, this was the reason Malik lived with Freddie. Their weaknesses that Malik was aware of came to benefit when they both were unable to change into black men who truly cared about those around them. And because they didn't, one knowingly and the other unknowingly, they both would pay the price.

Freddie scratched himself uncontrollably from the tension that was building up in him self. "Wh, what, what happened?"

Malik moved up into Freddie's face with force and power that almost went right thru him. "Nothing you need to concern yourself with anymore." Malik, filled with a controlled rage and only seeing J-Rob's dead body, glared at Freddie with out a blink. "Now, have you seen my all white short sleeve button down?"

Freddie moved away quickly to escape the heat, and began to search thru the closet. "Yea, yea, I wore it the other day. It should be in here."

Malik calmed himself down then slowly spun around and faced Freddie who emerged from the closet with the shirt.

Malik took it from the shaking hand that he observed and threw it in the bag. Freddie placed his hands in his pockets with his eyes darting all over the room. His thoughts were centered on what Malik was going to do to him and why.

Malik stood and looked at him one more time. He gave one last opportunity to come clean and stand upright. But Freddie refused. He remained a silent jitterbug.

Malik shook his head in disappointment and then headed off toward the backdoor with no emotion.

Freddie followed closely as he searched for the right words that he would never be able to find. "So um, where you going to lay your head?"

Malik stopped at the back door and slowly revolved to meet up with Freddie. "With good people."

"Leek, if there something you want to say, just say it."

"There's no reason. You already know." Malik spun back around and moved his hand on the doorknob. "Take care player."

"Well, um, let me get a number were to reach you at?"

Malik stopped and turned his head at Freddie and cracked a small grin. "No." He moved out the door and walked off into the night.

Freddie moved out on to the back porch and observed. "Well check it, hit me up. You got my number. The doors open any time. Take care. Umm, I mean, be safe." Freddie was only shouting out to the darkness. Malik was gone.

Lars' house was surrounded by medics moving in with black body bags and weak looking stretchers, over-stressed police who stepped in and out of the house, concerned neighbors that looked in horror at the dead body being wheeled out in their quiet neighborhood, and a few hyped up media people who talked to who ever would talk.

Captain Sagen pulled up at that moment, parked and observed the scene as he stood and lit up his flamed out cigar. "Now, what do we have here?" He made his way forward, past the various groups of people and once inside, he spotted Chief Albert Linzern, a bald Blackman in his mid-fifties whose eyes revealed he hardly slept. He stood and looked over one of the young men gunned down by the pool table.

Captain Sagen moved up next to Chief Linzern's side and stood for a quiet moment in observation. "Chief. What's happened here?"

Chief Linzern was not a man with patience. He was a lifer on the force who needed to retire but that was some years away. Plus he was far too valuable, to those who remained in the shadows, to allow to retire. The raggedy kept Chief took notice in the body that pulled up on his side. "What does it fucking look like Sagen? A fuckin' bloodbath." Chief Linzern gestured with his finger to follow him, which Captain Sagen did with a deep breath exhaled. The two arrived at the broken apart pool table. "You know what this means right?"

Chief Linzern didn't allow Captain Sagen to answer as he walked off toward the bathroom area. They passed another one of Lars' boys who was in a pool of blood in the hallway and arrived in the coke and blood splattered bathroom. Lars was face down in the toilet.

Chief Linzern moved over to the corpse and picked his dripping wet head up out of the toilet bowl and showed it to Captain Sagen. "You know who this fuckin' is?"

"Oh my god. That's Lars Rollins. He WAS a wanna-be big time supplier of dope to the streets. The word was he was about to move up in the world," answered a taken back Captain at the face that dripped thick, cloudy white water.

"Well, looks like that fuckin' advancement got stopped quick," said the hard voice that dropped the head back into the toilet bowl. He bent down and surveyed the coke spilled all over on the marble tile floor. He took a taste and realized it was good stuff then picked himself up and stood, facing Captain Sagen.

"Any leads?" Asked the two hundred pound, physically fit captain.

"Now if I had any fuckin' leads, I wouldn't be here making a fuckin' date with you. What we have here was a simple 'get fucked' that, I have to fucking say, was executed to precision by the fucks. Found no fingerprints, witnesses saw nothing and evidence is very little. The cocksuckers even left the fuckin' guns."

"I'll have ballistics check on it immediately," chimed in Captain Sagen.

"Some one pissed in my yard and I'm the only one that can piss in my fuckin' yard."

Captain Sagen walked behind a pissed and angry Chief Linzern who didn't know the meaning of restraint.

The younger Captain thought to him self about the scene at the deserted lot he just came from then looked over the house. As Captain Sagen slowly moved thru the shot up place, he fell behind Chief Linzern who walked out of the house and toward his vehicle. A message was handed to him from one of the police officers. He read it. His eyes enlarged at what he just read and he marched off toward Chief Linzern.

The Captain caught up to the Chief at his black Yukon. "I might have something Sir."

"Yea, and, what the fuck-?"

"I just came from an abandoned lot that was filled with shot up spots that all seem to be from out of state. All except one who Lt. Blackmon has identified as Junior Robertson, a local kid who is familiar with Lars."

"Beautiful!" Shot the Chief as the whole story came to picture. "So this Junior fuck hooks up with Lars and his people to make a deal that goes bad with the out-of-towners. Lars, Junior and his posse take out the spots at the lot, but not all of them. They quickly make their way to Lars' house and exact revenge then head back out of state with the product and the cash. That will about do."

"There's something more sir. It can't be that simple," interjected the questioning Captain who felt there was more to the story then what was relayed to him from his older Chief.

"Bullshit! It is that fuckin' simple cause we can make it that simple," hollered Chief Linzern who opened his truck door. "This was about competition for some table scraps that ended up getting personal. And that led to what we have tonight. So here's what we're going to do. We are going to wrap this up nice and tight so the law-abiding people of this city can see that we do our job. And if we have to, we'll swallow a straggler getting away for now. Aright?"

"I think there is a new player in the city Chief." Captain Sagen couldn't resist letting the Chief know of his theory.

Chief Linzern hopped into the Yukon, started the ignition up and then gave a mean business look toward Captain Sagen as he revved the engine motor. He wasn't in the mood to hear about theories. "We are talking about thirteen fuckin' bodies here. Thirteen CAPTAIN. That means that what ever we do, it has to be quick, precise and make sense. Fuck a wild goose chase and ghost theories you might have. I'm more concerned about what we do make sense. And what could be more sensible to the fuckin' people then what I just explained to you?" Chief Linzern searched for an answer on Captain Sagen's face that agreed with his assessment of the situation. After observing the investigative nature still present on the Captain, his face hardened and his voice deepened like a growl of a bear. "Screw your fuckin' head on and realize, the clock is fuckin' ticking." Chief Linzern peeled off.

Captain Sagen stood with a lowered head that he picked up and observed the Chief drive away. "Keep things simple huh? The old fuck is losing focus on the big picture here." Captain Sagen looked over at the house and the remaining bodies being carried out. This was definitely an opportunity for him, something he was waiting a long time for.

Tajaa did his thing in the kitchen as he fried up some organic extra firm Tofu in some olive oil, chopped up some broccoli, some peppers, and some garlic with some mushrooms that were added to the tofu he seasoned fully and checked on his side of brown rice.

Tajaa dished up a plate and brought it in to Divine who wasted no time in satisfying his built up hunger that he washed down with a glass of cold water. Tajaa returned to the kitchen and prepared his own plate.

Malik entered in the spot just in time, and dropped his bag in a closet near the front door. He walked over to where the smell of good food was coming from and observed Tajaa building his plate of food. Malik stepped into the small and cramped space, took a plate and began to dig into the food right beside the larger young man. Both exchanged greetings as they gracefully moved around the kitchen in unison, preparing their plates of food.

"Everything good?" Asked Tajaa.

"For sure. We're a go," Malik said with a content smile as he dished up the rice then laid the tofu and veggies on the bed of. He took a sniff, seasoned it right, poured a glass of water, then moved into the living room and found a seat near the television.

Tajaa followed right behind and sat down on the small couch that had a few rips in it. The two of them enjoyed the food and watched the news report on the price of gas, the state of the war in Iraq and the President's admission of spying on the American public.

"Do they really think that this spy shit he's admitting to is just started," spoke Malik in between bites. "They forget the Black Panthers, Malcolm X and too many to name Black people who have and still are under constant watch?"

"Ahh, it makes them feel better," thundered Tajaa. "I don't give a fuck though. They can listen to me all they want."

"We have nothing to be ashamed or scared about," Malik added. "The rest of these jokers will protest, debate and argue."

"While their being bugged," added Tajaa.

The two shared a small laugh. They continued to devour the plates of food that tasted too good, especially to Malik who enjoyed every bite he took.

"You see this gas shit son. Fucking ridiculous," said Malik sharply.

"That's why I'm happy I don't drive. The city's my home. I can walk anywhere."

"Yea but bus fare is going up, cab fare is going up and before long those that have rides are going to start charging, ya know. And this is bigger then just gas for a car sun, ya know. The thing is we have to understand that this right here, the price of gas, keeps us trapped in a specific area. Think about it. The majority that live in the city, remain in the city. We don't travel and get out and see what's beyond the border. We can't afford too. This has been made to keep poor people stuck in one area."

"And what is created is a cloud of depression," Tajaa chimed in with.

"True indeed, hopelessness, and violence acted out on each other due to resentment and anger building up each day in these small territories that these flower heads like to lay claim to. Accepted concentration camps."

"It's the nature of the beast," said Tajaa.

"And look, there won't be one word mentioned about the shootings tonight. They don't have any faces to show who did it or no angle to use it. They don't give a fuck about us. So we have to."

Tajaa turned his head and looked at Malik with a glorious shine in his eyes. He felt the same way and was aware of what Malik was saying when it came to the new institution of slavery that was being applied. His anger had turned constructive. Matter of fact, it wasn't even anger. It was pure love for his people. Tajaa didn't need to ask Malik what happened tonight. His only concern was taking care of Divine and providing a space to relax at this specific moment. That's what mattered. Doing his part.

Malik and Tajaa returned to the television news that reported on a Hollywood couples' breakup. They both turned to each other at the same time and broke out a knowing and understanding smile.

Just that moment, a knock followed by three quieter knocks was heard at the door. Malik and Tajaa knew who that was and sprung to their feet to open the door.

Born stood in the entry with a comforting grin on his baby looking face at three in the morning. He entered inside and exchanged hugs and handshakes with Tajaa and Malik, then Divine, who had heard Born's voice vibrate from the backroom, had to get up and show some love.

The lightening quick ball player saw the wound that had been clean and covered on Divine's shoulder area. He lifted the bandage up and got a look at it. "It stop bleeding?"

"Yea, Marcus Welby handled it."

Born turned to Tajaa and Malik. "Was he crying?"

"You know Divine. Like a teething one-year old," Tajaa said jokingly.

Born turned back to Divine. "You always did have trouble with that rough shit down in the paint. I could always post you up."

"Yea, yea, yea, whatever B. All of yall can kiss my lovely black ass."

"See, that's that gay shit right there," Tajaa said comically with a finger point toward Divine.

The four young men stood in the living room and shared laughs, smiles and playful jousts along with soft punches at each other. Malik slid out of the room undetected as Born filled his brothers in on his upcoming year on the court and what the team looked like.

Malik opened the bedroom closet door up and gathered the two duffel bags with the pounds of weed that he decided would not be put into play back in the city. That would be a disservice to what he was attempting to do. Malik was aware that it was time to start shipping out the garbage and this was the right move to go about doing even though weed was far from garbage, but it was abused, which ended up making it garbage in the end. He reappeared with bags in hand and looked at Born as all the laughing and talking came to a grounding halt. It was time to take care of business.

Born stepped forward and took the bags from Malik's grip and the two shared a deep and focused look with each other that communicated the importance of the task at hand. Nothing needed to be explained, asked of, or begged. It was known and fully accepted.

"You know what is asked of," said Malik with a straight and serious expression that communicated all the information Born would need.

"You know this, and it will be carried out all the way," Born made known.

"No doubt," Malik shot back with no emotion.

"One word when it's completed." Born met each ones eyes with no fear.

"Good. You better make motion out of here," advised Malik as he moved toward the door.

Born nodded then placed the duffel bags around his neck and shoulders and made his way toward the door. He came to a stop and exchanged love with each then moved out the apartment door that closed behind him.

Divine, Malik and Tajaa remained quiet as they each moved out into the apartment. Divine headed back into the bedroom and laid down. Malik picked his empty plate up, carried it into the kitchen and washed it off. Tajaa relaxed back on the couch and turned the channel to an old black and white movie.

Malik walked into the bedroom and laid down at the other end of the bed that Divine was laying in. He was still in some pain, but it was nothing he couldn't endure. Both laid back and stared up at the ceiling.

Divine moved his eyes from the ceiling on to Malik. "We did it bra. That's all over with."

Malik paused for a bit and turned his head down toward Divine at the other end of the bed. "Nah sun. It's just starting." Malik closed his eyes and found some rest as his words came to an end.

Divine took a moment and kept his eyes on Malik. He was right. This was just the beginning. Now came the hard part. They had to prepare them selves because what was to come would be more difficult and much tougher then what they just went thru. Divine moved his head to the side and closed his eyes with no doubts and no remorse. What they did was something that nobody else would do for the reason they did it. It brought great comfort to both of them. A feeling their fathers were never able to experience. And it was at that moment that it brought some of the best rest they got in along time.

CHAPTER SIX

Fear conquered leads to expansion and exploration in warm waters.

MALIK AND DIVINE sat at a back booth in the fine Chinese restaurant that was located off one of the main streets on the south side of the city. Harry Simmons, a prominent black businessman sat with the plainly dressed young men. Malik had just had his cornrows re-done and aligned perfectly in various circle patterns while Divine's short fro was lined up and leveled all the way around that hooked up with his full beard. The three discussed an offer that Malik proposed to the forty-three year old owner of various barbershops, cleaners, auto detail shops and corner markets to go along with an impressive stock portfolio. Along with that, Harry had a number of connections that were able to flip large amounts of cash thru various rackets, one being real estate. Harry was able to purchase million dollar homes for about four hundred grand that then in a short period would be sold off for one and half million, making three times the money in return. This was one time that Malik and Divine would be able to go half in with Harry on one of the houses he had in mind that was located outside the city. The only drawback that Malik saw was the timetable. It could take some time from the moment the money was passed until the house sold and the money made was returned. Malik was in no rush though. Him and Divine liked the idea of 200k in return for 750 k. Patience was definitely a virtue worth having when it came to achieving prosperity.

Rassa stood out in the night as the day came to end. An older black man in sandals that revealed his ashy feet and non-clipped toes, who ran a couple used car lots in the city, approached the tall and slender young Blackman. After some simple and short greetings, Rassa explained that he needed a favor from him and how he could benefit from it. The older man knew of some individuals who were willing to pay top dollar for European luxury vehicles and it just so happened that the older man would take a finders' fee to arrange those such vehicles, courtesy of the DMV, to fall into another's lap that then could be handed over to the right carrier. This was the type of information he had to offer. Rassa passed the old man who had little hair left on his scalp an envelope filled with cash and then nodded his head. It was a go and it was a chance that risked jail time and loss of money but the older man new that Rassa was on the level and that any bad business that should come from him, would find him self dealing with some severe repercussions. The old man took a look inside the envelope then with wide-open eyes and a smile returned the nod back. A time and date was set up and arranged then Rassa left quietly thru the back entrance as the older black man in a Miller High Life beer t-shirt felt good about the deal and confident that he could come thru and be of some help, both to Rassa and to him self.

DJ and Tajaa sat with a group of well-dressed black men from the suburbs who had started an on-line market that catered to Black people as well as a reputable fencing operation that was known in the streets. They gathered at the back of a pawnshop that was owned by one of the fellas. There, DJ explained the merchandise they had at their disposal and what they wanted for it. The well-groomed pretty boy's eyes lit up and were filled with the thought of the money they could make with their operations they had at their service. Tajaa slid a suitcase, with a steely glare focused on them, under the table. They pulled it up and took a look to find designer jewelry along with a sack of diamonds. The young men looked up at Tajaa and DJ in amazement. They had never dealt with such fine and expensive materials like what they saw in the case and DJ and Tajaa knew this. The only type of business that would be going down between them would be that which was on the level. The four men traded agreeing looks with each other as a piece of paper was slid to one of the men by DJ. They each looked at the figure written down then passed an approving nod at the two. To just hand over the case with out nothing coming back seemed from the outside to look dumb and naive but this was DJ and Tajaa. And the hustler new everything about the men he was dealing with.

If they were smart, they would carry their job out with honor otherwise things would start to happen that would affect everything and everybody in the suburban young men's lives. And Tajaa made that known with out saying a word.

Lt. Blackmon roamed the city streets in search of any answers that would at least give the perception of him doing his job. He shook down street dealers, talked with young, gum-popping girls and asked hardheaded, knuckleheads questions regarding any unusual business being done on the streets. Each face he encountered shook their head and gave the young Lieutenant nothing but stop signs. But for some reason, he didn't mind and wasn't disappointed by the lack of information. He admired the rare site of his community taking care of their own business instead of allowing another to think, do and protect for them. The closed mouths filled him with a sense of inner satisfaction that definitely contradicted his job. Too many times, lips were quick to move and give up information for the smallest little gift that when seen in the light was basically nothing. So after thirteen bodies dropped, he was sure heads would be talking non-stop to secure a little something for themselves from the outside authorities. But that never happened. Not one mouth opened to deliver the slightest hint of direction. Lt. Blackmon looked around the rundown buildings, garbage filled streets, cracked up sidewalks, patchy brown grass, and lifeless broken branch trees, and smelled a new aroma in air.

Captain Sagen took a moment inside his vehicle and observed Malik share words with a couple young men, who had to be in their late teens, in the city park. After seeing the teaching session had come to an end, Captain Sagen exited his ride and approached Malik who sat on a park bench and enjoyed the night breeze that blew with a bottle of water. No introductions were necessary, each knew who the other was. The Captain attempted to spark up a friendly conversation that eventually led to him asking about J-Rob. Malik expressed his displeasure with the murder but only revealed the fact that he was a friend from around the way. And then Malik hit reverse as he turned the tables and asked the Captain if they had any leads on who did it or what they were doing about it along with quizzing about what's going on. In all, the Captain came away with nothing while Malik walked away with tiny tidbits of info on their direction. The most important thing Malik learned that evening was the difference of opinion that existed between the Chief and the Captain on the 'who' and the 'why' in regards to the recent activity. Malik was the type of being who turned water to wine. The tightest lips always opened up to him and provided him with what was necessary. It was hard to say no or walk away. His conversations were fun, exciting, and thought provoking and they were all involving. In the end, Malik had you checking yourself. Captain Sagen didn't even realize what had slipped out of his mouth in the course of their one on one that went in the way of the wind that blew the gate open and allowed Malik to take it in.

A few days passed with relative calm and peace due to Lars' operation being temporary shut down. Then on a clear night under a full moon, Malik, Divine, Seven, Pops, Benji, DJ, Tajaa, Rassa and Lite gathered at the cemetery and stood over J-Rob's grave.

Their soldier had done his job well and they we're not about to let him return to the essence in vain. Respect was shown fully.

Captain Sagen sat in his unmarked vehicle across the street and observed the group of young men gather and show their love for J-Rob. Seeing that the streets were dry with any info and no one was talking, he thought to camp out at the city cemetery and see who visits J-Rob's grave. And this right here looked like more then just an around the way friend or associate to him. The Captain picked up a camera and snapped off a number of shots of the individuals present at the dark and isolated graveyard.

Captain Sagen entered the police station in a hurried rush with a file in his hands. He blew into Chief Linzern's office unannounced and slapped down the photos of Malik, Divine and the rest of the group that he had taken in front of the staring Chief.

Chief Linzern slowly took his time and took his glare off his over excited Captain and on to the photos that lay scattered on his desk. He picked up Malik's photo shot and gave it a quick look over then turned to the wired captain. "What do you want me to do with this? Wipe my ass."

"I think we should strongly consider that these are our shooters," said Sagen with hands on hips.

Chief Linzern looked at the meagerly dressed young Blackmen with no jewelry, no expensive clothing, and no bulges. "You're reaching. Big time. And I don't like it. These boys are nothing more then spectators. Sideline operators who don't have the backing or the necessities to carry out those operations," said the disheveled older man whose authority was exercised.

"Chief, I think – "

Chief Linzern could take no more and he rose from his chair and leaned over his desk toward Captain Sagen. "Look, that's it. I want this stopped right now. I'm ordering you to close the case and put an end to this bullshit. It was a group on group slaying with a straggler or two that got away. Hell, we even got one of the spot's at the lots gun that was left at Lars' place, which shows that these two had contact. What more do you need?"

"But Chief . . ."

"No but, no how about this, no nothing. Close it up. Now." Chief Linzern demanded.

Captain Sagen and Chief Linzern locked eyes. The Captain felt a pass was being given here. That eyes and ears were being closed to the possibilities. But why? How come with such flimsy evidence was the Chief letting this go? It seemed to Captain Sagen that more and more black killings were just being swept under the rug and ignored until it was useful. It wasn't like he cared about the young men killing each other, but how was he going to get to be a Chief, a congressmen or a state senator or a judge if all he did was allow those that could be of help to his own aspirations fly the coop? He wanted to make a name for himself in the system and Malik, Divine and this group right here gave him the avenue to make some real money as well as position himself for a power play move.

Captain Sagen gathered his photos up from the Chief's desk and left out the office, slamming the door shut.

Seven arrived at the door of a cheap hotel room across the state border in Tanisha's Honda Accord. He knocked on the door, room 111, and was immediately grabbed and pulled inside by his six foot two, hundred and ninety-pound uncle who wrapped him up and gave him a huge bear hug that tossed Seven from side to side. After the hug that would never end did finally come to an end, the two of them took a seat and shared some small talk about the man's brother who was Seven's father. After the 'getting to know' talk finished, Seven passed his uncle a box with a couple guns in it. Seven's uncle looked and inspected the semi-automatic weapons that must have been used only once and were in top shape. He picked his head up and observed a key that sat in the middle of Seven's palm. He took the locker key in hand slowly and then nodded with a knowing smile. He rose up from his seat and gave his nephew another big hug. It felt too good to see his nephew who he hadn't seen in awhile. Seven had heard his mother talk down to his father about his criminal brother and how he was mixed up in so many bad things. She disallowed Seven from seeing him as a little boy but as Seven grew up, he slowly came to know of the uncle he was shielded from. The fifty-something year old dark-skinned man who looked just like his father, was no choirboy for sure, but it goes deeper then that. Seven found out about his robberies, his gun running and his con games that he ran on various wealthy individuals. And as he looked at his uncle's activities closer, he saw that he robbed from the greedy, he ran guns out of the city, and he conned those who refused to aid in charity in the right direction. These were things his mother never told him, if she knew at all.

Now, Seven felt, he was picking up the torch and running with it that his uncle saw and appreciated with an unbridled joy. That was why this meeting was so special and loving for his bald-headed uncle. He was pleased and satisfied to see that his brothers son saw that shit is not all pretty in this world and it takes action to really get things done.

Pops stepped out of the airport terminal and into the hot Las Vegas air and gave a look around at the lights that lit up the desert night. Just as the older man's eyes caught the sites of lovely, sexy ladies in little clothing, a drop top corvette pulled up were an old friend from back in the days yelled out Pops' name. He noticed Gary immediately. He noticed that he hadn't changed much as he moved into the passenger seat with a comfortable smile. Gary was one of them cool white dudes, hippy style, who like to talk about his French background. Gary and Pops had attended college together that included much partying, women and various hustles to feed their bellies. Gary was a straight up gambler. He loved sports but he loved betting on it and winning even more. On campus, Pops was aware that he got a number of important players to throw games and shave points. After college, he expanded his operation, linked up with important help like lawyers, agents, bookies, casino managers, sport officials and ladies. Gary used everything in his power to know the angle and find an edge. One of his plays was to cozy up to the players girlfriends where he would be their best friend and that shoulder to cry on and boy did those tears pay well. When he moved up to the big lights, he just transferred his game to the players wives who loved having Gary over to their parties and other functions. Who better a person to call on, Pops thought, as they drove down the strip. He would do just perfect for what he had in mind.

Just as Pops was getting situated in Vegas, Malik and Divine finished playing a game of basketball at an indoor fitness club with Harry, who was a member.

A few weeks had passed since the last meeting when a phone call from Harry came for Malik that asked to meet up. So here they were. With everybody catching their breath after a game, getting a drink of water and arguing about who got next, Harry took a seat next to Divine and Malik. Without drawing eyes or attention, Harry began to gather his things together and reached for an item in his duffel bag as he exchanged some small talk. Accomplishing his task, he rose up, extended his hand to both Divine and Malik and then headed to the exit doors.

Divine and Malik exchanged a quick questioning look about the nature of this meeting. They didn't discuss a single item or even been updated to the progress on the pending deals. Then Malik moved to his duffel bag that was underneath the bench he sat on. He reached in for his towel that he pulled out but he saw a shoebox that the towel covered up. Malik lifted the cover and saw nothing but neatly stacked hundred dollar bills fill the box. He picked his head up and looked toward Harry who gave an approving look toward Malik before leaving out the gym. The real estate came thru and so did Harry.

Rassa arrived on foot, ball cap backwards, short white towel with gold edges to wipe the heavy perspiration that dripped from his dome laid over the shoulder, at the used car lot and met up with the beaming older man who was feeling good. With no words, no greetings, and no questions, nothing but business, he tossed some keys to Rassa who moved toward a 1988 Honda Civic that sat near by to the back and opened the trunk. He found a small brown shopping bag with a slip of paper that had an address and a name written on it. He put it in his pocket, closed the trunk, got in the car and dove off.

DJ and Tajaa, in jogging pants, t-shirts, and high tops with no jewelry, stood at the pool table and played a game of pool amongst the host of young white and black faces that littered the suburban bar that was packed tight on this night.

The two young men from the group of suburbanites that they met with some time ago at the pawnshop, walked in and eyed the two in the back of the place. They arrived at the pool table where DJ finished sinking the six ball. A Macy's shopping bag with a cardboard box inside was set down beside DJ who only nodded his head and then took his shot. These guys knew better then to cross Tajaa whose rep was known and respected. It was a wise business move by the suburbanites.

The young men in name brand clothing, long chains and cell phones were invited to join Tajaa and DJ in a game of pool for some pocket money. The challenge was accepted and the game commenced as the sack with a brown box sat to the side, close to the pool table.

Pops and his old college buddy, Gary with slicked back hair, slick clothes and slick ways, exited Caesar's Palace with cool smiles on their faces as they caught up on old times and hopped into the cherry red corvette that then pulled and raced away, down the busy and packed Las Vegas blvd. Gary had made his last of a number of pickups with his guys at the various spots.

Pops took in the sights as they passed the Bellagio, New York, New York and MGM casinos. Gary pulled out a fat manila enveloped and handed it over to Pops. He looked inside and realized this was one of many envelopes that Gary had passed to him that had more then doubled his money, almost tripled. He closed it and tucked it in his suit jackets' inside pocket.

Gary had done well and Pops gave a reassuring nod in the direction of the pasty Frenchman who had made America his home. He pulled into the Luxor with a cocky grin. All he did was lay down some sure bets for Pops that paid nicely and promptly. They sat in the ride, waiting on the valet, and puffed on a couple cigars as a couple sexy vixens passed in front of.

Seven returned to the same cheap motel and met up with his still excited uncle who couldn't get enough of his grown up nephew. The tall, older man showered Seven with a bunch more hugs and back slaps. He felt honored to be a part of his brother's son's life again. And he showed it by dumping on the bed a waterfall of rubber-banded money. Seven looked at his uncle and flashed a smile in a pleasing fashion. He had come thru in grand fashion. The key was not for a locker, it was for a garage and it was there that the guns were passed. Seven's uncle had sold the guns for a fair price to a militant organization that was tired of the constant police abuse that was taking place and had decided to stand up to it in another, more confrontational form. As Seven and his uncle sat at a table and talked, a young lady with a body that banged in every dimension and a face that defined pretty entered in and began to throw herself at Seven in a seductive nature. She took a seat in his lap, caressed his face, gave gentle kisses to his neck, and basically thru her bubbling breast area into his face. His uncle watched in amusement as the younger man attempted to halt the tempting and sexually attractive young lady as well as fighting his own urge to rip her clothes off right there. His uncle had paid for her service. It was his gift to his nephew but Seven quickly put a stop to the strong advance and explained his situation and Tanisha to his understanding uncle.

The older man then gathered up the young lady, admiring his nephews loyalty to his one woman, and headed into the separate bedroom but not before they said goodbye to each other with a deep hug engaged in.

Rassa drove up and parked at a busy warehouse that was full of activity in the night with loading, unloading, stocking and packing in full session. He went inside the cluttered office and approached a small-framed man who stood at a worn out desk. He extended his hand and passed the note to the middle-aged white man at the desk in the small room that over saw all the operations. The frail thin with a receding hairline man read the note closely then looked at Rassa for a moment. His clothes showed that he was not all concerned about fashion but his face was clean-shaven and his fingernails were spotless which revealed his job was to push papers inside the air-conditioned office. He was expecting this visit so he reached underneath the counter and pulled out a key that he slid along the counter top area to Rassa in a small white envelope. He gestured in the direction that Rassa should go.

Before Rassa left he asked for the piece of paper back that was given freely by the blue-eyed man. He then stepped out of the office and approached an eighteen-wheel car-carrier that was stacked with Mercedes, BMW's, Volvo's, and Audi's. Rassa got in the truck that was parked in the back and after a few moments of getting the hang of driving a big rig and how to work the clutch, he pulled out and drove off, thru the gate that was opened by the same white dude who passed the key.

A couple hours outside the city limits, Rassa pulled into the back of a large salvage operation in a little town and parked the truck.

He got out and was met by a large bearded, tattooed up white man who, with no words spoken, handed over another car key to Rassa and a head gesture. No smile. No words, No handshakes. Nothing but a grim face and a fat belly. Rassa didn't care cause this was all about business. Get in and get out. Fuck finding a friend. He walked over to the Nissan Altima, opened the trunk and inspected a black duffel bag that was filled with clothes that sat on top of wrapped up money that layered the bottom of the bag. After checking the bills and making sure the proper amount was there, he shut the trunk and gave a nod to the sloppy man in a pair of dirty jeans. Rassa hopped in and drove off.

As he moved down the road, Rassa pulled out a CD of his that was in his jacket pocket and slid it in the CD player. He started to bob his head and say his own lines that played.

> *We sun'in you cats/when We turn on the brights/We gunnin at cats/when We grab the mic/do a heist for ya cargo/ rob the stagecoach/money, crystals, diamonds and gold.*

Malik sat in the lone chair at Tajaa's apartment and mellowed out with one of Rassa's music pieces playing in the CD player.

'Everybody lives in hell/but We rockin' ice style/Liberace lifestyle/faggot with a nice pile/he'll always burst good/best rappers in the hood/but We die to get out/officers and big mouths/want us in the big house/so we do'in more dirt/niggas smokin' rain drops on this planet earth/its so pretty/man, how pretty is this shit, tell'em yo/its so pretty/man let them kids know, let them kids know/We got guns and hugs and love and hate/animosity and harmony, real and fake/We got guns and hugs and love and hate/animosity and harmony, real and fake/its so pretty/its so pretty'

Tajaa entered in and set down the shopping bag with the brown box in it at Malik's feet and then made swift movement to the bathroom to relieve himself. Malik took a look inside and saw the cash that laid inside neatly stacked and rubber banded up. Tajaa was followed by Pops who sported a Las Vegas t-shirt. After a hug and a handshake, Pops handed over the suitcase filled with hundred dollar bills. He took a seat next to Malik as the two talked about the college basketball season and his own high school team that he coached. Pops was a stickler for discipline and fundamentals, two qualities his players, and players these days in general, severely lacked.

As the conversation continued, Seven entered in and exchanged love with Tajaa, who returned to the living room from the bathroom, Malik and Pops. Seven opened his backpack that he was wearing and dumped out a mountain of cash on to the floor. Pleasing looks were exchanged and hand slaps to each were traded back and forth with congratulating words that spilled out in loving and appreciative motion. Divine entered in the door next and joined in on the animated conversation that took place amongst the bodies of young men and the money that laid on the floor.

Rassa shuffled in to the apartment to his music that was playing in the room. "Its so pretty," Rassa sang along with his words that came from the speakers. He noticed the mountain of cash on the floor that he began to move around with a smile and an upbeat shuffle. He came to a stop, moved over it, opened the black duffel bag and emptied the money out of it that spilled on to the floor. The mountain of dough had grown and was lying, scattered on the thin, stained carpet as the group of men stood, talked and thanked each other with smiles at what they, together, had produced along with a few punches shared between each.

While his brothers were doing their thing, in a neighboring state, Born sat at his kitchen table alone in his campus apartment and bagged the weed he had been given in a variety of weights. A scale sat to the side of him on a smaller table that was filled with plastic bags and white, pouch-sized envelops. Stacked on the table in piles was half pounds, ounces, quarter-ounces, twenty-sacks, dimes and nicks. As he checked the scale to make sure the right amount was about to be bagged, a knock came at the door. Born, non-chalantly and calmly, got up and slowly moved to the entryway. He looked thru his door hole and found out that it was a young white man in an addidas t-shirt and flip flops who was a sophomore standing in the warm night air. Born revealed his intentions and returned with three twenty sacks.

The hippie-looking white boy with long hair and corduroys handed Born a hundred dollars and a word that he would be back for more.

After finishing up the transaction, Born returned to the table but as he bagged a quarter-ounce, a knock came at the door again. He answered it and found a few of his guys from the football team standing out, their voices carrying loudly. They were looking for an ounce, which Born supplied to them with no hesitation.

The no-shirt wearing, corn-rowed, young Blackman again attempted to finish the bagging process but was interrupted soon again, this time by Sally, an all-American white girl with blonde hair and blue eyes. She gave her order to Born of what she desired from him who supplied her with a smile. Sally let him know that she could bring him more customers if his stuff was of high quality. Born and Sally parted ways with an unspoken agreement between each other. She would assist and he would supply. It was a risk to involve her but Born had an idea that would keep the risk to a minimum.

The following night, Born left the gymnasium after a workout session and walked thru the campus area that was near his apartment. Two young ladies he knew who were cheerleaders approached him. They made a request for an ounce of weed that he supplied with ease as well as passing a number to one of the pretty-women with nice legs.

This was no come on. This was strictly business.

Born took a couple steps and was quickly run up on from behind by Sally. She cheerfully told him about her day and the things she got lined up as they walked toward Born's place. Sally made a buy in the process and as him and Sally left each other, another young man who played for the tennis team, picked up an ounce. Everybody smoked in college as Born was finding out. It was just as much of a part of the college life as alcohol was, matter of fact, it was a bigger part cause there was no hang over. And when the potency of this product that he was selling got good word of mouth. It was a feeding frenzy that would be non-stop, and the price would not matter.

The weekend came and in college that meant party time. Born stepped thru the doors at a house party given by a teammate in a solo state. The moment he entered the place brought great happiness to a lot of people who greeted him immediately. Born roamed around the two story house and met all the faces, from white party boys, to black football players to cheerleaders to A students to dopers. Everybody had respect for Born. He was a stand up dude. If he said something, he meant it and he always carried out his intentions to the fullest. There was no half-stepping in the young man.

Sally, who spoke with her girls in one of the many rooms, spotted Born and quickly made her way towards him. She pushed the throw-back jersey wearing young man into an empty bedroom and closed the door. Once alone inside, she found herself extremely attracted to the star basketball player. She purchased a couple twenty sacks that she tucked in her pocket of her jeans that revealed her hips then took her hand and sensuously placed it on Born's chest. She was definitely turned on by her nipples that Born felt the perkiness push up against his chest.

She was looking for something more then a bag of weed and the beer she drank gave her the courage to express herself toward Born. She backed him up against the wall and planted a kiss on his neck as her hand slowly slid down his chest.

Born caught himself and stopped her cold by taking her by the arms and leaning her back, away from him. This was something that he couldn't do to her, especially since the state she was in. Born gave her a kiss on the cheek and moved out of the bedroom.

He made another sale as he stepped out of the room and thought about Sally for a moment. Maybe he should go back in there and get at least some head. But Born knew that would be bad for business and that's all that mattered at the moment. Besides, the attraction to her was limited. He was still thinking about Cessy who he was unable to find at the party.

A few nights later, Born walked into one of the many dance clubs that lined the main street in the college town. After greeting the various faces, sharing words with a few of his friends and exchanging hugs and kisses with a couple of the lovely ladies near the DJ booth, Born saw a certain face that he approached and asked for what was owed to him. The young black man, who was buffed from the weights that he lifted, pulled out some cash, counted it off and handed what was owed with no problem, then bought some weed with what he had left over. It was at that moment that he sensed a pair of eyes on him. It was Cessy. She stood and watched with a serious expression of displeasure on her face. With no words, she turned from his sight and rejoined her girls at the table. Born put the money in his pocket as the thought of approaching her and explaining entered his mind. But this piece of work he was doing need no explaining, not to his teammates, his fans, or her. She would just have to learn to live with it and see the bigger picture – if she could.

Born rotated from Cessy's lovely sight and moved to the outside of the club where he joined his teammate, E, who stood up against the wall, close to the club entrance. E was having fun as he flirted with the many young ladies that passed by and returned the flirt back. Born and E exchanged a handshake and a hug then both leaned back against the wall and observed the main street at a little before 2 in the morning.

"What's it looking like with you?" Asked E.

"Seeing faces and getting love kid," Born said calmly.

A few gorgeous Asian women passed by that E's eyes took hold of and wouldn't let go. "You see Cessy in there?" Asked E.

"Yea," answered Born as he thought about what her eyes said to him.

"Yea, and it looks like she wants ya bra," E said as he turned with one of his big ass grin.

"Looks can be deceiving."

E thought for a moment and realized this was the perfect moment to let out what has been on his mind. "Like ballplayers who are really dealers?"

Born turned his head and cast a serious 'mind-your-business' look at E. Born thought he shouldn't really speak up on something that he doesn't fully know. Both him and Cessy were jumping the gun with their quick judgments of him. After a moment of pause, he broke out a little chuckle just as Sally approached from down the sidewalk and stopped in front of E and Born.

"Hey Born. Hi E," said Sally with a sort of sadness mixed with anxiety in her words and face. "Born, do you have anything?"

He took a moment, stepped back and closely looked on the disheveled young lady whose eyes darted in all directions. He noticed that her clothes weren't laying on her body in the same seductive way. And her skin was very pale.

Born stared at her with curiosity. Something was wrong with her. She was always bubbly and kept herself looking neat. But not tonight. Something shot thru him to walk away from her at that moment. Instead, he picked his eyes up off her and looked around the area. "Dam girl, you aright?"

"I'm fine. I have the money. I just, I just need something, bad."

"Forget about it. Maybe you should just go home and rest."

"No! Please, don't do me like that. Just this once. Help me out," begged a visibly frazzled Sally. "Come with me to my car. We can do it there."

Born took a moment and stared at the young girl who was nervous, tense and off balance. She did need to relax. "Aright girl, come on." Before he stepped away, he handed a wad of money to E that went unseen in the public eye. Even E was surprised at the dough being pushed covertly inside his palm. He took it in hand and stared at it for a moment then realized what Born was doing. He stuffed it in his pocket quickly so to not be seen and turned his attention to Cessy who had just stepped out the hole in the wall nightclub and was observing the server and the servee walking away. E and her shared a knowing and concerned look with each other. They cared deeply for Born and only wanted the best for him, and what he was doing, they felt, was not it. With no words to E, she moved off and disappeared in the opposite direction.

Born and Sally moved off toward her vehicle that was parked around the corner from the club. Born was about to round the corner when he turned his back and caught the site of a disturbed E who met up with his pupils in a concerned fashion.

Born and Sally arrived at her vehicle in a remote area. He reached into his backpack and pulled out a small envelope that he handed toward Sally. "I'm not going to do this for you again. Either you come correct or nothing," said Born in a demanding and serious tone.

Sally's hands shook as she took the little pouch in her fingers. "Thanks, thank you." She leaned into her car and flipped on the headlights then off that Born failed to see.

"Are you and your girls going to have another party?"

"I don't know," answered Sally who handed over the money.

"The last one you girls had was wild," said Born as he noticed a nervous and shaking Sally whose head was on a swivel. Something was definitely on her mind he could sense.

"Wild girls. I'm all out by the way so you're going to have to find another source after this," added Born with ease as he prepared for some trouble. "I'm outta here. Take care of your self sweetie."

And just like that, Police rushed in from all directions and swarmed on the young man in the all black outfit with a black sweatshirt over the George Gervin #44 Spurs throw back jersey. He was surrounded and apprehended by four police officers. They searched Born with vicious intent and only found some food receipts, a couple phone numbers, change and the money just given by Sally. The backpack only had a couple folders, a notebook, pens & pencils and an electronic organizer.

Sally sprang out of the hands of one of the officers who held her away from Born and moved toward him. "I'm so sorry! Please, believe me! They busted me and I had to! I had to! They made me Born, I'm sorry! I'm sorry!" Sally cried out as the officer moved back over and drug her away from Born. He was placed inside the cramped backseat of the police squad car.

The four white officers gathered right by the car window that Born sat near, and looked on, mocked and laughed at him as they held the small envelope of weed in their hands. They were filled with pride at the nights catch. They couldn't wait to make out the report.

As Born was about to be transported toward the station, E stepped out of the crowd of gathering people and watched him drive away with eye contact between the two held. He slowly lowered his head in disappointment toward the sidewalk and shook it.

"Fuck," said E to him self silently.

Born sat in a steel chair at a solid wooden, square table in a small room with marked up cement walls. After about an hour or so of waiting, he was joined by two of the arresting officers. One of the officers, a big, burly red headed white man, paced back and forth behind Born. The other officer, a thin set white man with brown hair and a thick mustache, took a seat at the table, across from him with a serious but calming facial expression.

The pacing officer rubbed his knuckles while he yelled and ranted about Born and what he wanted to do to him and what he had committed.

Born sat calm and cool and observed the walls were he could see the blood stains from some other victim that these two had in here before.

The redheaded officer stopped and grabbed Born by the neck and demanded his attention.

The other officer who was playing 'Good Cop' put his hand up toward his overheated partner. "Calm down Rich. That's enough," said Jake who then looked at Born. "Look, all we want from you is the person who supplied you. We don't want you. We're not here to mess up your season or your career." The pale skinned cop sharpened his glare on to the realizing young man whose expression was pure stone, unmoved, as he turned his eyes down on to the scribbled up table.

Born kept his mouth shut. He was wise to the game and the tricks that went down when it came to the police. He picked his eyes up from the table and stared at Jake and saw that he was trying hard to stay calm and not go ballistic like his partner was.

"Come on Wallace, be smart. I know you don't want to do ten to fifteen, especially with the season around the corner. Rich, that's about right, ten to fifteen?"

With spit foaming at the corner of his mouth, he leaned down to the side of Born. "I think that's about right. It might be twenty. We got you dickhead. Your ass is ours. If you don't help us, you can kiss your season goodbye and start puckering up for hairy Lonnie."

Born continued his silence as Rich let out a wicked and deep chuckle from the pit of his stomach and took a step back and looked down on the young man whose face was emotionless.

"Let's look at your situation. We got you with the product, making a sale, one of your customers who will testify and when we toss your place, I'm sure we'll find a lot more. Now, just give us your supplier and play ball with us and I promise you, we'll help you out in any way we can."

Born rubbed his nose and closed his eyes as he massaged the bridge on his nose. He dropped his hand down on to the table and glared in silence at Jake.

"How about it? Write a name down for us," said soothingly. Jake slid a pen and pad across to Born. He looked down at the instruments for a moment then eyed Jake who sat with a smile and a nod. Born refused to make any effort to pick up the pen. He just sat and stared across the table at Jake.

"Enough of this bullshit!" Rich erupted. He pushed Born, matter of fact he threw Born off the chair that caused him to hit the floor with a hard thud that was produced when a body hits cement. Rich moved over him and begin to beat on him with punches to the face and kicks to the stomach and dick area.

Jake leaned back in his chair, lit up a cigarette and watched the beat down progress. "No marks, remember," cautioned Jake.

As the blood and spit were flying from out the nose, mouths and open wounds, the Lieutenant walked in and viewed the vicious beating Rich was giving Born. The silver haired older white man with many deep wrinkles in his face pounced on Rich and separated him from Born.

Jake quickly rose up from his chair so to make it look like he was stopping Rich from getting at the young college student.

"What the hell is this!?" Screamed the Lieutenant.

Jake calmed Rich down and yelled at him about his actions. He looked at the older Lieutenant with a fake concern for Born. "We were just questioning him sir."

The Lieutenant walked up and looked at a sweaty and out of breath Rich in his face. "Interesting method of questioning," said quietly but with force. He took a few steps back and looked at the middle-aged officers. "Now get the fuck out of here! I'll deal with you sons of bitches later!"

The two officers slid out of the room. The Lieutenant looked down at Born who lay on the ground with a busted lip, a bloody nose, various bruises and was holding his mid-section. Born got up on one knee and took a breath. The Lieutenant gave a hand and helped the composed Blackman to his feet and in to a chair. "I apologize for those two."

Born wiped the dust and dirt from the black no-name brand sweatshirt and polo sweatpants. He uses his sweatshirt to wipe the blood that was running from his nose then brought his hand to his mouth and realized his lip had been busted open when he saw the blood on his finger. He was prepared for the accusations, the threats and the beat down. He licked his lip then spit out a mouthful of blood on to the floor then gave another wipe to his nose to make sure the bleeding had come to a halt.

"Yeah, well, your free to go. Your coach is out in the front lobby waiting for you," said the Lieutenant with a touch of remorse. But for some reason, Born knew how the words came out, that he was being forced to release him. He stood up out of the chair with no help and quietly moved to the door.

"Hey!"

Born slowly turned his head and looked at the smiling Lieutenant.

"Good luck on the court this year," the old man said as he cracked a crooked grin. "Go get'em."

Born spit another mouthful of blood to the floor and moved out of the room and into the lobby area were Coach Ray Harris stood and looked at him with an expression that had mixed feelings. On one hand he was angry with the police when he saw the busted lip and the pain on Born's face. But he was also disappointed at Born for putting himself in this position. He was unable to understand the reason why Born would do this. What he saw was a young man who had great athletic talent and a bright future. What he failed to see was Born saw basketball as a game and life as something bigger.

Coach Harris was a forty-six year old black man who played pro ball back in the days. He was a bench player on a number of teams who was known as a sparkplug that charged his team up. He put together a thirteen-year career by being able to do the little things that helped a team as well as staying out of trouble and was known as a great guy and a team player. Ray Harris was about six two and skinny as hell but

was extremely agile. Now here was a guy who played by the rules driving his star
player home who had just broken the rules. They sat quietly in a white Cadillac CTS
that moved thru State College on its way to Born's place.

Coach Harris glanced over at Born a few times. He was angry but he had to remain
cool and find a way to reach out. "You going to tell me what that was all about?"

Born took a breath and exhaled it out as he leaned back in the leather seat.
"Nothing coach. Don't worry about it."

"Worried? You dam right I'm worried, and you should be too. Especially if they
found anything else at your place."

Born cracked a small grin at the corner of his mouth and turned his head to the
passenger side window. "They won't find shit," softly said that Coach Harris was
unable to understand.

"Huh, what did you say?"

"How'd you get me loose?"

"Now you know the program supporters don't want to see the star player locked
up before the season has even begun."

"Only until the season is over."

Coach Harris spun his head toward Born and glared at him. "Why are you
doing this?"

Born continued to relax in the seat. "Coach, I'm tired."

The bald black man faced forward and thought about the pressure that may
be building on Born. Was there something he did that caused this? He searched for
the words that could communicate his concern and would offer his hand of help.
"Son, you better remember something. There are only a few players who are in the
position that you're in. But there are many that can take your place." He turned to
Born and observed the young man resting in the seat with his eyes closed. "Do you
hear me?!"

Born opened his eyes and looked at his agitated coach. "Yea, yea. That was
beautiful coach."

"I'm not playing B. The more strikes you get in this game, the harder it gets. I
know. I been around guys who thought they had the tiger by the tail. Only come
to find out the tiger had their tail and kicked that ass everyday. This is some real
life stuff here."

"Real life huh?" Born said as he picked his head up and looked forward. "Coach,
I appreciate your concern and all your words of wisdom, but don't sweat about this,
aright."

The luxury vehicle pulled up to Born's apartment complex and entered into the
parking lot. Coach Harris put the ride into park and then took a moment and looked
at his star guard with a little concern and a lot of irritation. Why was this kid acting
like nothing just happened?

"Come on Coach, please," said an exhausted Born who did not want to hear
any speech.

"This is our year. Our year! There is not a team in the country that can match up with you and E," exclaimed an excited Coach. "The only one that can stop us is us."

"The only one that can stop us is us," repeated Born. "I like that coach."

"I'm not play . . ."

"Coach, I hear ya. For real. Now, can I go?"

Coach Harris, after a moment of searching Born's eyes for any answers, gave a head motion. "Get out of here."

Born moved out of the vehicle and into his apartment that Coach Harris observed each step of the way. After Born disappeared inside, Coach sat in his ride and stared straight ahead. "Stay good young one. Stay good and you'll have it all."

Coach Harris pulled out and drove away.

Born's neatly arranged and moderately decorated apartment was filled with friends & acquaintances from and around the college area. All except Cessy. The gathering had young people drinking, talking, gambling, playing cards and socializing with each other around the two-level loft in various rooms.

Upstairs in the bathroom, one of Born's teammates threw up chunks into the toilet that he hugged up on as a couple of other teammates, with their girls, looked on and laughed at the site.

In Born's bedroom at the back, Born and one of his hippie boys who he was cool with completed a transaction. As far as being out of product, well, that was just for Sally. E approached the bedroom door that was slightly opened and observed the activity that increased his anger toward Born. As the money exchanged hands, E entered into the room. The young hippie with a tie-dye shirt and bandana wrapped around his head to hold his long hair in place and out of his eyes, headed out the room, giving a pat to the back of E. The tall and slender ball player entered in the room as he looked at Born and tossed the duffel bags he held in his hands to the floor in front of Born who opened them up that revealed the large amount of cash that was in both of them that he had made and added what he just collected to it.

"Thought you were out?" Asked E with an attitude.

"I am now."

"Look it you," E said with an air of disgust.

Born shimmied his shoulders and took a drink from a wine cooler bottle as he moved his body to the music playing in front of a staring and standing E. "You ready for the season?"

E set his glass down and took a seat across from Born. "The real question is are you going to be around for the season?"

"Stop buggin star."

"I'm not the one fuckin' up."

Born stopped his shimmy dance as he sat down and looked at E with a serious face for a brief moment. "You know," Born paused and cracked a questioning look. "Is everything alright with you, cause, you've been on some funny shit lately."

E grabbed Born by his 'Billy Sims' Oklahoma #20 jersey and pulled him up from his chair. The two young men stood, face to face, with Born looking up at the taller E. "Fuck no, I'm not aright! This is our opportunity right here B. A chance to make history. And instead, your fucking off around here, trying to be Tony fuckin' Montana!"

A quiet and calm Born looked at E's hands that gripped and ruffled the jersey then lifted his head up toward E and smiled. "Tony Montana?"

E released the grip that he had a hold of and gave a shove that sent Born a step away from him. "What for B? It's so unnecessary. You need money, I got you."

"That's sweet of you but, do you really believe that this ball game they throw us is all there is?"

"For me – yes."

"That's sad E. That is fucking sad," said Born with a straight and serious expression. "Do you know that the average tenure of a pro basketball player is six to seven years? Six to seven years, that's all."

"Coach had thirteen."

"Yea, and what did he have to do for that thirteen years?"

"Hey, seven is enough for me to get paid."

Born picked up his wine cooler and stepped toward the door. "Is that why you play? Too get paid." Born faced up to E and met with his eyes. "Don't you want to do what you love to do? You know, what makes you feel alive and free. I know I do. You better step back and see the new slavery out here. It's real kid. If you only play for the money, then how are you going to be part of something special?" They shared a moment with no words, only focused eye contact that spoke louder then words. Born had made his point. Then just as quick as he is on the court, he broke out a smile. "Gotta use your truck tomorrow night bra, alright." Born moved out of the bedroom, exiting out the door, and down the hall. "And learn to relax stiffwood!"

Born shared a few hugs with some of the young ladies and started to do his shimmy dance with a couple of them.

E sat and observed Born from the bedroom for a moment. The words rang in his head. The game of basketball had changed since the days of balling at the park and how he loved it so and now how it had become a sufferable job of sort. He definitely wanted that feeling back. Born new what he was talking about, but what did he mean then by long money?

Divine and Malik sat on the concrete apartment steps underneath the night moon and each enjoyed a bottle of juice and the warm breeze that hit their face. They picked their heads up and looked in the direction from were some music was coming from.

Born, in E's Chevy Blazer, pulled up in front of the two with a smile and his Dallas Stars ball cap pulled low. "Yo! You two waiting on me?"

Malik and Divine got up from the steps and made their way toward the vehicle without answering the question. Divine took the wheel as Born hopped in the back seat with Malik taking shotgun. The blazer sped off.

After greetings were exchanged and a little small talk threw back and forth, Born reached into the rear of the four-door truck and grabbed a large shopping bag with a few shoeboxes in it. He took out one of the shoeboxes and handed it to Malik. He flipped the cover open and observed money stacked deep and thick inside. Malik turned to Born in the backseat and cracked an approving smile then leaned the box to Divine who took a glance then faced forward and nodded his head. Malik handed the box back to Born who had another shopping bag right beside him on the backseat. He turned his head and looked out the window at the run down apartments, the going-out-of-business shops and the wandering young people out in the streets. Malik turned the music up as the three moved their head to the verse as the ride motored thru the city.

> *'We franchise like Randy Moss with Garnett/We hot steppin' in erotic city with out Prince/Jimmy Jam and Terry Lewis ain't giving this hip hop shit/Morris Day and JeRome was the realest/remember them fish nets/Vanity 6/Appallonia I'm a sex U to shootin' this dick/we cuttin' corners/mashing in the streets of passion with full clips.'*

Divine, Malik and Born arrived at the front of Benji's house. The Blazer sat still with the three inside holding a discussion. Malik informed Born on the money made by each one, the reason for this, and the course of action that would now be taken from this moment along with his part to play. Born listened and understood completely. He was committed with out saying a word and Malik and Divine were well aware of this.

Benji stepped out his front door and observed Malik and Divine who continued to go over all the corners to the situation. Born nodded in agreement at what they had proposed and added a couple of his own plans that was well received. The three got out of the truck, exchanged hugs and hands with parting words. Just as Born was about to get in the Blazer, he spotted Benji's sight. He quickly sprang from the opened side door and met up with the young politician. They brought their hands together followed by their arms embracing their shoulders. Benji and Born had much love for each other despite the various physical differences in their lives. They respected each other. They admired each other. They looked out for each other. They stepped back with smiles and spoke briefly on what each had been doing. Malik and Divine, both with a shopping bag in hand, walked up and passed Benji and Born who gave each other one more handshake before Born darted back to the Blazer and drove off. Benji turned and joined Divine and Malik who at that moment were moving inside his home.

The three young men, one in cornrows, one sporting a baldhead and the other one with a short afro walked into Benji's bedroom and threw the shopping bags on the bed. Malik got on the phone and started to dial numbers.

Divine picked up a 'Fortune' magazine and flipped thru it at Benji's desk as he took a break and relaxed in the chair.

Benji fell on the bed and took notice of the shopping bags filled with shoeboxes that laid on his bed. He pulled out one and observed the box and how heavy it was. "Did you all get enough shoes? This doesn't even feel like shoes. See what kind you got." He opened the box and stared at about fifty thousand dollars packed inside. He swung his head to Divine and caught his eyes. "What the . . ."

"Nice huh."

"Where did this come from?"

Malik hung up the phone, finishing his phone call, and looked up from the number pad on the phone and over at Benji. "What's more important then were is what are we going to do with it?" Malik dialed another number and got an answer that he turned his attention to. "Peace. A, yo, get up with us. Ruggz, Knowledge. True. Yea, get him too. One." Malik hung up and observed Benji opening another shoebox and staring at the money.

Divine fought to keep from laughing at Benji's reaction. "Dam, rest your eyes B."

Malik and Divine both broke out in a small laughter that Benji joined in on as he lay back in the bed and looked on his two brothers.

Ruggz Bowling Alley was located in the uptown area on the south side of the city. The seventy-year old Blackman, who owned the place, was good friends with Pops and he arranged for Malik, Divine and the group to use it and meet at.

The gray-haired Rugs sat and conversated at the table with Malik and Divine who patiently waited for the rest of the young Blackmen to arrive.

Benji sat at a table to the side and enjoyed his cranberry drink with a newspaper.

Seven walked around the place and observed the action with a few late night bowlers knocking pins over and keeping score.

Pops entered into the plainly furnished place with a cheap, thin carpet that didn't match a thing in the joint. Pops took a seat with Malik, Divine and Rugs at the table.

Rassa sat at the bar with a drink and spoke with a lovely, older-looking, brown skin woman who had good teeth, Rassa thought. The forty-something year old woman was finishing up her night in search of sugar daddy to treat her and her babies to the American dream that was a black family's nightmare.

DJ played one of the arcade games with a couple youths that couldn't be no more then seventeen-years old and out way past their curfew. Hard heads that didn't care about shit, and refused to listen to elder people's rules.

Tajaa and Lite entered into the place, strong and steady, and shared handshakes and hugs with each of their brothers in attendance.

Malik turned to Rugs. "Is everything ready?"

"It's all yours."

Malik gave a nod to Divine who faced out to be heard. "Let's go fam!"

Each left what they were doing and walked to the back room that was located in the arcade area, past the set of pool tables. One by One they moved in to the mid-sized room that was just big enough to hold all of them. In the center stood a table with one chair at each end and four lined up on each side. An incense burned in a holder that sat in the middle of the table.

Pops moved into the room with a tray of glasses, a bottle of cognac and a bottle of grape juice.

Rassa broke out a half-ounce bag off weed and immediately began to roll a few blunts that Seven gave a hand with.

Benji watched Rassa roll one and he then tried to roll one himself that fell apart, didn't hold the weed and ripped apart.

Drinks were poured, words were shared in various spots thru out the room, and blunts were lit up.

Malik stepped into the room last and took his place at one end of the table. Divine took a seat at the other end and the rest of the guys grabbed and filled in the other seats as the room calmed down.

Rassa exhaled the blunt smoke and looked over at Malik. "Aright Leek. We're all here God. Now, what's the deal with pulling me away from a night with a sweet little mommy juice?"

DJ poured some of the cognac in his glass. "Yeah, you know Black don't get to taste that honey very often."

The room exploded into laughs and expressions at the crack by DJ.

"Ahh here he goes with his comedian act. The playboy bunny."

DJ made a funny face with a centerfold pose then flashed a middle finger to Rassa. Laughter continued to rain out and a number of voices rose up to add in on the fun with Rassa and DJ.

"Yo! Yo!" Malik stood up from the chair, getting their attention.

Heads turned and quieted down.

"Regardless of what it is, it should be enough just to be here together," Malik added as he took his seat and leaned back.

"True, true," Tajaa thundered.

Lite took a drink then looked around the room. Everyone was there, except for Born which each understood the reason for. "It's just, on the phone, you made it sound urgent."

"Yea, so, what's up?" DJ said calmly.

"First things first," calmly said Malik as he took a swig of his drink. "I have nothing but love for the work that each of you put in to get what we got," Malik felt the strength building in him as the words came in remembrance of what had just been accomplished. It felt good to do something with these young men who he grew up with and had the same aspirations as himself.

Divine nodded as he relaxed and enjoyed his drink. "That was beautiful. Yall better know that. We proved to selves, which is all that really matters, that we could come together. Now, on to the next step in this and it's going to take a total commitment."

Smoke filled the room and the drinks tasted sweet as each set of eyes acknowledged the thankful words and were appreciative of the accomplishments made. No one was talking about where was their cut or what they were going to buy or questioning each other and their part. Each one was dedicated and firm with the group in that room and the loyalty that was necessary. But what was this next step Divine spoke of?

"I spoke with Born and there's no doubt about his involvement after the shit he just pulled off. He's in – all the way," said Malik with no hesitation or question.

Divine moved up in his chair with his facial expression stone. "All the way."

Rassa pushed up on to the table that he set his arms on. "He's in to what? What's this all about? Spit it out."

"What do you think son? What have all of us been talking about for the longest about doing out here? And what do we see each day out here? You all know what this is about," said Malik casually, nodding his head.

"And it's going to call for stepping on a few toes. Naah, fuck that. A lot of," added Divine with a serious tone.

"I'm talking about doing what our fathers were unable to do or unwilling to do. And for us to do this, you all have to understand that we're going to get bloody. Real bloody, bruised and battered," Malik said sharply.

Each one in that room, at that moment, knew precisely what Malik and Divine were talking about. "So if you rather not go thru what is to come, then you're free to leave us now. Take your cut and go peacefully. Cause there can be no scarecrows and no cry-babies in this what we're about to do," Divine said with an intimidating and unflinching expression.

The room went quiet for a moment as each exchanged eye contact with each other. No one moved from their seat. They all new what they were getting into and they accepted it fully.

Divine leaned back in his chair and shared a moment of eye contact with Malik. They were right. This was what they each had been waiting, preparing, studying, cultivating and experiencing what they each had for. This was the time.

"It's good to see that you all feel the same way," Divine said that broke the silence.

"That's why you were all called and so," Malik said and he started to rub his hands together. "Here we go. Are you all ready?"

In various tones and volumes, all faces answered back in the affirmative.

Malik cracked a confident grin and looked over the powerful faces that stared back at him. One face in particular he kept a longer glance. Benji's. "We're going to see. Aright," rang Malik as he turned from Benji's sight. "Now, on to other things. I got a Cee note on Divine and Self against any challengers on those lanes."

DJ jumped up. "Ooohh shit! Give me some of that action." He turned to Lite. "You up for it L?"

"You ain't got ask me twice," said Lite who stood up from his chair.

The room quickly turned into a place filled with excitement as hugs, handshakes, drinking and movement around to pass the blunt and speak about this or that took over.

The door opened to the back room and DJ, Lite, Seven, Rassa, Benji, Pops, and Tajaa stepped out and moved back into the bowling alley, lounge area.

Malik and Divine remained in the backroom and stood still, face-to-face.

"Let's make history G.O.D.," said Malik.

"I agree," said Divine.

"It's going to be hell son. You know they've been waiting for this."

"Then there will be no excuses Original Man."

"And no regrets."

Malik extended his open right hand that was taken by Divine's right hand and pulled them close to each other with a confident smile beaming on each of their faces. They pulled back and looked into each other's eyes for a moment then slowly made their way out of the room.

Each new their role. Each new there part. Each new what was to come and what had to be done. And now came the application process to be put into play. A family in the city that the city badly needed had risen and been born.

With the venom of truth/inject troops/let loose with the fists of fury/severe and sincerely/bury fairies/to where He takes it all from the first law/to the day We maul/sprawl/never hold back/open the door/catch it like a Kodak.

THE BEGGINNING

Order out of Chaos.